A graduate of Warwick Business School, Heath Tredell is now a hard working director of two family companies. In the past he achieved much as a promising racing cyclist. Now in his limited spare time he enjoys spending time with his three children, playing squash, scuba diving and learning to fly.

An early hours ponder over life's mysteries was the inspiration for the biggest conspiracy theory the world has ever seen. He is now working upon two further novels, one of which brings closure to **H^ea v e n** and Zak's story.

H^eaven

A haven, a place
just *dying* to meet you.

HEATH J TREDELL

H^eaven

A haven, a place
just *dying* to meet you.

Vanguard Press

VANGUARD PAPERBACK

© Copyright 2007
Heath J Tredell

A CIP catalogue record for this title is
available from the British Library.

ISBN 978 1 84386 316 8

*Vanguard Press is an imprint of
Pegasus Elliot MacKenzie Publishers Ltd.*
www.pegasuspublishers.com

First Published in 2007

**Vanguard Press
Sheraton House Castle Park
Cambridge England**

Printed & Bound in Great Britain

This book is dedicated to my family without whom this book would have been impossible, and also to a man I used to know.

Imagine there's no h^eaven, it's easy if you try,
No hell below us, above us only sky,
Imagine all the people, living for today.
Imagine there's no countries, it isn't hard to do,
Nothing to kill or die for, and no religion too,
Imagine all the people, living life in peace.
You may say I'm a dreamer, but I'm not the only one,
I hope someday you'll join us, and the world will be as one.

(John Lennon)

Prologue

They say that God moves in mysterious ways, and as Zachariah sat in his doorway watching the hustle and bustle of New York's pedestrians walk by, he pondered this maxim. There weren't many mysteries left for Zachariah. He had witnessed everything the world had to offer, and much more than most people even dared try to imagine. He had seen the highs that love and joy can bring to someone; and felt the lows that only desperate loneliness and heartache can show you. He once considered himself invincible, God-like in his power over people and their lives. He had the world at his feet. Where wealth fuelled excesses and greed; where people would go to any lengths possible to help feed your ego, so that they in turn may feed on you. He had witnessed first-hand, people like Yelina, who possessed a level of kindness almost saint-like in its honesty, openness and generosity. But mostly he had witnessed greed, greed and passion. Not passion in a loving sense, but an angry, obsessive passion, the kind that takes over your life and consumes you in a sea of insatiability. The passion of avarice, one of not needing what you have or deserve, and yet demanding and searching for more than you could ever cope with. If the Lord had meant for someone to witness these extremes, he had chosen Zak Sharpe. Zak was that man and this is his story.

Growing Up

They fuck you up, your mum and dad.
They may not mean to, but they do.
They fill you with the faults they had
And add some extra, just for you.

Philip Larkin – 1974

MARCH 2000 - Zachariah sat on his step, watching the thin, early morning orange mist that encompassed Empire Boulevard, slowly brighten away. He reached his roughened hand into his inside pocket and pulled out a dog-eared notepad. It was his latest edition. The previous three books had disappeared, or more probably, had been stolen from him. This one had a small elastic band wrapped neatly round it. A small, freebie biro, courtesy of a catalogue store, was between the notepad and the elastic band. He carefully stretched the perished elastic band enough to take it off the notepad and wrap it over his wrist, he did not want it to break, it was the only one he had. Opening it, he looked at the first page.

Remember your Number one priority – Prove to them you are not this person!!

Without a thought as to whether he was going to

follow this piece of advice, he continued. His dirty thumb then searched through the top right hand edges of the paper, about two-thirds of the way through, his thumb stopped. As he filled each page with notes, he tore off the top corner as a kind of bookmark. It was a simple system he'd learned from when he used to have a diary with a perforated corner. This had no such perforation, nor was it even a proper diary, but it worked.

He took a look at the biro, half broken, and with the once clear plastic now partially opaque with scratches, cracks and wear. He began writing the date and time down carefully at the top of his diary. He considered, as he often did, whether to write a memoranda note – just in case.

By eight o'clock the mist had all but disappeared and been replaced by a warm, bright haze. The street was now alive with people busily making their way to work, hurriedly collecting their lives together for another day in New York. Watching this daily tale unfold, he reflected on what was, and might've been. Despite his headache from last night's overindulgence, he contemplated the people he could be sharing his life with had he had the foresight that hindsight makes look so obvious. Why didn't they teach that at school? Why didn't they have it on the curriculum? He turned back to his notepad and wrote,

'*Life Skills – Being Happy With What You've Go*t'. THEY SHOULD TEACH THAT AT SCHOOL!!

Zachariah considered the words carefully and decided he still agreed with them. He'd have never have fallen foul of life's experiences had he stayed for *that* lesson. Mind you, the kind of school Zachariah went to would certainly have not shown an interest in anything remotely as civilised.

The weather was certainly getting warmer but, being spring, the morning could still offer a biting chill. Zachariah always rose early as the overnight frostiness woke him in the early hours. He had known a lot worse, yet was now regretting discarding his thick, brown, second coat a few days ago. A flea-ridden fleece, it had stunk of its previous owner and the booze he'd consumed. A rancid sickly smell of beer, wine and spirits, all worn into the thick grunge of countless cigarettes and dirt that had accumulated over the years. Its most annoying trait was its small pockets that were neither use nor ornament. It did however possess a good zip and that had kept him warm and quite dry for the last few months. Zachariah had decided to dump it though, a tramp he may be, but he still tried occasionally to keep up his appearance. He had opted therefore to keep the thinner, cleaner trench coat with the added practical benefit of deeper pockets for his worldly possessions.

He reached inside and gathered its contents into his dirty, hardened hands. He looked through the contents. A dime, unspent money from yesterday's earnings; a plastic, blue lighter with a good bit of life left in it; thin, hard, grease-coated toilet paper courtesy of the local public toilets; half a pencil, and a cufflink he'd found under a bench a month earlier; all shared their space with a half bottle of white spirit, unfortunately with only the smallest of dribble left. Zak took a pitiful and slightly disappointed glance at it, and undid the thin metal cap lid. He pitched the bottle towards his mouth and savoured the sharp pang it gave his taste buds. He looked back at the bottle to confirm what he already knew; it was empty. He tossed it aside carelessly and gazed out into the world. Zachariah sat and compared today's weather with that of his native country... England's.

***

Zak had been born in the winter, on 'the coldest night of the year', as his father had once told him. It was the December of 1967 and Warwickshire had been covered in snow. Edwin G. Sharpe, his father, a person Zak had called 'Sir' for the whole of his life, had made all the preparations for the first and what was to be only new arrival to the Sharpe family. A bonny baby of 10lbs 1oz, he had his mother's jet-black hair and blue-grey eyes and father's nose. Blissfully unaware of the elation that he brought to his parents, his mother Paula named him Zachariah.

Few people recall their foremost five years in this world, and Zachariah was no different. Edwin and Paula had tried a number of times to add to the family, but without success. So, happy and contented, the soon to be called 'Zak' for short, wanted for nothing. Paula loved him dearly and spent an almost exclusive amount of time with him. Zak's first real memory of any sort was from about this age, when he remembered his father telling him that he'd love it there and Zak not fully understanding what he meant. This seemed to be a time when father and 'mommy', were at odds with each other. Later in life he suspected that this was probably a time when his parents diverse upbringings clashed.

Edwin, Zak's father, had enjoyed a very privileged upbringing in the more leafy parts of Leicestershire. Born into a very wealthy family, Edwin had been raised somewhat at arms length by his parents, who seemed preoccupied with the family business and fortune. Boarding school had followed prep school, had followed nanny. Edwin had been systematically cultivated into a man who had all the necessary skills to further the family fortune and yet none that some of us would consider essential to an ordinary upbringing. It is argued that children are much like a

18

photograph and develop into a reflection and product of their own environment. Edwin was being developed into the cold, hard businessman where money, influence, power and greed reign supreme. It is this that his parents hoped for and dreamed of – a highly successful entrepreneur who could only promote the rapidly growing family company. Edwin had not expected anything back in return for this. Starved of genuine love from birth, Edwin had found the giving of affection and love a stranger to him. He had courted a few potential companions in his time but had found the majority of them either not appropriate to the family or not suited to him. Most suitors for this position seemed to have needs that he couldn't possibly meet. Many had aspirations, hobbies and even careers, they simply wouldn't do for a self-centred Edwin. What Edwin had grown to appreciate was not what many were offering. Once vetted by his parents for suitability, he wanted a partner who was stable, dependable, loyal and able to organise his house and private life. He wanted someone in whom he could depend to be there to support him and offer him the psychological, personal companionship that, periodically, his company failed to provide.

It was a relief to Edwin therefore, that he met Paula at the 1965 Lloyd's of London New Year's party. Paula had been seated on the same table as Edwin due to a financier knowing both families. Paula had seemed quiet, shy, and had none of the absurd demands or interests that others had displayed. Miss Paula Jameson had been born in 1947 and was very attractive, and considerably younger than Edwin. Of obvious Irish descent, and no peerage to speak of, Paula had grown up in Kent. Her Irish parents were obviously 'new money' and had moved to England just after her birth. Using their contacts in Ireland they had established a very lucrative building business that was rapidly expanding in the post-war race to re-build London.

Paula had experienced a very different upbringing to Edwin. Her parents, at least it seemed to Zak, appeared to have a much calmer and more composed approach to home life and work life. Paula's father had become very successful but had maintained that more rebellious side of his nature that allowed him to enjoy, arguably too often, the relaxation methods often only found in public houses.

Had Edwin been younger than his thirty-five years when he met Paula, he would've probably found it nigh on impossible to court a girl from such a background of informality; particularly one so young. As it was, Edwin's parents had reached a stage where they had neither the fight to argue nor the expected respect that parentage of a younger son would've automatically given them. Their views had become less important as Edwin had grown older and the 'disagreement of '64' was the final nail in the coffin of unquestioning compliance. 1964 had seen an opportunity for the family firm to take over what Edwin had seen as a rapidly growing company in an equally expanding market – electronics. He had heard that due to cash flow difficulties, a forerunner of the electronics world was going 'belly up'. Edwin had witnessed the growth in television and radio first-hand and believed it to be only the beginning. Indeed, this business opportunity had already invested heavily into research, and development into new products. This overspending into what was as yet a very small market, was partly its downfall. His parents had advised against it, 'stick to the knitting', they had said.

"You know nothing of the industry, we have prospered very well in textiles and there we shall remain."

Edwin, who had company control by then, due to a transfer of shares for inheritance tax purposes, looked at his father. The old man's kind, grey eyes and white eyebrows now looked at

20

him sternly.

"I can't, Father. I can't stand by this obvious opportunity and let it slip through our hands. Please, I implore you to have faith in my decision. I promise not to fail you." Edwin's father finally conceded. Edwin took the complete overspend by the previous owners of the electronics firm on innovation, and harnessed it. He took the textile industries' management system's focus on attention to detail and customer orientation, and threw it the company's new electronics arm. This refusal to tow the line and wishes of his parents had caused ructions and arguments such as the family had never seen. But Edwin's quality and customer-first approach won many followers, and the company and industry grew exponentially. Programmes like Benny Hill, The Hitchcock Half Hour and Jack-a-nory all became public favourites. The colour television was in its infancy, but was growing fast. Profits soared as public interest in television fuelled sales. The future looked far more inviting than the textile industry.

It has been said that man's experience of life is first mediocrity, then boredom, then fear. Edwin had become so excited with life running the business, that he had become bored with life outside of it. Only when he did look at his personal life, did the boredom change to fear. As possibly the biggest motivator to act that a human can have; it was perhaps the fear of not having children to pass his empire to that motivated Edwin to court and propose to Paula that year. The wedding had been organised for the February of '67 and invitations posted to all of the important people. Edwin had asked a manager of one of his companies to help organise his wedding. Edwin argued that with invitations being sent to people who influence the business, the whole ceremony and celebrations needed to be very well, planned and organised. What Edwin had thought was something

21

relating far more to strategy or politically motivated planning.

By the day of the wedding, the absurdity of contrasting perspectives was very evident. Most of the groom's invitations had been mailed to business associates, politicians or other wealthy families. Friends of the groom not connected with the business were in short supply; most had lives of their own to be getting on with or had lost contact with him over the years. Most of the 'friends' that *did* make the effort to attend were of his parents, "old money" and similarly wealthy people… aristocracy. In contrast, the bride's invitations had been sent to all parts of England and Ireland and almost exclusively to family and friends. Very few of these couldn't attend and even those had quite valid excuses. Paula's family invited very few business associates, and their attitude, enjoyment and celebration at the wedding was noticeably different to Edwin's 'family'.

Paula clearly loved Edwin in a way that would have been incomprehensible to the workaholic businessman. Her parents had worked hard for their success and she was to be the first of the Jameson's to marry into the upper classes. Paula became pregnant soon after and Zachariah arrived in the December of '67. The rest, they say, is history, and 'Zak' developed much of the mischievous personality from his mother's side. He was nurtured on a mixture of genuine love from his mother and kind formality from his father. His mother won the first of their marital arguments and had insisted she nurse and raise Zak herself. Edwin had clearly felt that this duty should be left to the staff, leaving her to attend functions and organise the household more effectively. This was, after all, the way in which Edwin had been brought up and had served him and his parents well. But with a new bride and other more lucrative business interests to occupy his attention, he had yielded to her motherly aspirations. The caring for Zak was undertaken equally between

Nanny and Mummy, until he finally left for boarding school. Caring for Zak was a pleasure and experience Paula found uncompromisingly instinctive. She had witnessed and retold to her husband all the growing up landmarks that accompany the role as a parent. Indeed, during this time she had encouraged Zak's mind to imagine, and his heart to burn with a passion for life.

Boarding school life didn't really suit Zak. His school days bored him and he found himself more than once on the wrong side of both the institutions and family expectations. Edwin mainly conducted any chastisements over his antics. When Zak had been younger his father's commanding voice had pierced him like a hot poker, forcing him to move in the line of least resistance or be burned. This had, to all recollections worked for a considerable time, but like his father had found through the 'disagreement of '64', the parentage poker loses its heat over time and its effectiveness wanes. Zak had braved the heat far earlier than his father... parenting, or modern day aspirations, perhaps? Paula showed a far more relaxed mannerism, she had a much more subtle way of encouraging Zak to do things. It seemed in retrospect that her love conquered all. Zak hated letting her down, and this personal interior fear would last Zak all his life. Merely the thought that he had worried or upset her seemed a much greater stimulator than the poker of consent or formal expectations of his father.

Like many institutions, the Winston Stanley School for Boys had its holes; where those in attendance could tweak the system to their own advantage. Zak had always been close to his mother, and she often gave the impression that life offered much more than the formal home or school surroundings that encircled and protected the young Zachariah. Because of this, Zak had always been of a curious nature. When at home, he had often

23

sought the areas of the house and grounds that he was not supposed to venture into. Once, whilst at home, he had wandered around to the gardener's shed, a completely forbidden act in itself. The idea that the master of the house knew where it was and was even so curious as to venture there would have been unthinkable to his father. Zak had risked going inside and had found there a dusty place of wonderment. He'd expected to find a neat row of spades, rakes and hoes, and instead had discovered a secret world. It was like stepping into a goblin's den.

A torn, dusty-brown armchair took pride of place and sat facing the mucky window. The sun strained through the dust and grime, past the cobwebs, and washed a mustard-yellow light over the shed's interior.

Below the window and to the left was a small table and a small wooden packing case with old newspapers and magazines inside. Zak would, on a subsequent visit, find some of these to be pornographic and took great pleasure in the shamefulness of looking at them. The pictures were of obvious delight but, as Zak found he had more time, he found himself reading some of the articles with such titles as, 'Are you sure you're normal?' or 'Children in prison'. In the 'Special Edition' there was a very old article about, 'What wacky weapons the Pentagon wished it had'; but that was too dog-eared to be worth reading.

The back wall of the shed held a plethora of different tools, hanging from rusty nails in the wall, all were well used and some in desperate need of replacement. He would also notice on future visits that there was always a bucket of clean water stood next to the armchair. He would work out many years later that this was probably used to keep bottles of beer cool in. Opposite the chair, on a shelf, stood an old transistor radio, quite dusty and well used but certainly ok for listening to a bit of 'Earth Wind and Fire' or Blondie, with her 'Heart of Glass'. Zak's inquisitiveness

24

had rarely let him down and a chance wander had taught him a great deal about the mysterious goings-on in the 'hidden world'.

It was this inquisitiveness that helped him find the institutional holes in boarding school. The Winston Stanley School for boys had a manner of formality that Edwin would have (and Zak thought must have) cherished. Large high ceilings and oak-panelled walls were, 'oh so typical' of the décor of their house in Leicestershire. Zak was not much taller than normal and found athletics more interesting than football, rugby or cricket. All of these team sports did nothing for Zak. He just *wanted* to get stuck into the action all the time, and found that the level of involvement these gave him, just wasn't enough. He excelled instead at running and long jump.

But school life never really appealed to Zak. He craved a new surrounding, and was delighted to get one at university. Here the institutional holes were much bigger and the rewards better! University allowed him to experiment with alcohol, pornography and cigarettes. Even soft drugs were all available should you know the right people, and although Zak rarely dabbled in such schemes, he was always well informed about who supplied what. University gave Zak the space his inquisitive personality craved. It was though sadly short-lived, and dramatically life-changing.

The Good Times – Parties
(1986 – 1991)

Sweet is pleasure after pain.

John Dryden – 1697

Zak had not excelled at boarding school. It seemed to him to be a tale of two cities in one camp. There were those students that loved the strict disciplinarian ethos that characterises many boarding schools. There were others that excelled at the demands placed on them from lectures. There were finally those who gained pleasure from fighting the system; those who saw those institutional demands as excessive, restricting and punitive. Zak was in this minority group who attended the Winston Stanley School for Boys, he was in the more elite group who made up 'The Rivals'.

'The Rivals' had consisted of him and a few others from his year. Their determined destiny was to be the forerunners to modern leadership and entrepreneurship. Sebastian Peddar was the son of a wealthy financier. He was physically the largest of the Rivals. With his brazen ginger hair to match his outlandish and very extroverted personality, 'Seb' was often the generator of ideas. Hugo, was a small, wily youth with pointed features and a chiselled jaw. Hugo hated his name and 'H' was often the person to find the finances to turn their ideas into reality.

'Jimmy' or James Michael Edwards, was definitely 'old money' type. His parents constantly hoped for him to 'find himself' and lose his childhood antics that caused his parents so much grief. The Rivals were the ones who didn't need academic excellence to succeed; it was just destined for them regardless of their actions. Their ability to tweak the school system allowed them the confidence to believe that the world was their oyster and theirs for the taking; and take it they shall. Time would prove them woefully wrong, but to these pubescent schoolboys it seemed providence.

Home life with his parents had paradoxically mirrored the boarding school ethos. Zak quickly learnt that his mother was that part of his parentage that he could influence more easily to his own advantage. From her he would receive the most desired return of emotion. Paula was an easier target. Her love for him was unquestionably sincere and permanent. Zak was her little boy. His father's love was more restrained. Edwin's aristocratic stiff upper lip followed his own upbringing and had meant that he and Zak had always respected each other's role both in family and society life but never really got beyond this. 'Son', and 'Sir', related amicably if not distantly from one another.

Youth and wealth make ideal breeding partners; their offspring are often arrogance and selfishness. 'The Rivals' had enjoyed combining their youth and wealth and had at times epitomised these theological offspring. Wealth had made them very self-absorbing, self-centred and uncaring and they loved it. Zachariah had sat in his doorway near Prospect Park and witnessed on many occasions, reminiscences of his youth. His tool, during school, had been money. The tool he witnessed all these years later on the streets of Brooklyn had been streetwise bravery. Zak had not needed to be brave when he was younger, he had simply bought whatever he wanted and bribed whomever

27

he needed with his money. The kind of compliance he had witnessed from his doorway was gained through bravery. Bravery fuelled, not by arrogance or selfishness, but by need or greed. Teenagers became leaders or followers and the followers were those not brave enough to face adversity against the odds. The mere thought or threat that their opponent would go one step further, take slightly more risks, was often enough to secure a person gang leadership status. Rarely did Zak witness actual gang violence. He was sure it went on, but didn't care to venture down the alleyways where it did.

In essence, Zak's boarding school years were a broken roller coaster ride towards adulthood. One wheel on the truck appeared to be working fine; sturdy through a good upbringing, and reliably kept on the track by the fear of letting the family, and particularly his father, down. This was the wheel that encouraged him to be resolutely good mannered, respectful, wholesome even. This was the wheel that optimistically pushed him into the classrooms for study and told him which subjects or activities would benefit him most. It was the part of him that said, '*Zachariah, be the best that you can be and earn the respect of your peers*'.

Cricket was a real favourite for boarding school. There seemed to be a great contention between his school and another in a town not ten miles from theirs. Tutors seemed particularly interested in students that showed a talent for the sport. The subject of the competitiveness between rival schools often arose during lessons as examples for mathematics, geography, science and even history. As politically desirable as this sport was, it was not the one that Zak chose. He had listened instead to a far bolder wheel on his cart that told him that there was far more pleasure to be had elsewhere.

The other wheel of Zak's emotional roller cart, seemingly

over-greased by a desire to experiment, be wild and push the system, looked destined to throw him crashing to the ground. Like an unseen impish devil on his shoulder, this wheel told Zak that life didn't get better than this. Life is one big party and his money and growing notoriety made him the star guest. This was the wheel that told him: '*Forget what the world wants you to do, and do what the hell you like. You have the money, so why do you need to chase acceptance from others? You have no need to be the cleverest person in the form because you have enough money to simply employ the cleverest people when you need their help. All YOU need, Zak, is the ability (and wealth) to see when you need help and not be afraid to take it when offered. Why spend hours in boredom, studying, when you will ALWAYS be rich? Intelligence and academic success are NOT the be all and end all in life.*' There were many occasions Zak was a hairsbreadth from being caught listening to this wheel. This was the one that said it was ok to drink and smoke the odd cigarette.

As Zak grew older he often fondly reminisced to himself the time when Jimmy introduced them to Pot. They met near Hampton Block where there was an old bench. Hampton Block had once been used to house large school equipment, and so was really little more than two large, partly run-down buildings joined by a walkway. The bench at Hampton was a popular place for grabbing a crafty fag because it sat in a slight dip in the grounds, and was out of sight.

"Well, come on then!" said H.

Jimmy grinned and reached into his blazer pocket and triumphantly, like a magician with a rabbit, pulled out a rolled cigarette.

"Whoa!!" bellowed Seb. "Cool beyond!"

Jimmy's face brimmed.

"Def! You got a match? Come on, let's get it lit!" said H.

29

Jimmy reached his other hand into his pocket and pulled out a purple plastic lighter. He put the cigarette to his mouth and used both hands to shield the wind. The four Rivals gathered round closely. Zak's excitement was intense as he watched the yellow flame catch on the end of the cigarette and turn the thin Riz paper and tobacco to an orange glow. Jimmy breathed in eagerly. Taking the cigarette from his lips, he continued to breathe in deeply. Zak knew he could never do that without an embarrassing bout of coughing. The roll up was passed round them in turn. Zak's cigarette experience was minimal but he was determined to experiment, his defective roller coaster wheel wasn't taking no for an answer.

It didn't taste much like the cigarettes he'd had before; it had a strange smell and tasted sharper. Zak breathed in as much as he dared and taking the cigarette away from his mouth, held his breath. He held his breath until the cigarette was in H's hands. By the time Seb had hold of it Zak's head was swimming. He let the smoke out and stifled a sensation to cough. Jimmy, by now was on seconds, and Zak knew it'd be his turn again in a moment. Without recovering from the first draw, he pursed his lips again and took another drag. Seb was grinning at him. His stocky, plumpish face and wide smile reminded Zak of the Cheshire Cat from Alice in Wonderland. His draw was cut short by a laugh that just refused to stay down. Zak began coughing and passed it on to H again. Jimmy was also laughing by now as H took a huge draw on the spliff. H was just passing it to Seb when Zak heard someone coming, and spun round to see Sparrow, the Technical Design lecturer, coming.

"Mmm!!" Zak turned round and looked wildly at Seb. Seb flicked the cigarette behind his back as far as he could, where it landed in some dry brush.

"What's going on here?" asked Sparrow.

"Nothing, Sir!" replied Zak.

Zak knew that cigarettes were seriously frowned upon, dope would be unforgivable.

"No, nothing, Sir!" repeated Seb.

Zak turned to look at his friend as he spoke, but his eyes were drawn first to H, who had turned a very pale version of his former self.

"Smoking?" asked Sparrow.

"No Sir, not at all, we were just talking."

"Talking, eh? Let's look in your pockets."

Knowing he had nothing to declare, Zak started first. Jimmy had apparently dropped the old lighter on the floor while Sparrow was checking H's pockets. He had by now turned a very strange shade of green and looked like he was about to throw up. Standing it into the mud, Jimmy was safe. He needn't have bothered though as before Sparrow had a chance to check his pockets, Seb had drawn Sparrow's attention to the now obvious start of a fire in the brush. They all received a most serious of warnings about their conduct for that incident. Seb always said that a bollocking never hurt anyone.

This more energetic side of Zak's personality certainly won the battle of wills, and so it was this side that he listened to when picking pastime activities. This wheel won over, and pushed him into gymnastics and weight training. Both very individual disciplines and gymnastics was particularly advantageous when one wanted to get to know female gymnasts better! Zak loved the idea of being able to do a back-flip on the floor programme or be able to hold himself in the infamous crucifix position on the rings. This also meant that events and competitions were often held outside the confines of the school and ALWAYS with a lot of female presence.

Gymnastics competitions were a great opportunity for Zak

to show off his physique. From the moment the auditorium or hall audience marched them in, Zak felt like the bees knees. As he became better he started to get the odd medal, and then he positively brimmed with pride. His mother would always be there cheering him on, and willing him to succeed.

It was through these competitions that Zak met Sophie. A student of Tile Hill School for Girls, Sophie caught Zak's attention simply by the way she asked for the time. Zak was simply resting until his floor routine.

"Have you got the time?" asked a dark haired girl next to him.

"Er… I can find out," replied Zak. What a stupid question, Zak thought to himself. Who on earth would be wearing a watch at a gymnastics competition? No competitor in his right mind would wear a … Her laughing interrupted his thoughts.

"You don't get it, do you?" she asked, smiling. "You're supposed to say, have you got the energy? Then I say, why, have you got the place, you would ask position, and so it goes on until one of us runs out of things. We see who wins!"

Zak's realisation of her antics had him smiling with her. After introductions were made, Zak and Sophie struck up a very friendly conversation that would be repeated every future time they met. Gymnastics competitions were organised about every two months, and each time they met, Zak and Sophie would always start off their hello's with this strange game. A good deal of waiting around is done at gymnastic meetings and they spent this time chatting, laughing and joking around. On the fourth time of meeting, neither wanted to concede defeat.

"Hello, Zak, do you have the time?" Sophie smiled at him.

"Do you have the place?" he replied.

"I would if you had the energy!"

"But do you have the position?" Zak smiled.

"Do you have the desire?"

"Do you have the nerve?"

"Yes! Do you?" Sophie exclaimed, with a beaming smile across her gorgeous face.

"Of course!" Zak replied, no, wanting to give in.

"Come on then! ... or are you chicken?" Sophie glared at Zak mischievously, her emerald green eyes glistening.

"Me? NO!"

"OK, come on then!" Sophie began walking away. As she did so she looked back over her shoulder, and looked at Zak again to see if he was following. Zak looked around, making sure no one had overheard their conversation nor realised where he was about to go. Everybody else seemed preoccupied with their own preparations. Zak followed.

Sophie led him out of the main hall and along a series of corridors that led to an equipment storeroom. Once inside, Sophie immediately began pulling a large blue exercise mat off a pile and onto the floor. What followed was to become a regular event at future meets. Zak's last hurdle from boyhood innocence into young adolescent manhood had finally been conquered.

The stolen moments with Sophie fuelled a yearning to be attractive and desired; consequently, Zak took pride in his physique. Alcohol and smoking were purely party pieces to help him mix in with the crowd he'd learn to relax with. This hormone-driven distraction in full working order, Zak managed to keep the rest of his roller coaster cart generally on track, and graduated for university. He had avoided the drugs that were available and, ironically for him, had found their way into the hands of the prim and proper lot that had taken up cricket. University life slowly saw the end to Zak's desire to be a better gymnast and although a short-lived experience, became the end of a chapter of many parts of Zak's life.

Learning and Life

Here's one I made earlier.

Christopher Trace

1986, and the Warwick Business School, offered many attractions. One might suspect these to be the worldwide reputation for providing very good teaching; but in Zak's case it was a superb coach, and better than average facilities for gymnastics. The numerous bars, women and good nightlife were purely a coincidental, additional attraction. Zak's additional attraction was a somewhat friendly girl called Becky. Zak never really took Becky too seriously however, as Becky wasn't always choosey who she was friendly with. Other times, Zak would often find himself 'chilling' with other students in the Airport lounge, sat propped up against the wall talking to a girl, or talking to another lad about the girls on view. It was a cattle market and Zak's physique and good looks made him a prize bull. His notoriety as being a multimillionaire's son also helped.

Barely into university life, and within his first year, Zak's education came to an abrupt halt. Zachariah would later often recount the laughing and joking of students at the appearance of Simon, the family's smartly dressed butler. The executors had sent Simon as he was considered the closest person emotionally to Zak at the time. As Simon stood in the small corridor in

34

Radcliffe waiting for Zak, students had sniggered childishly and made fun at his formality. Zak's friends, whose names and faces were now merely a blur in his mind, had been walking with him back along the corridor to his room.

"Bloody hell, Zak, got yourself some private tuition?"

"Ha ha," replied Zak, sarcastically.

"No, it's Simon, he looks after the house."

"Holy shit, you got a butler?"

"Yeah, hey look, if he's here, I'd better go and see what's up, I'll see you later, ok?"

"Don't forget to ask him to sort out your room in the dorm before he goes back then!" Zak smiled as he walked away and towards Simon.

"Hello Simon! What are you doing here?"

"Good afternoon, Master Sharpe. Could we find a private place to talk?"

"Sure, we can use my room." Zak led the way inside his small study room.

"What's up?"

"Take a seat, Master Sharpe I have some important but disturbing news."

Zak looked Simon in the eyes. As he did so, the seriousness of his demeanour dawned on Zak and frightened him.

"What's the matter?" Zak asked.

Simon had rehearsed this statement for the past two hours and however he had planned it to sound, the plan had gone out of the window.

"I am afraid I am the bearer of terrible news. I don't think there is an easy way to explain this but I would like you to prepare for some shocking news. Master Sharpe. Zak. Your parent's plane was involved in an accident on its return from Japan. It seems that a storm forced the plane to crash land. Zak, I

35

am afraid there were no survivors." Simon looked at Zak earnestly, trying to decipher what was going on in the young man's mind. Zak's eyes were wide as he blankly tried to comprehend what Simon had told him.

"Zak, I am truly very sorry."

Zak's heart fainted at these words, such was the enormity of the situation.

"What…. How? I don't understand?" Zak's mind busily tried to cope with the many questions it had and the all, consuming, competing emotion of despair.

The weeks that followed remain a hazy memory; Simon first telling him of the news and urging him to pack up some essentials so that arrangements could be made. With solicitors, barristers, directors of the family businesses, all but Mike Underhill offering seemingly cold expressions of sorrow, Zak never did return to university. Seemingly endless meetings as people around him tried to offer advice on the best course of action. The funeral was a completely depressing affair with Zak suddenly realising how alone in the world he was. Even through his grief, Zak had other directors urging him to become involved in business meetings. He had the best legal and organisational brains around him and yet felt alone and helpless. If it weren't for Mike, life would've been so much harder. Zak's father had chosen Mike some years earlier. Mike was a true self-made high flyer. The sort of man who could make millions on his own if he only had the courage and self-confidence to try. Zak had been sickeningly worried that he would have to pick up where his father had left off and did not have a clue what this might entail. He was relieved to find that Mike handled most issues brilliantly and could easily see why his father had made him Group Managing Director. Unbeknown to Zak, Mike had a lot of sympathy for him. Mike could empathise with the comparative and oddly hard life that Zak, regardless of the family wealth, had had to learn to live with. Zak found Mike to be very trustworthy and easy to talk to. As the wave of meetings subsided, Zak was advised that he should take a break, but with wealth comes depressive loneliness, as friends made at university couldn't afford to jeopardise their education and go with him. Self-consolation would be found in a bottle.

***

The morning sun was out now and Zachariah sat in his doorway pondering the reasons his father chose Mike Underhill. The possibility that Mike was the sort of son his father never had was quite a real consideration. Eloquent. Attractive. Intelligent. Had it not been for the ability the man had of putting you at ease and gaining both his trust and confidence, Zak might have found Mike to be a threat. Zak wondered whether Mike had actually achieved everything Zak hadn't. Sure he didn't have the wealth that Zak had enjoyed, but he had been a lot more successful finding a loving and devoted wife who had given him two of the most gorgeous looking children Zak had ever seen. Zak had been less than successful at this and, rather than uncomfortably ponder on his own inadequacies too long, he drifted into thinking about the effect time has on human memories. He clearly remembered his initial holiday following the death of his parents. It was the first in many that he would take. He had decided to relax on the French Riviera.

Monte Carlo offered many discoveries, a highly cultured place with its many places of interest. Zak had been there before with his parents to mingle with business associates and to watch the Grand Prix. The Hotel de Paris was beckoning, its extravagant and luxurious surroundings were an ideal point from

37

which he could take in the cultures and begin to enjoy this Monegasque lifestyle. He had initially decided to spend a quiet few weeks looking around the museums or relaxing by the pool. What occurred to Zak many years later in his doorway was that this was the vacation that would unhinge the last nut that held the bolt of sensibility onto his roller coaster cart. A stay in the nicest of hotels in the world with its sumptuous gastronomy quickly bored him. He tried relaxing by the pool but with no one of his age group to talk to, he quickly tired of this. Renowned for its restaurants and museums, Monte Carlo offered much, but delivered little to a twenty-year-old lonesome tourist. Mind you, tourist would probably be the wrong word for Zak's state of mind at that point in his life. He was more like an explorer searching for a purpose in life and for all its glory and splendour, this was no place for a restless soul. So out of a mediocre attempt at entertainment, the rare gambler decided to chance his luck at the casinos. What transpired was less to do with gambling and more to do with finding a playmate.

***

Stefan was at the roulette table and clearly had the wealth and inclination to gamble hard. Zak found that he too was a person looking for more than just roulette. From a similarly wealthy background, Stefan was the youngest son of a German family who owned a company that made industrial compressors. They quickly got on well due to a fine twist of fate that saw them both win from the 19. Stefan decided to quit whilst he was ahead, and Zak was delighted to accept Stefan's invitation to a party. This arrangement became the blueprint for the next two weeks. It would always remain in Zak's memory as a time of life that was full of fun, excitement and joyous, seemingly endless episodes of delight. Had he ever written a biography, Zak would reflect this time to be a stage of his life never to be missed.

The majority of holidays he took after that contained only snippets of excitement worthy for his brain to recall. However, desperate to re-live the experience, the next few years, his social scene altered completely, formal social gatherings slowly gave way to alternative opportunities to meet younger members of the social elite. Opportunity, lifestyle and inexhaustible money meant endless exclusive parties; Zak revelled in the attention that came his way. His social calendar grew and drew him into a world of drink, soft drugs and women; all attractive and eager to feed his obsessive desires for pleasure. With this partying came media interest and public notoriety. Zak began to notice and accept this interest and even build professional friendships with the reporters and photographers. He might even hint as to where he might be, to save them the often laborious and tedious task of following Zak's every move. Zak meanwhile developed a tabloid reputation for philandering and outrageous actions. Should he arrive at a party with a woman, seldom was it with the same as the previous week. Should Zak arrive alone, rarely did he leave without being drunk and with a woman or women on each arm.

Zak eagerly fed the media interest and revelled in the scandals. Stories continued to flow in and as the press soon realised, Zak Sharpe was hot gossip. Rarely did a week pass by without his name or photograph appearing in the gutter press about his behaviour and womanising. A photograph appeared in the press, after Zak was seen leaving a high-class nightclub with two models and taking them to his yacht in the port.

'Two ladies join millionaire, Zak Sharpe, for a night of Passion', much to Zak's enjoyment, hit the headlines the following day. The Hercule Harbour often held Zak's yacht and he had invited two stunning girls back to it for a 'nightcap'. The press had witnessed this and had made great length on his assumed antics. As was often the case, rarely did two ladies act like the stars of porn films and sometimes jealousy even stopped proceedings altogether; but to Zak's insatiable desire for attention, these were small risks. 'Two ride the SS Sharpe', were sometimes the headlines, or 'Happy Hippie Zak', referred to his interest in soft drugs and 'Shag Sharpe', became a tabloid play on his name. Undeterred, Zak continued to ignore the real effect of the stories and instead took pleasure in feeding the media with increasingly outrageous mannerisms.

Known for his millions, his party lifestyle and endless womanizing, Zak had attained playboy status, and he loved it. Women followed him to venues and bribed whoever to ensure that they could meet him. Their desperation to grab his attention often amazed him and they appeared to revel in the challenge to bed him. He was only too delighted to oblige and discovered how much of an aphrodisiac money and youth were for nubile, ardent, attractive females. Many of these simply wanted to be the next girl in the tabloid press. Here they would bare all and earn money from their story of lust and passion. Zak didn't mind, why should he? He'd taken the flower long before the press got a hand to it. Zak was now a famous multi millionaire playboy.

Today's the Day

The tree of liberty must be refreshed from time to time.

Thomas Jefferson – 1787

Turning left, Zachariah began his journey down Empire Boulevard and along the path towards Washington Avenue. The houses here were tall, three or more storey apartment blocks with maybe half a dozen steps to the front door. Zachariah eased his legs into action after what felt like premature aging had set in; his legs ached, he felt a lot older than his 36 years allowed and remembered how he used to enjoy sports at school. He had taken a great deal of pride in being able to excel at most sports whilst not having to train at all. "Bloody legs," he murmured to himself. His morning cough was back. He'd picked it up some months back and it did not seem to want to go away. His head was thick and groggy, still reeling from his nightcap the evening before. Whilst he walked he tried lifting his heels to kick his backside. He thought it might alleviate the ache, but it didn't work. His futile efforts now only received mild attention from his seemingly arthritic knees. He continued to walk past the apartment blocks and up to the junction with Washington Avenue. He decided to breathe deeply and force some life into his lungs and body, hoping the dull sensation of uselessness would leave him feeling refreshed and ready to face the day. It

41

forced him to cough again and Zachariah decided that time would heal and not to force a speedier recovery.

The constant battle against people's preconceived ideas had worn him down, but he was determined he wasn't giving up on his fight. He ambled across the junction and saw the park further ahead. In a place like New York, the trees, grass and wildlife in Prospect Park were a rarity, and one that gave him comfort. For a man who grew up in leafy Leicestershire, New York was definitely a concrete kick in the face. A large GMC Yukon barked its horn at him in a futile attempt to make him walk across the road quicker. In a fashion Winston Churchill would have been proud of, Zachariah defiantly stuck his fingers up and carried on at his own pace. 'What is it with this God forsaken place anyway that makes people want to build roads this wide?' he thought.

Mind Games

Is this the real life, is this just fantasy
Caught in a landslide, no escape from reality.

Freddie Mercury

From 1991 to 1993 things changed. Slowly but surely invitations to some events began to wane, and Zak found that invitations to the better social gatherings began to elude him. Sensationalism and high publicity were fine for newly-opened café bars in London's West End and his money guaranteed him entrance to the nightclubs; but increasingly the invitations to join exclusive private clubs were being offered to equally crowd-pulling alternatives. The worm was turning and Zak started to develop a slightly irritated sensation whenever he saw an assemblage of reporters and journalists. Their personifications altered from an admiring, mildly welcome assembly of comrades of opinion to a troop of secretive, malevolent beings whose single-minded function was to beget his demise and humiliation. They seemed to welcome him out of his apartment in London every morning like a lavatory stench that would follow him wherever he went.

Once too often they were there and Zak gradually developed an annoyance with it. But rather than leave him alone they seemed to feed upon his frustration.

"Hey Zak! How's it going, son?" asked the plump reporter,

with his photographer.

"How's what going?" replied Zak

"Well, last week you were out with a mystery woman. I did some sort of research and I came up with a name of Natalie Wilson, daughter of Lord Wilson. How is it going?"

Zak pondered the situation as he continued to walk towards his car. Natalie had become infused with shame that their picture should appear on both the front page, and a number of photographs, not all very complimentary, on page 3 of a cheap tabloid. Natalie had been compared to a number of conquests, and her long lasting suitability questioned. She had decided to not endure any more comparisons and didn't need to be judged in such a public way. She had told Zak it wouldn't work with them… proving the tabloids right.

"Look, it was just a date! It was just two friends having a night out," Zak replied.

"Yeah… we know all about how friendly you CAN get… but did it?" asked the reporter, laughing

Zak's patience held no more.

"Look, what the fuck has it got to do with you? Just fuck off."

The reporter moved closer and right in Zak's way.

"Come on Zak! What's the matter? Too much beer? Shit in bed, were ya? Come on! Why did she dump you?"

Zak's patience snapped. Pushing the reporter out of the way, he headed for his car.

"Stop being such a twat, Tom. Fuck off. I'll let you know another time."

The reporter repositioned himself between Zak and his Bentley.

"How did she dump you? In the morning? Or half way through your shag?" asked the reporter, smiling his sickly, smug

44

grin again. Zak's emotions overtook him, and he harshly pushed the reporter out of the way. Flashes from more than one camera clicked and light exploded in the vicinity. The following day's headlines, and even the weekly tabloids, noted Zak's brutal handling of the media and blamed poor sexual performance for the outburst.

Their initial appearance had been a welcome if not unorthodox start to his day, but as resentment grew about the stories they wrote, both their welcome and appearance changed. They began to develop a personality more akin to devilish gnomes than friendly journalists. Zak began dreaming about them, and had twisted nightmares about how they were affecting his life. His one recurring dream was where he was being asked to open something or other, and as he began to offer his now well-rehearsed opening speech to the audience, he would notice a pretty dark-haired woman smiling at him. She had fantastically mysterious eyes that smiled at him. As he started his speech he would smile back and only then would notice that she was not just smiling but actually beaming at him. The man stood next to her he recognised from his driveway as one of the tabloid reporters. He was laughing in her ear, and as Zak looked across the room to compose himself, his voice was fading and he'd noticed that all of the people were smiling and laughing. But they weren't just laughing with him. How could they? He'd hardly started. They were laughing AT him. Zak would look around the room more and notice familiar past photographs of his drunken and shameless nights out. Large black and white or sepia photographs all around the walls. The crowd would by now be in fits of laughter, pointing at him as he stood there alone. Their laughs getting louder and louder and more callous by the moment. Fearful of what he might see, but unable to stop himself, his gaze would be drawn back to the woman with the

45

alluring eyes. She was still listening to the tabloid reporter in her ear and laughing out loud now. The dream had often ended there, but occasionally had ended suddenly, when the reporter would suddenly flick out his tongue into the ear of the woman and glare at Zak with bright green eyes, waking Zak suddenly.

With these twisted nightmares about the press, Zak began to undertake a little bit of investigation. Zak started buying books to help him interpret his dreams, but most told him of poor performance in love. Not the answer Zak was looking for. His pleas for privacy fell on deaf ears and Zak decided enough was enough and he would socialise for solace elsewhere. England was suddenly far too small for him, the rest of the world was waiting.

From this point followed three years of travelling, partying and learning what the world had to offer but seldom being able to fully enjoy it. Zak wanted a relationship, a family, and these were both so very elusive to him. Too many women knew of him and his reputation and decided to give him a wide berth. His reputation followed him, and so did the entourage of paparazzi, media and gossip column photographers. Zak had matured and grown out of his devil-may-care attitude. The media however, didn't.

At first he could cope, he just had to look good and keep up his appearance. Zak had always loved keeping fit and working his biceps into some sort of fashionably masculine shape. In an effort to stay desirable he began plucking, then dying out the premature greyness of his sideburns. However, their presence was an ever-greater reminder that his life-clock was ticking. Their slow but persistent advance up each side of his head made Zak ever more aware of this. Huge mountains were made out of minor nothings in his life, and these began to take their toll.

Pressure was also mounting at work. As much as Zak

owned the company, its directors were always, and now increasingly, concerned about his media association and its effect on share price. This culminated in an occasion when Mike had taken him aside and as tactfully as possible had told Zak about the effect his headline chasing was having on the company. Apparently the board of directors, of which by now Zak only knew four by name, had voiced concerns that Zak was not exactly gaining the company a good reputation. 'Not exactly Richard Branson', was the comment. Mike had told Zak that in his opinion, any advertising that didn't damage particular brands was good advertising. Still, he had bravely asked Zak if he could at least bear this in mind and keep a slightly lower profile. Zak tried to explain that this would be futile, as reporters earned far too much money by photographing Zak to simply stop following him. But Zak couldn't help but agree with the one man for whom he had a lot of respect in the company, and secretly wished for it himself.

Zak had tried taking columnists to court to force them into printing the truth, but found this to be pointless and foolhardy. Magazine and newspaper sales outstripped the amount of damages that he would be chasing by six or ten to one. The figures just didn't add up. Having fun was starting to be not much fun at all.

Realising that life was more than just one long party, Zak began the more sober task of looking for a partner who would give him a chance. Zak quickly learned that most 'potential suitors', as his father would have called them, fell into three categories. There were 'The Sex Pests' – playboy hunters who just wanted sex with someone, indeed anyone with a high profile reputation on which they could build a career. 'The Money Grabbers' were drawn to him for his wealth and the gifts and holidays he could buy. Finally there were 'The Fame Dames'.

These just wanted the media attention gained by his high profile media image to boost their own fame. This happened four times in a row, and Zak not only became very wary of women, but also began to despise the tabloid media and all it stood for.

Stories of their night of passion would be spread across the front pages like some descriptive sequel to a soft porn film. The real damage to Zak's ego occurred when a woman called Sheena rated him quite poorly. Not only did she do that, but she also spilled the beans on the lengths Zak went to so that he kept his good looks. His embarrassment of that hurt a lot and changed his relationship with both the media and women forever. He had tried to look at the situation objectively and figure that Sheena would have been paid handsomely for telling and showing the readers exactly what he'd had. But when even Mike had dared to joke with him about her version of his performance, the wariness and hurt stuck.

When Zak had started university, his mother had said to him to look after women and not play around with them like some toy.

"Zak, now you listen to me," she had said, in that richly soft Irish accent of hers.

"Good women are like a Linehan. Treat the sweet well, savour it, taste its flavour and it'll last you a whole long time. Play around with it and its liable to fall outa your mouth and onto the carpet below. From that moment on, Zak, you can only look at it from a distance, remember the pleasure it brought yea, but never taste it again." Zak had smiled mischievously back at her "Yes, but there's more than one sweet in the sweet shop!" "Ay, so there is son, so there is… you just make sure you hold onto a good one… or it might be that when you go back for more, the best ones are gone. And no amount of money will get you those sweets back. So don't be spitting too many out, and

48

don't go trying to taste two at the same time! That's a recipe where you don't enjoy the flavour of either. No son, I'll tell y'now, pick a nice sweet that's gonna last. None of these fancy ones that are all packaging, but one you like and that's going to stay with you. Otherwise you'll end up with chewing gum!" Zak's mother smiled at his bewildered look. "Eh?"

"Fresh and exciting, long lasting even… but ultimately tasteless."

It would not occur to Zak until much later in life that his mother's analogy was right. The women Zak desired now had to have wealth of their own. This would remove the Money Grabbers. But as Zak looked into the shop, wealthy women in there were either Army & Navy or Lemonade Fizzballs, neither of which appealed. The Jargonelle Pears simply wanted to be as far from him as possible. Once again in his life, and by Zak's own actions this time, Zak was lonely and bitterly so. With no immediate family, women who only wanted him for his wealth or fame, he was fast becoming a person the world seemed to love to pick on, use or abuse.

***

Zachariah walked down across Washington Avenue towards Prospect Park. He was considering his chequered past when his eye was drawn to the billboard above the corner of the Italian restaurant. It advertised a new film showing. Zachariah smiled to himself. The poster displayed a recently released film. *Marks out of Ten* was a recently released romantic comedy about three thirty-something women. The Sheena revelation came back to his mind as he walked. That woman did nothing to make a young playboy feel good about himself he thought.

He looked up again at the billboard, and as he did so was

surprised to recognise the woman on the right hand side of the poster. Underneath her photograph was the name, Suzie Gibbs. Zak recalled hearing that she had married a film producer a number of years earlier. Suzie Gibbs was her stage name. Zak had known her before the big screen, when she was plain old Suzanne Chambers. Suzanne had been a rapidly rising starlet struggling to get onto the 'B' list in America. She was one of the many women, before his introduction, to decide that he was just too immature to form a relationship with. Zak had met her at a film premiere. Not hers, that was sure, she was not a big star back then. They had been introduced, talked, laughed and he had managed to charm his way into an all-too-brief relationship with her.

While Zachariah contemplated and considered briefly whether she was indeed a boiled sweet or chewing gum, he remembered her very attractive body, soft hair and magnetising eyes. He had got to know her just long enough to appreciate her before the tabloids caught them on camera. While her picture in the newspapers as, 'Zak's latest conquest' was bearable, Zak's photograph coming out of a Los Angeles nightclub with another woman a week later was not. Zak tried in vain to tell her nothing went on and had blamed the sensationalist media. A girl was indeed on his arm for all of thirty seconds, a media plant no doubt. Photographs had been taken and published to great effect. The press had once again sold many more copies.

His explanation fell on deaf ears and Suzanne decided to wash her hair and herself of him, permanently. She flew to Los Angeles and very publicly had gone to the same nightclub to prove whatever he could do, she could better. This, to Zak, was an irony of biblical proportions. Zak knew she craved press attention and had used it to not only rid herself of him, but also to further her own career. Zak found himself missing her dreadfully. He remembered wandering around his flat for days with a yearning in his stomach that put him off doing anything. For the first of what was to be many times he passionately found himself wanting a soul mate and someone with whom he could settle with. Suzanne was definitely high on his most wanted list, in hindsight a definite boiled sweet. He had tried to call her to play down the tabloid pressure, telling her that it would soon die down. If she would only stay with him long enough for them to realise that she was not a new conquest then they could be together, happily loving each other's company. But it was not to be. Suzanne either rebuffed his calls or found other more pressing opportunities. "You know how important my career is to me, Zak," she'd said. "I just can't meet you, I have to be there, if I don't show, I'll never get another chance like this again," and like that she was gone. Out of his life. The reporters didn't know this of course and had not cared either way. They'd got their story; they'd got his picture, his life, his very soul laid out for public scrutiny. Another chance foiled.

1992

Now H^eaven knows anything goes.

Cole Porter – 1934

1992 was a year that would change the life of one Norwegian woman by the name of Katarina Hansen. Her long-time violent drug dealer of a lover was to find the time away from his wife to take her on a boat trip to Italy. He had some work to do there anyway and had managed to at last find the time she demanded from him, to include her in his life once in a while. Not that she could ever demand anything from him, but she could at least moan a little. Elian was certainly the master of the relationship, through his power and money. He had married into one of Cuba's larger families, that dealt in drugs of all persuasions to many parts of the world. Locally, his family was treated with the respect normally reserved for gods.

The trip started pleasantly enough, Katarina stayed in the salon or galley, rarely venturing out on deck without sun block. Not far into the journey, and heading towards Bermuda, Elian decided to make the most of his new-found time with his sex mate. He had been attracted to Katarina because of her fair skin and blonde hair. Her slender hips and small bum were also in stark contrast to the dark-skinned big-bottomed girls of his native country… and boy, could she fuck. Elian could live out his wildest fantasies, and knew full well that she had little to complain about. He provided the apartment, the driver, the money; all she had to provide was pleasure for him.

One of the fantasies that Elian had developed between them was domination. He found distinct gratification from treating Kat like a whore, making her pleasure him in whatever fashion he wanted, and even beating her if the height of his pleasure didn't match his expectation. Now well on their way, and with the yacht on autopilot, he sauntered downstairs. Kat was busying herself in the galley. She turned to look at him, and immediately recognised the look on his face.

"Get me a drink," Elian barked, with a sly grin on his face.

Katarina made him his favourite and took it to him as he sat on the sofa. He tasted it.

"This isn't very cold!"

"It's got ice in it," she replied.

"No, I am sorry, this is not good enough. For this, I will have to ask you to distract me until it is cold enough to drink," replied Elian, smiling, and rubbing his crotch. Katarina had played this role and had these conversations many times before. Faking a smile, she dropped to her knees in front of him

"Will this do?" she asked, as she undid first the buckle then the button of his brown denim shorts.

"I don't know; what did you have in mind?"

Katarina knew exactly what he had in mind, as she slowly undid his zip, and played along with his thinly disguised demand for fellatio. Elian leaned back in the mulberry leather settee as Katarina lowered her head. He hardened, as she worked her lips and tongue on him, and after a short time grabbed her hair, pulling her off him.

"Sorry, that's just not good enough! I think I want a little more from you!" he said, with a cruel grin on his face. "Get up!"

Had Elian not been in such a menacing mood, his penguinesque walk, with shorts and Y fronts around his ankles, and erection, would have been comical. As it was, Katarina was pushed over to the dining table and forced over it. Lifting up her light blue chiffon dress he exposed her lily-white bum cheeks. Elian held her down with one arm while he ripped at her G-string with the other. As her entered her, his hands grasped at her hair, pulling it tightly as though it were a reign for him to hold. Her head in pain, Katarina hoped it would end soon so that she could go back to enjoying the trip. But she was not in luck. Elian continued, and moved his hands around her neck. Hot, sweaty palms clung to her, tightening as they scrambled for grip. She began to feel herself struggle for breath, and in view of his current rhythm he was not yet near to coming. Katarina started to panic and tried to force his fingers off. Terror struck her like a bolt of electricity as he seemingly derived pleasure from her now frantic efforts to let her breathe. His thick, strong hands held fast and tightened ever more.

Rough sex had often played a part in their love making, but never to this extent, and Katarina now feared for her life. Unable to speak or even moan, she swung pointlessly behind herself trying to hit him. She stamped her foot down hard on his. Elian yelped and jumped back in shock. A look of horror spread across his face, but was soon replaced with anger. How dare she, he thought.

"You fuckin' bitch!" he spat at her, angrily.

Before Katarina could utter a word Elian punched her in the face. The force swung her back round to face the table and once again she could feel a hand grab her hair, and another, her arm, and force her face against the mahogany tabletop. Elian held her there while his foot dug itself between her legs and forced them wide apart. Hoping he would just hold onto her hair, Katarina lay there waiting. Elian let go of her arm and spat on his hand, then rubbed the spittle between her legs. He spat again and Katarina supposed, applied it to his erection.

Nothing prepared Katarina for what happened next.

"I'll teach you, ya BITCH!" Elian shouted, and forced his member deep into her anus. Pain seared through her body and she screamed out, as tears forced themselves out of her eyes. Elian had never done this before and even though he had been rough, he had always done it playfully. This was an angry man, determined to rape her. Elian let go of her arm and grabbed her neck once again. The hands she had often held and loved were now cruel, and callously around her neck. As Elian drove deep into her, he began grunting like an enraged bull, and biting her neck like a wild dog. His hot panting in her ear and the smell of the garlic from lunch they'd shared, billowed towards her nostrils.

"GET OFF YOU BASTARD!!" she screamed... but the man was not for listening. Tears streamed down her cheeks, and as the agony tore through Katarina's body, she could feel the gap through which she could breathe getting smaller as every second passed. Desperate, she looked ahead of her and saw an ornament of a brass dolphin. Grabbing it with her right hand, she swung it as hard as she could over her shoulder. It didn't travel as far as she had thought it would, but instead came to an abrupt halt against Elian's head. The thud stopped the bull in its tracks and instead of pounding into her, Elian slumped on her, and his blood began to trickle over her shoulder and onto the tabletop.

Dropping the brass ornament, Katarina pushed back hard against the table, and the large man fell away from her onto the floor. Turning round, she kicked him several more times in the head, stomach and groin. Exhausted, her heart in her adrenalin-fuelled body thumped hard against its chest cavity. She stopped,

55

then stood there panting and unaware of the faint trickle of crimson blood that had started down the inside of her right thigh towards the floor. She looked down as her Cuban sugar Daddy lay helpless in front of her. Katarina kicked him again.

"Jeg hater De, De fucking bastard!" As she did, Katarina felt a warm trickle down her calf. Elian had made her bleed. Rage quickly turned to fear however as Katarina realised the consequences of her actions. What to do?

She couldn't radio for help, as undoubtedly, questions would be asked about why she was there. Katarina thought for a moment and decided her life was almost certainly over when he did come round. She makes her choices.

The Introducer

*The secret of gathering in the greatest fruitfulness
and the greatest enjoyment from existence
is living dangerously!*

FW Nietzsche

With the billboard behind him, Zachariah continued to shuffle slowly to the park entrance and down the steps towards the grassed area. As soon as he could he stepped onto the grass, it still held the morning dew and it cooled and awakened his feet. He stopped and looked down at them, and saw a couple of toes poking through the tops of his left shoe. The ragged, serrated slit of a cut on the other that told him it would not be long before his big toe nail on his right foot made its debut through the roof of its imprisonment. He wiggled his toes and could just make out his nail underneath. Walking on he came to the pond in the centre of the park and found his usual bench reliably waiting for him. He sat down at it and looked out across the calm water in the pond towards the trees the other side.

Just over to his right was a young girl of about twelve; she walked up and began feeding the ducks at the poolside. Zachariah wondered if she should be in school, she didn't look the truant type; her hair was tied neatly behind her in a ponytail and shone in the developing morning sun. She delighted in the fact that the ducks were splashing around her feet vying for attention and more bread. She laughed, and looked towards her mother who was sat further around the poolside. Truants certainly didn't feed ducks, nor wear feminine dresses like the one this girl wore. Brooklyn was far from being the kind of neighbourhood where femininity prospered, an often harsh and brutal area of New York it could certainly show a person the hard side of life. The girl seemed oblivious to hardship around her. Turning towards him, he noticed that she had Downs Syndrome; her widened face and slightly slanting eyes told of her mental condition, and Zachariah realised her mind would be less critical of the environment around her. Zachariah thought over the poster he'd seen earlier of Suzanne, a very attractive thirty-something with similarly blonde hair to the girl now before him. But for the grace of God go I, he thought. His mind meandered through the memories he had of Suzanne and somehow arrived at the day of, The Introducer.

***

Zachariah's memory of names never was very good, in the past drugs, and more recently alcohol had seemingly not improved things. He couldn't even recall how he'd come to meet this man. Who was it now? How did he manage to give this man an audience even? It would return to him, he was sure, but for now, all his mind would concentrate on was the man himself.

The Introducer. No name, just that an appointment had been made to meet someone who could help him. Yes, that was it. Help. He had mentioned to someone that the media pressure was becoming too much to bear and that he needed a break from it all. The next thing, he was going to a hotel to meet an introducer. No, not an introducer, 'The Introducer' a one-time and very confidential meeting about those issues that troubled him.

Thursday 25th February 1993. The meeting had been arranged in a small coffee lounge at one of London's finest hotels. 'The Introducer' had arranged the little tête-à-tête and although the room seated around forty people, it had been exclusively booked for the meeting. Two leather settees, separated by a glass coffee table that stood in front of the big floor to ceiling window, which overlooked an overcast city centre. Zak sat waiting; the coffee lounge was eerily quiet.

Exactly on time, the door to the lounge opened, and in strolled a man in his middle fifties. Of obvious wealth and good living, he wore a black Brookes Brothers suit. The dark blue patterned silk tie was in stark contrast to the purest of white, silk shirt. Zak thought he looked a little like a high-class club worker, but the small details told you he wasn't. The half-inch cufflink below the jacket and intricate matching lapel buttons told you this was more than a well-dressed man. This was a man who knew the difference between good-looking and best taste. Zak noticed his black-patented leather shoes as they click-clacked on the polished wooden floor towards him. Removing the almost black, designer glasses and placing them into his top pocket, he introduced himself.

"Hello, Mr Sharpe." His voice was calm and dark. He smiled. "So very pleased to finally make your acquaintance."

He continued to walk and held out his hand, and looked directly at Zak with piercing blue eyes that were cold, and were it not for the kind laughter lines around them caused by his smile, they would have been very unnerving. Closer up now, Zak saw the dark blue contrast of the mandarin suit collar. On each side of his neck lay a small button in the shape of two hands shaking each other

The Introducer spoke with a slight American accent, the

area of which, Zak wouldn't have known. Zak rose from his chair, and walked towards him to greet him.

"Hello, I have heard a lot about you," replied Zak, realising how thin his attempt at reaction was, but still hoping to make an impression. The Introducer gave no clue in return and Zak led The Introducer back to the chairs, beckoning him to take a seat.

"Not too much, I hope," replied The Introducer flatly.

His smile at Zak, huge and slightly pretentious, was the sort a car salesman uses to show you he's interested in your presence whilst he determines whether you have the cash to buy his exclusive models. It quickly disappeared and he continued:

"I have read an awful lot about you Mister Sharpe, and heard that I might be of assistance. Your introduction, via Mr Jackson, was very interesting. Please, tell me about yourself. I want to know all about you and the problem that you are finding so difficult to solve." His mannerism was very pleasant and Zak felt at ease with him almost instantaneously.

"Well, I don't really see it as a problem as such, just part of the lifestyle and position I have drifted into," Zak replied

"And what sort is that, Mr Sharpe?" asked The Introducer.

"Please, call me Zak. Well, I guess that having the privileges I have makes me an easy target for the media, and I find it difficult to just relax and do what I want to do, when I want to do it and without thinking, Who's in the bushes taking snap shots of me for tomorrow's front page?"

"By privileges, you mean money?" asked the Introducer.

"Well yes!" Zak exclaimed.

"Why do you see having money as a privilege, Mr Sharpe?"

Zak looked at The Introducer and noticed the lines and creases in his face. Most spread from his eyes that were still cold but intent. Zak might have found them strange and slightly unnerving but yet bizarrely he found them increasingly those of

60

an old friend... trustworthy and comforting. He would later struggle to recall many of his features at all but would always be able to picture his eyes.

'Where are you from? Your eyes are so piercingly blue, and yet even if I look close I can't make out contact lenses... who are you?'

Zak had been studying this so intently he'd forgotten the question

"I'm sorry?" he said, springing back from his thoughts. The Introducer, seemingly oblivious to the fact that he had been ignored, simply repeated his question

"Why do you see money and notoriety as a privilege? Is it something you feel everyone would want, Mr Sharpe? Or is it potentially the cause of the burdens that you speak of?"

The Introducer had asked his question using words and a mannerism that complicated Zak's mind enough and made him feel that he would need concentration to not feel he was being left behind. Zak thought for a moment and considered what had been suggested.

It never occurred to him that The Introducer hadn't called him by his preferred name. Zak was never one to stand on ceremony. Regardless of his immense wealth, Zak had rarely traded on it or let it get to his head. He had used it to attract people, women primarily, but had rarely let it affect his perspective on life. His father was a prime time, one hundred percent pompous aristocrat and Zak had loathed him for it from a young age. He had gone out of his way to not talk or act with, the pomp and circumstance that his father found so comforting. Instead, he followed his mother's sense of humility in this world and to choosing to still enjoy life.

"I guess so," replied Zak.

"Not that I would do without it you understand, but I

suppose you could be right. It brings me many of the comforts that I have enjoyed. I can buy whatever I like. I've bought the fastest of sports cars, the most exclusive of yachts, have six wonderful houses and have never had to worry about the cost. I can go wherever I like, I've been all around the world and visited every country I can care to imagine, and I've done it without a worry or care in the world."

"Without a care? Then why am I here, Mr Sharpe?" asked The Introducer.

The Introducer looked at Zak as though he were intricately studying Zak's every move and word. He had sat in the leather seat opposite, and the setting of the afternoon sun formed a shadow over half of his face. Zak noticed that he was not smiling now but considering Zak carefully. His ringless, well-manicured fingers were intertwined and hands were clasped in front of him. His thumbs played a game of chase around each other and Zak thought, 'He's a shrink! That bastard, Jackson's got me to see a shrink!' The Introducer raised his eyebrows and tilted his head a little as if motioning that he was waiting for a reply.

"Sorry, I missed what you were saying."

"I asked that if you didn't have a care in the world, then why am I here?"

Zak reconsidered this question carefully and finally conceded,

"Ok, I admit that it's not that I don't have a care in the world, I do. I guess a lot of who I am is down to losing my parents at a young age. I was devastated. Both my parents dying in such horrific circumstances and so suddenly, really freaked me out. I didn't know which way to turn. I was so lucky that the company was doing well. I really have very little involvement and simply withdraw whatever funds I feel I need to live on. I guess I was young and inexperienced at handling the lifestyle such wealth allows and kind of went off the rails a bit, you know, went a bit wild!" On the word wild, Zak raised his eyebrows and flicked his hands into the air.

The Introducer never answered but just sat listening. Zak continued,

"…Well, you've probably read all about it in the press anyway. I guess I sought solace in my wealth and in the parties that I could and did get invited to. The only problem is, is that regardless of my wealth, I'm really yet to find a great deal of happiness. My mother was my rock. With her gone I felt lonely and without a friend in the world, abandoned if you will, by her death. My father and I were never very close; he was a typical English gentleman whose sense of duty came well before any sense of love for his family. Anyway, following their death, I decided to get away from it all and went on holiday to Monte Carlo."

Zak had never opened up like this to anyone, and sought reassurance by periodically checking to see if The Introducer was looking at him, taking an interest, or simply falling asleep.

"Isn't it funny how these things happen, and you never realise at the time what a profound effect it is going to have on your life? I mean, there I was in Monte Carlo, minding my own business, I guess I chose there for the fact that I had some great times there with my mother. We had a holiday home there, up on the hill. We used to walk along the bay and look out at the yachts coming in or we'd get an ice cream at Giovanni's. Well, there I was and I was trying very hard to sort my head out a bit. My parents had recently died and I was all alone in the world, and just wanted to get my head straight. If it hadn't have been for me choosing that red 19 I doubt my life would be quite where it is now. It's silly isn't it, the run of a roulette wheel ruling your decision on life for the next three years. Well, as it was, I was sat

63

there with this frumpy woman to my left and this guy nearby, called Stefan. He's German, and from a very wealthy family who build compressors or something. He was there and bet on the 19 just like I did... and we won! I was convinced it was going to drop into the four. Anyway, without trying to bore you too much with the finer details, Stefan and I got on extremely well. Absolutely brilliantly, and from that holiday I never looked back. I still stay in touch now; I send him emails and invitations to parties in the UK. As it is, he's rarely able to attend as he's being doctored into the family business, and is being forced to calm down somewhat." Zak looked for sympathy for the loss of his playmate from The Introducer. Finding none he continued.

"I, on the other hand, have avoided such responsibilities and been able to party!" Like a child recalling a day at the park, Zak developed a wide, approval-seeking smile. The Introducer joined him in his excitement with a smile of his own.

"I have been to some wonderful places. I can tell you where some of the finest nights out are to be had. My only problem now though is... the press. Well... the press AND women." Zak lost his smile.

"You wouldn't believe how much they go hand in hand! When I was younger, not too long ago, but certainly when I had less worries, I used to party all night long. I've had a greater sex life than most men could only dream of. I've had beautiful women *PAYING* guards to get introduced to me. Can you believe that? And they're great looking. The thing is... that after a while they all seem to drift away. Usually to tell the Sunday tabloids how it was, when it was, and what they did with me. Now don't get me wrong, I didn't mind too much at the start. It's only now I'm sick and tired of it. In fact it's getting to be more of a problem than a bonus." He looked and thought about what he had just said.

64

The Introducer leaned forward, and carefully untwining his fingers, he lowered his hands. "How much of a problem is this, Mr Sharpe?"

"It's hardly a problem, is it? I mean, I can't make them go away 'cause there'll always be people out there wanting to sell for loads of money what they can't be bothered to earn properly. So even if you could help me, it would only be until the next new reporter came along, ever keen to get his name noticed as being the one that took THAT picture! As much as it's a problem, it's a way of life for me, which I'm just condemned by. I couldn't possibly become a recluse, but I've even considered going for plastic surgery to make myself less recognisable. How extreme is that!?" Zak widened his eyes as he emphasized the ridiculousness of his situation.

The corner of half of The Introducer's mouth rose a little in a knowing smile. A Mowgli smile, as Zak would've called it, a smile from the corner of one half of his mouth.

The Sale

If there were dreams to sell,
What would you buy?

Thomas Lovell Beddoes – 1830

"Have you got long, Mr Sharpe?"

The Introducer leaned closer and spoke both slowly and purposefully. Zak gave a slight nod

"For, what I am about to tell you, I tell you only once, so you had better listen carefully, and learn quickly. What I have to offer you shall only be offered once. No amount of money sometime in the future will tempt me back, on that you have my promise. If you decline, you will never see me again nor be able to ask for my services; even if you find me I will deny ever even meeting you. This is a once in a lifetime opportunity, whose terms are non-negotiable and based completely on your word being your bond. Do you believe in your word being your bond, Mr Sharpe?"

Already intrigued and mesmerised by the fantasy of this conversation, Zak was very interested. This sounded like a Dan Dare episode or a meeting between a secret agent and an informer. Disappointed with himself at not having the concentration levels needed to stop his carefree mind from asking insignificant questions whilst this man spoke, Zak jolted back into the conversation.

"Yes! Course," Zak replied.

"I sincerely hope so," said The Introducer.

Zak listened more intently. The Introducer continued,

"Then let me take you on a journey from yourself. Your problem, Mr Sharpe, is not with the media, nor with your wealth. It is with YOU. YOU are your biggest problem and I have seen it many times before. You are like the passion flower, your passion attracts. People are drawn to others who display unusual characteristics. You attract people who decide to give you fame and expect you to relish in its ownership." The word relish rolled off The Introducer's tongue like a coveted piece of literature, all of its own.

"Metaphorically, these people are parasites. They are like the Longwing butterfly." The Introducer looked at Zak, considering if he knew what he was talking about

"The Longwing butterfly, beautiful at first, attractive to you. You, the delicate passion flower, watches as this butterfly approaches. Fame dawns on people with the same attraction, Mr Sharpe. You look forward to its attention. Then, the Longwing, or fame, lands on you. Beautiful at first, it then begins to feed on you. You begin to realise it's eating you alive. Fame, like the Longwing butterfly to the passion flower, is but a poisonous predator and will kill you if you do not escape it." The Introducer checked Zak's understanding.

"You see, Mr Sharpe, People adore, worship and love others who display personalities, traits and skills not shown by the wider population. People desire these special people for the very fact that they have these unusual characteristics. Unfortunately they demand far more from these people than they can hope to provide. These characteristics often bring these people fame, wealth and notoriety that can make that person's

67

life a living hell.

"What right do people have to punish skill, wealth or personality with the pain and anxiety they happily call fame? Some people say they're lucky, I would suggest that fame rips the heart and soul out of your body and leaves you empty inside. Exhausted from the endless giving that persistent demands on you exact. Like the Longwing and the passion flower, fame WILL consume you. Like I said, Mr Sharpe, I have met many people with your problem and you may know of whom I speak. I've met men whose voices changed our world; their music altered our lives most profoundly and gave us years of joy and pleasure. I have met people who all they ever wanted to do was serve their country. To be an example of what others should be. To change our views, question our morals and shift our prejudices from the often hurtful, degrading and insignificant hole into which they've slipped. These people were GOOD people, people whose nobility made grown men weep, whose kindness fertilized the good in all of us, and whose souls we sought to destroy in the name of fame." So far, to Zak, this made complete sense. He liked this man.

"So what right did we have to interfere in these great people? The media is often heard crying, 'it's in the public interest'. Why is it then that the child abuser living next to a school is allowed peace and privacy? The media determines that the fact that all you might have done is to try to stop whites hating blacks, tried to stop a war, tried to bring happiness to others through your films or songs, means that we should and MUST know about what makes you tick. Who you talk to. When you go to bed AND who with. It's a disgrace to treat these great people like this. I have met grown men whose public persona is one of a strong man who would never bow to anyone, would never give in and never let anyone question his honour. I have

68

met people like this who have sat and wept about how unrelenting the pressure is, and how much it hurts them. The pressure has made them turn to drink, drugs or comfort eat. They have become less and less of the person that they were that made them great, as a way of telling the world to look elsewhere for solace. But it doesn't happen. It often kills them. They often go to H^{e}aven…"

The last of his words rolled off his tongue and sounded like Ye-avon. Zak had not thought of his accent much until now; the American slant on most of his conversation had given way to a Mexican tinge on this word. Zak couldn't decide what he had said. Was it heaven or haven? If it had been haven then he would've used the word 'a' before it, and Zak couldn't recall him saying 'a' haven.

"Did… Did you say Heaven?" Zak asked, confused.

"What I can offer you, Mr Sharpe, is a once in a lifetime opportunity to seek sanctuary. To seek safety in a retreat so remote you can never return. A chance to seek refuge from your life in a place where you can be yourself once more. The only chance in your life when you have the choice to be whomever you like being, without fear of ever being hounded by the press or media. Wouldn't it be wonderful to have the opportunity to live in exactly the house you want, in a place where the sun shines all year, where people aren't behind bushes taking photos, but are your friends? Where women don't want you for your money, they want you for YOU!"

That point caught Zak's attention. He had often met women who were attracted to him purely for his money or notoriety. This had been nice when he was younger, but as time had gone on it, had scared him.

"How often have you met someone and later discovered that all they wanted to do was use you? Use your fame? Use

69

your money to simply help THEM? When was the last time you met people who accepted you as a human being? Who didn't judge you on your colour, your money, or the prodigy that the press created? But simply accepted you as you, no strings nor history attached?"

"But surely everyone reads the papers, everyone watches the news. How could you do this?" asked Zak.

"Simply, my friend, because the people there are either in the same boat as yourself, or don't watch TV or read the tabloid tatters." As he said this, The Introducer pulled out a large Cohiba Cuban cigar.

"Would you like one? They're very good!" He held it out for Zak, who declined.

"No thank you, I try not to smoke, and only do when I've had too much drink to care." The Introducer gave a small smile and tilted his head in a nod of understanding. He took out a shiny, double-bladed guillotine-style cutter. Lining it up with a thin red line on the cigar, he quickly and efficiently chopped off the tip, and put both the cutter and tip back into his pocket. Zak watched with interest as The Introducer took out a small, silver windproof torch lighter. The cool green colour of the flame from the lighter camouflaged the heat it produced, and was slowly engulfed in the red heat and smoke from the tip of the cigar. Taking a look at the end and putting the lighter back, The Introducer proceeded to pull out a small silver box. It was a little bigger than a matchbox and had been engraved with an intricate pattern of lines that combined to make up a circle.

Whilst he did this, Zak tried not to stare, and instead looked aimlessly around the room. He noticed the mobile bar that had been placed near the large window in the room, and became instantly attracted to the thought of a Bacardi and Coke. Zak rose.

70

"Would you like a drink?"

"No thank you, Mr Sharpe, I'm fine," replied The Introducer. Zak continued over to the mobile bar and poured himself a large Bacardi and Coke whilst The Introducer enjoyed his Cohiba.

"What do you mean by the same boat?" asked Zak.

"Consider how the press has fuelled notoriety, legend almost. Sometimes this pressure has proved too much for the icons of this world and for some of them, H^{e}aven has provided sanctuary." There it was again... the name whirled around Zak's head.

"When did you last read the tabloid press, Mr Sharpe?" enquired The Introducer.

"I read them perhaps once a week, why?" said Zak, as he sat back down with his drink.

"Do you really read them?"

Zak hadn't thought about this and watched as the thick cigar smoke rose steadily from the tip.

"Well, I suppose so, do you mean the articles? Well, I guess not really, I mainly flick through them to see what sort of rubbish they're printing."

"You didn't read the article last week then, about the engaged celebrity giving his lover a goodbye kiss after spending the night with her, rather than his fiancée?" asked The Introducer, who had opened the box and was using it as an ashtray

"NO!" Zak scoffed, "I can't be bothered with it. Who the hell he wants to sleep with is up to him, that's exactly what I'm often in the press for. Who's he sleeping with now? Who is she? Where does she live? It's a bleedin' liberty! I let them get on with it. I'm only bothered when it's my name they're printing."

"Exactly, Mr Sharpe. Now imagine if you can go to a place

where no one cares who you've slept with! A place where there's no need to hire body guards or hide behind bullet-proof dark windows. Why? Because no one there gives you that sort of attention, besides… no one has a gun!"

The very pleasing aroma of the cigar had wafted across towards Zak. He found its fragrance very pleasing, solid, relaxing.

"Wouldn't it be fabulous… if you could walk around your house or garden and be certain that no one was hiding there, trying to get your picture? What about going out? How much would it be worth to you Mr Sharpe? If I could take you to a place where you could go out every evening and NEVER see a photographer, NEVER be hassled by people wanting you to join their god-forsaken religious cult or balmy army?" Zak smiled as he remembered being approached by just such a religious cult only a few months earlier.

"What about being accepted for the person you are and not what the press have twisted you into?" Zak breathed in more of the pleasing scent of The Introducer's cigar and a growing realisation of wilful deliverance dawned upon him.

"What's more, Mr Sharpe, imagine if you can, a place where it is sunny all year round, everywhere is clean and fresh. A place where your home is only moments from the warm tranquil sea, or even on the beach itself. Where you could wake up in the morning, enjoy breakfast on the beach and spend endless evenings making love to your sweetheart knowing that you two are the only ones there. Does this sound like heaven to you, Mr Sharpe?" Zak nodded and smiled back at The Introducer.

"But let me say this, let me be clear, you are not alone, Mr Sharpe." The Introducer was shaking his head and Zak's head automatically mimicked his head movements. "No! That sort of world belonged to Robinson Crusoe. He was a very lonely man. At H^{e}aven, Mr Sharpe, you will have neighbours, friends near by. Not the friends you have now, for sure, but friends who because they too have wealth and a desire for happiness and tranquillity, accept you for who you are and not what you can give them." The Introducer sat back.

"They are the people with whom you can talk, interact, play, entertain and be entertained."

"Like who?" Zak asked.

"Your neighbours in H^{e}aven could be any of the people you can think of, who in life were damned like you by the press, society or people... Who can you think of? Who when alive suffered the same public-eye damnation that you do? The same interference when all they wanted to do was get on in life?"

Zak's mind ironically remembered a quote he'd heard that John Lennon had said: 'Listen, if anything happens to Yoko and me, it was not an accident'. Zak truly believed that Lennon wanted more anonymity before he died. His thoughts were just turning to Elvis Presley when The Introducer interrupted them.

"Well, it is likely, Mister Sharpe, that they are already at H^{e}aven." Zak considered his thoughts.

"Mister Sharpe, you will be able to walk through the town and shop without a single person demanding your attention, taking your photograph or asking you for money. The health and education system is unparalleled, its doctors and teachers are among the best in the world, and come evening, the town lights up and offers entertainment until YOU want to stop. But let me ask you, Mr Sharpe. What stops you from doing the things you really want to do?"

Zak had been busy imagining past stars of stage and screen who were now dead all walking down the street.

"...Well, I guess if it's not the problem of press and

photographers everywhere, it's the law. I mean not many places in London stop open until six or seven in the morning, especially where I'd want to go"

"Then Heaven is going to be your saviour, Mr Sharpe. For at Heaven, there are no rules. No planning laws, you can build whatever house on your land that you want, big, small, round, underground, in the open, surrounded by trees, on the beach, near the road. It matters not because no one will care. At Heaven crime doesn't exist so the law doesn't exist. People will only steal if they can't get what you have. But everyone at Heaven has exactly what he or she wants! What is wrong with this place you live in now? Look!"

The Introducer motioned towards the window where the smog, hustle and bustle of London city life were mapped out before them.

"This place is too crowded! If you want to ride a motorbike you've got to have a license because they don't trust you to be responsible. Why don't they just teach you how to ride it and let you get on with it? If you want to live with a dog you've got to have a dog licence! You've even got to get a licence to catch a goddamn fish. Now how crazy is that?" The Introducer didn't wait for the answer.

"They don't even trust you to have a pet! How often have you been to a night out and had to wear a black tie?" Zak thought this over and imagined thousands.

"Who says? Why should they have regulations on what YOU wear when it's YOU paying THEM to eat there? At Heaven, we do not have laws. We have no regulations. We live a peaceful life without stress, rules or even religion."

"No religion? Why?" asked Zak.

"Why!" exclaimed The Introducer, with a look of astonishment on his face "Look at history, Mr Sharpe. Just about

74

every war in history has been over that pompous farce they call religion. People are born in the name of one religion or another. Some determine their whole lives around their interpretation of transcripts long lost. They will eat, sleep, work and rest in the name of it. They will form deeply held beliefs that other religions are mistaken, become so entwined in the concept that God is watching them, and not the other six billion people on the planet, that they will pray for deliverance and fight, destroy and kill in the name of it!

"People use it and abuse it for their own benefit. How often have you read about priests, vicars, nuns and bishops abusing others with their so-called 'status' as religious leaders? No, Mr Sharpe, religion is the worldwide mechanism for the destruction of what should otherwise be a harmonious place to live. It is like a cancer, it affects all corners of this planet and gives very little back in return for the pitiful amount of pleasure it brings to a select few."

The Introducer leaned back in his chair and looked carefully at Zak. Zak looked back, busily thinking over what had just been said.

"So how do you make sure then that people don't act recklessly? Or go around making life hell for others? Surely you do have crime at Haven?"

"H^{e}aven, Mr Sharpe and no, we don't." Zak looked at him, not convinced with this at all. The Introducer took the last breath in from his cigar and put the remainder of the stub into the silver box and shut the lid. The cut glass ashtray between them remained unused.

"H^{e}aven has no crime to speak of as it has no laws, only rights and wrongs. What is a wrong, Mr Sharpe?"

"What is a wrong?" Zak repeated,

"Well, I guess there are hundreds, otherwise there wouldn't

be all the laws. Murder, rape, torture, arson, drugs." The list suddenly started to dry up and Zak found himself searching hard for others.

"Er... speeding, disturbing the peace, I've been done for that one! ...Er bribery, bigamy, there's, there's quite a few."

"But which of those are true wrongs, Mr Sharpe, and which are our interpretation of how others should live?" Zak thought this over.

"Bigamy is only not allowed because ugly men decided that good looking men would have all the women! Bribery and corruption exist only because men with power and money often seek more than they deserve but have neither the skills nor energy to get it. Drunkenness and drugs often only hurt you. No, Mister Sharpe, people do get drunk and some may disturb your peace from time to time, but our selection of candidates ensures that these disturbances are normally only celebrations that everybody enjoys. As for bribery or corruption, everybody already has all they want so there's no need to bribe someone to get it!"

"Candidates?" asked Zak.

The Introducer had put the silver box back into his pocket.

"Oh yes! Mr Sharpe, H^{e}aven is a very exclusive place. You not only need to be very wealthy to live there, you must satisfy The Group that you are of the right social stuff. That you have the right personality and that it is right for you. It is not simply somewhere YOU choose to be. Like I said before, no amount of money will bring me back to talk to you about this, let alone offer you a place unless WE are convinced you are right for H^{e}aven." Zak had never experienced this before. Never had anyone so convincingly told him his money didn't matter and couldn't get him something. This made him want a place – badly.

"Well, what do I have to do?" asked Zak.

"My main concern, Mr Sharpe, is that I must be convinced that you want to come. Remember, it is a one-way ticket and an expensive one at that. My main concern is for your happiness and whilst there are many females already there and many people who come to live in H^{e}aven arrive alone, some bring partners or arrange to meet others there, sometimes as much as a year apart. I note that you don't have a partner, Mr Sharpe. Do you see that as a problem?" The Introducer's face was as serious as Mr Graham's was at Zak's prep school. Mr Graham had been the head tutor at The Blythe Preparatory school and Zak had often made jokes with school friends about how Mr Graham couldn't possibly smile, and they had imagined him in many funny situations with his completely straight face. The Introducer looked ever so Mr 'creepy' Graham at the moment.

Smiling at his thoughts, Zak replied, "A partner? No I don't, but that is part of my current problem. How can you be sure these women won't be after my money like the rest? What makes these different?"

"Women at H^{e}aven will have no interest in your money, Mr Sharpe, as they are already there. It's a one-way ticket, Mr Sharpe, they can no more leave and return to spend your money than you can. So if a woman likes you, loves you, it is for YOU, Mr Sharpe, nothing else. Give it some thought, Mr Sharpe and I will meet you here again in one week. I will need a decision from you then. Please remember, this conversation must not be divulged to anyone, not even your closest friends. If it is found that you have, Mr Sharpe, I will not be here next week."

The Mr Graham look was back and Zak sensed that when he wanted to be, this man was as serious as life gets. The Introducer's face changed in an instant and lit back up like a tungsten bulb. He rose from his chair and offered his hand. Zak shook it. "I trust I'll be seeing you next week, Mister Sharpe. Do give it some careful thought."

The Introducer smiled and walked away, his heels clicking as he went. Putting his dark glasses back on he walked through the door and was gone. Zak felt suddenly alone in the empty coffee lounge. He stood there for a moment and realised there was no trace the conversation had even taken place; no ash in the ashtray, no witnesses, apart from his own, no glasses of drink with fingerprints... nothing.

Zak made his way to the reception. A tall, attractive teenager stood behind the desk. She smiled at Zak through thick, rimmed glasses.

"Can I help you, Sir?" she asked.

"Yes, hi, my name is Mr Sharpe. I've just had a meeting in the top floor conference room. Can you tell me who booked and paid for it?"

"Yes! One minute."

Zak stood at the desk waiting anxiously. A couple in the corner of the reception area had clearly recognised him and were talking about him. He faked a smile at them and turned to face the desk.

"Mr Sharpe, it says here that you booked and paid for the room for today."

"I did?" asked Zak.

"Yes. Three days ago, by cash. Is there a problem?" she enquired.

"No. No problem." Zak turned away, confused. The couple were still staring at him.

"Sir!"

Zak turned round to face the receptionist again.
"Yes?"

"You have already booked and paid for the room again next

week, Mr Sharpe!" said the puzzled receptionist.

"How did I pay?" Zak asked.

"Let me see, er yes, it's fully paid for, for this time next week. Cash, it says here."

"OK. Thank you," replied Zak, as he left.

The Plan

If you fail to plan, you plan to fail.

unknown

Zak cancelled most of his appointments the week following the first meeting with The Introducer. The weather failed to improve much beyond its monotonous recipe of rain, clouds and the grey overcast blanket that seemed to prevail not only the skyline, but also his whole life. He wondered, what had he achieved so far in his life? Had he really made anything of himself? Here he was, a twenty-five year old man, who had all the trappings of a very wealthy and very successful person, and yet he felt almost dropped into an intolerable position. The company was doing extremely well and had even braved expansion into the now, thanks to a Mr Gates, rapidly growing microcomputer market. But he hadn't made that choice. That had been an expansion idea left to the board. Profits and turnover were both up, and Zak found his disposable income was reaching an unquestionably obscene amount. Yet this thought gave him no satisfaction. What had HE done? What had HE achieved? He found his questions wanting and it worried him. Having money was simply not enough. It brought joy yes, but sadness too. Rarely now could he wander out into the street without being harassed by people. Virtually never now could he enjoy a pint of beer in a local pub with friends, or even go shopping! He had wanted to do just that when he had finished his meeting with The Introducer, and found to his dismay that some girl had waited with her friend outside the hotel for a picture taken with him, and his autograph. Why? Why should someone who has never met him want his autograph? This crazy display of childish obsession troubled him. He wasn't what he would call famous; he simply enjoyed the good life, the nightlife, the social life that his wealth brought him. Of course he knew the answer deep down. The girls simply wanted to brag about how they'd met him and talked to him (or more?) and had a photo with him to prove it.

With only a few days to go before he knew he would meet The Introducer again, his attention turned to what sort of new person he could become. He pictured a new him, fitter, drinking less and eating better foods, taking up an active hobby, rock climbing perhaps.

Zak had always been apprehensive about heights and yet Zak had many times wished he'd overcome his fears. Perhaps he should become more spiritual? No, that was not allowed. Lifestyle, yes he thought, I'll change my whole lifestyle and become a better person, and with the new start I'll be able to find myself someone who loves me for who I am, a better me. I'll be a better person and find a soul mate… a family.

Zak arrived excited and psyched up for his second meeting with The Introducer. He had hardly slept the night before and arrived a full fifteen minutes early. The outlook from the window was considerably brighter than it had been a week earlier and Zak found this to be symbolic of his decision. A fresh start, brighter climates, a new dawn… a new beginning in H^eaven.

He had been careful not to mention the meeting with anyone, he did not want to jeopardise such an opportunity. Eager to hear more and get the ball rolling he sat in the sofa like an anxious teenager waiting for a first ever date to arrive. He sat watching the door carefully, looking for the slightest sway that may suggest the air in the foyer beyond had been disturbed.

At ten o'clock exactly the door to the coffee lounge opened, and in walked The Introducer. Wearing the same dark blue suit with its mandarin collar, Zak considered that The Introducer looked like he'd got a whole wardrobe of exactly the same clothes. Elegant, stylish and strangely formal in style.

This time however, The Introducer was carrying a slim, silver briefcase. It looked like a pearlescent sheet-steel, or possibly even polished aluminium.

"Hello, once again, Mr Sharpe," said The Introducer, holding out his free hand. Zak shook it enthusiastically.

"I guess that the reason you are here, Mr Sharpe, is because you would like to take the step?"

"I've given this more thought over the last week than I have many things over the last few years… and yes I would," replied Zak.

"Good, although in all honesty, Mr Sharpe, if I had thought you wouldn't be interested I wouldn't have met you last week." He smiled before continuing. "Okay then, we have lots to agree and lots to organise. For many reasons that will become apparent, Mr Sharpe, our meetings must be kept to a minimum. Let me begin by assuring you, Mr Sharpe, that I am a very honourable man. One's honour is the last bastion between men and their woes. I shake your hand, Mr Sharpe, because I consider you worthy of my attention. When I shake it, I show you my honour and give you my sincerity. For you to see and live the life of your dreams you must trust me, Mr Sharpe, and in return I will place my trust in you."

This to Zak would've sounded like a well prepared speech

had it not been for the sincerity in The Introducer's voice.

"No one must know you are going to H^{e}aven, Mr Sharpe, and no one must know you have prepared to go there." The Introducer had Zak's full attention, this time there was no hint of his mind wandering to consider. This time it was data retrieval.

"All transactions must be cash. All cash given by you must be untraceable to H^{e}aven. You must hibernate your spare money and store it with us until you arrive. You can bring with you as much money as you like. I would suggest a minimum of £30 million." The Introducer stood watching Zak's face carefully, analysing his response.

"Thirty MILLION!! Why in God's name would I want that much?" asked Zak.

"Like I have explained, Mr Sharpe, H^{e}aven is a one way ticket. You are a young man and are happy with the comforts you have. Once you abscond to H^{e}aven you cannot return for more funds later, and so this is my best estimate of the minimum amount of money you would need to build your home, furnish it, provide transport for yourself and keep yourself in the luxury to which you have obviously become accustomed." The Introducer had emphasized the word obviously and motioned delicately toward Zak's designer clothes. Zak always wore clothes from designers renowned for their flair and industry-leading designs. Made to measure bespoke clothing like this never came cheap.

"The only thing you can buy before you reach H^{e}aven is your land on which you build your new home and make your new life. There is a plot of land available which is approximately, let me see, in English, nine and a half acres. It has its own beachfront of which thirty metres are completely hidden from other properties. Many of our clients insist on this privacy but it is not always easy to guarantee. The price for this land and a lifetime of protection from outsiders is ten million

83

pounds. You will need to purchase this before being accepted. There are, of course, larger sites if you wish, with prices going up to fifty-two million pounds for a sixty-acre site with its own lagoon. Like the saying goes, you pays your money and you takes your choice." Zak looked horrified as the extent of his decision dawned on him.

"Do you wish to continue, Mr Sharpe?" The Introducer studied Zak carefully as he said this. Like a cat studying a cornered mouse, The Introducer carefully looked for signs that Zak was too afraid to continue.

"Mr Sharpe?"

"Yes, I do," replied Zak. The deal was done, the plans made and Zak was on his way to H^{e}aven.

Washing

Opportunity makes a thief.

Francis Bacon – 1598

Nearly a year after that meeting with The Introducer, Zak had managed to 'hide', indeed invest his money in his future at H^eaven. He now stood nervously outside the same hotel's lift doors where they originally met. He hadn't set eyes on 'The Introducer' for over ten months and he wondered what the next step was.

***

The previous year had started like the scene from the very best from a secret agent movie. His meeting with The Introducer had ended, they had shaken hands and that seemed good enough to The Introducer.

The Introducer had handed Zak the briefcase and, almost comical in his formality, had introduced it as 'The Advisor'. The Introducer told him to only ever open it when alone and bring it with him to the next meeting planned. Zak was to follow its advice to the letter, pressing the red button whenever The Advisor asked him to 'press the button'. He should never push the green button unless specifically told to do so. Zak had no idea the next meeting would be this far coming. The case had won his admiration, respect, loyalty and even friendship over the last ten months and was now firmly and tightly in his hand. He nervously waited for the lift to arrive to take him up to the coffee lounge.

The silver metal case was kept shut by two sets of combination locks that The Introducer had set for him, and housed a laptop computer. The case, so very stylish in appearance, had a small side panel on its left hand edge, and also a blank panel.

The other side had a small round plug socket, possibly used for earphones. When Zak had opened it in his bedroom ten months earlier, he had felt like The Jackal from the Frederick Forsyth book. This secret world of bluff, lie, deceit and the most cunning of plans lay before him… and he loved it! The pre-programmed computer turned itself on and booted up whenever he opened the case. Set in the lid was a colour screen and where the keypad was only a standard QWERTY keyboard, separate number pad and the red and green buttons. No function, no caps lock, no shift LAT or CTRL keys.

The letters h, e, a, v, e, and n were in blue and the letter 'e' was slightly raised as though it was set in superscript. The red button was located towards the top and centrally, about where the function keys would have been. The green button was under a flip-type clear plastic guard. Zak had no idea what this green button did but knew it was an inviting temptation to press. Bright, green, warm in colour, inviting and even tempting, with a childlike simplicity, Zak figured that when the last stage was reached, it would be that button that would be the final stage to H^{e}aven.

The screen flickered into life and a computer-generated, featureless but plumpish face came on the screen.

"Hello, Mr Sharpe," he said, "I am The Adviser. Please press THE BUTTON." The voice from a small speaker was a computerised male voice. Zak thought for a moment about The Introducer. It was at this point that Zak realised The Introducer had never given Zak neither a name nor indeed any way of tracing him and this secrecy thrilled him. He nervously pushed the red button. The screen froze for what was probably only three or four seconds but felt more like ten to Zak. The face reappeared.

"I am going to tell you how to guarantee your place at H^{e}aven and help you save the funds needed. Listen very carefully to what I have to say. You can ask me to repeat certain instructions or tasks, but only three times. Ask me a fourth time to repeat my instructions and I will end, and so will your chances of ever seeing H^{e}aven. You do this by pressing the letter R, three times. Please remember that R, three times is repeat. However you only have THREE chances. NEVER write down any instructions. If you understand these rules, press the button." Zak thought for a moment, but more confidently pressed the red one.

"Thank you, Mr Sharpe. Please slide back the small panel door on the left hand edge of the case. Place a finger in the slot located behind the panel and keep it there for 5 seconds." Zak did as he was told. Behind the panel was a small dome shaped hole. He placed his finger inside and a green LED light drew across his fingertip, reading its grooves and contours carefully. "Thank you, Mr Sharpe, you can now remove your finger and please close the panel. Remember the finger you used as this will be used to log you into this system in future. Now, before I continue to help you with your task of organising your path to freedom, I need your help."

"My in-built battery will not last what might be a long time before you return me to The Introducer. In the mean time I will need you to go to any mobile phone shop and purchase a standard 2.4volt adapter. The symbol in the bottom right hand corner will tell you how much power I have left; I do not like feeling tired and would appreciate you keeping me above the 20% power line. Is that ok?"

"Yep," replied Zak. He then realised how stupid he'd been to answer the laptop verbally and began looking for the 'Y' key.

"I believe you said yes. If this is correct, please do nothing. If no is your answer, please press the N key and say no again." There was a short pause. "Thank you," said The Adviser.

Zak looked at the case, amazed, and studied the aluminium and plastic casings. He made out a small hole in the centre and just above the screen and decided that must be the location of the microphone.

"...When you have purchased one of these I would be grateful if you would log back in and we can continue. Do you have any questions, Mr Sharpe?" Zak started to look for the letter 'N' and then decided to chance his luck and speak. "No!" he said, as clearly as he could.

"I believe you said, no. If this is correct, please do nothing. If yes is your answer, please press the Y key and say yes again." There was a short pause. "Thank you," said The Adviser. "In that case, Mr Sharpe, I will conserve my power and meet you again soon. Goodbye."

"Bye," said Zak. The computer then turned itself off and the screen went blank.

Zak's excitement took the better of him and without a moment to lose he closed and picked up the case. Looking around the room he decided to hide it carefully under some jumpers in a drawer in his dressing table. He picked up his keys and carefully checked the room before closing the door and walking quickly out. A full, but short, fifteen minutes later he was walking back towards his apartment, a new telephone charger in hand. He had literally run down to the high street and to the nearest mobile phone shop. Plugging it in, he waited. Nothing. He closed the lid and opened it again. Again the screen flickered into life and Zak breathed a sigh of relief.

In green appeared the words, PLEASE LOG IN. Zak studied the three words carefully before opening the small panel and placing his finger inside. The green LED inside the small dome-shaped hole passed slowly over it reading his fingerprint. The plump face of The Advisor appeared once again. "Hello, Mr Sharpe, that was very quick of you. Thank you for your promptness. Please press the button to confirm that you have completed the last task and are sat with me alone." Zak felt a sense of complete joy at the fact that his log in had worked and that The Adviser KNEW when they'd last met. Extremely impressed at being able to interact with what was clearly a very professional and technically advanced piece of equipment, Zak's enthusiasm to follow commands was growing by the second. Fuelled by his own importance in this interaction, Zak began a relationship that was to be the most intimate and private that he'd ever had. The green button was never mentioned.

This was the first of what would be many conversations he would have with The Adviser. The Adviser told him where to go, what to do, who to ask for and how to get the results he wanted. He followed them all to the letter. Among many other things, it meant opening up bogus companies and putting some transactions their way. It was fortunate that this was very easy, as Zak knew he didn't have long. Zak took most pride in the dummy management consultancy business he had set up. He decided to call it, 'Sweeping Hard Management Consultants'. 'Sweeping Hard', was chosen as it was an acronym of his father's name. Zak spent some time thinking carefully for not only a name but also an advertising slogan. He even organised dummy literature about how the firm would show their customers how 'Sweeping Hard' stood for the way that the consultancy would introduce you to 'sweeping changes', that would revolutionise company performance. He booked dummy appointments in his diary, and instead went for long drives into the countryside. He created the extortionate invoices based on their meetings and when such extravagance with the board was cleared and paid for, felt a sense of smug satisfaction.

Board members are only as brave as their jobs allow and with Zak being the main shareholder, no one asked too many questions. When he was asked, Zak often passed it off by explaining that he needed the help of the private training in company management. This ironically earned him a good deal of respect as board members saw how the untimely death of his parents, as he had only just begun university, had affected his education. The board could hardly argue with this logical line of thought and seemed quite impressed by his initiative and eagerness to become a better contributor to the company.

One of the tasks prescribed by The Adviser was a holiday trip to the Cayman Islands. Here he was to open a number of bank accounts. One by one, names of companies were given to him plus post office addresses at various locations around the world. He was to find a local printer and have business cards produced in the name of each of these, as and when requested. This would secure enough confidence from the banks to open an account. Completely amazed to find how few questions they asked, opening several bank accounts in the Cayman Islands was easy. Once each account was completed, The Adviser told him to destroy all business cards used to gain the account, and get new business cards printed for the next.

Zak had never until this time questioned his conviction,

belief and faith in what he was doing. However, being asked to forget where he was going to be putting millions of pounds in untraceable cash made him feel nervous. For the first and only time during his journey of guidance, he decided to ignore The Adviser and hold onto just one business card from each. He wrote in ink the name of the bank, account number and sort code on the back of each after he'd entered it, and kept it. Security, he told himself. The first account he opened was in the name of the dummy company he'd established, 'Sweeping Hard'. As time went on, Zak stopped trying to invent clever names and instead just thought of the first relevant thing that came to mind.

Early on in his interaction with The Advisor, Zak suspected that the suitcase had a built in modem, as after he'd set up each account it would pause. A small pop up window would appear with the words 'Please Wait', and an hour glass would appear on the screen and slowly drip sand from top to bottom before turning itself over to start again. During this process, Zak thought he could hear dial tones. They would then fall silent and shortly afterwards Zak would be told the details of the next account, the next step. The messages of advice would then appear like whispers from afar urging him onto his final destination. Zak discovered to his surprise that the Cayman Islands had hundreds of banks. The Adviser chose the banks and types of accounts and once established, Zak was told to give instructions to the previous bank he'd visited. He was told to instruct them quite specifically to undertake an immediate bank transfer into the account of the latest bank should any awkward official pry into his details. They were to ring a phone number and leave a message that they had been 'forced to be prudent with this investment', and hang up. Apparently this sort of account was quite common with foreign investors in the Cayman Islands. It surprised Zak to discover that The Cayman Islands is one of the world's largest financial markets for this very reason. Such were the laws in The Cayman Islands that this layering of accounts was designed to slow any investigation into the funds or their origin to a speed where they would never catch up with where the money really was and who owned it. By the time each bank had fought its case of client confidentiality, the money was long lost into the next account.

Once Zak had returned to the UK, The Advisor would give Zak details of more plans with methods of hiding cash from his business and authorities. Each plan was worth between £500,000 and one million pounds. It was left to Zak's discretion how much was invested. All The Advisor would say was 'The greater the investment the better life you will would enjoy in H^{e}aven'. The Adviser had told him he had less than a year to invest in his future at H^{e}aven. Most of the funds involved schemes relating to private investments. The Adviser told him it was neither illegal nor traceable that private investments went bad. Zak was to take as much money out of the business as he saw fit and invest in whatever scheme The Adviser told him. Some were more believable than others.

This string of poor managerial decisions attracted muted, then increasingly more vocal attention from The Board. Mike Underwood had been given the none too enviable task of approaching the company's not only main shareholder, owning over fifty percent of the company, but also someone who had become increasingly protective of his privacy. Mike invited Zak to see him.

"Hi there, Zak, how are you? Please, take a seat, sit down. Would you like a coffee?" asked Mike.

Zak followed Mike's motion towards a black leather office chair.

"Fine thanks, Mike. Yeah, I'd love one, the drive over was

horrendous," replied Zak. Mike pressed on his intercom. "Cheryl, could you organise two coffees please, one for myself and the other for Mr Sharpe?"

"Certainly, Mr Underwood," came the metallic and crisp reply. Zak both wondered and doubted that Cheryl called Mike, 'Mr Underwood', very often and considered that it was for mainly his benefit.

"So, I see you've been busy with Executive Renewal. How is that going?" asked Mike.

Executive Renewal was a dummy company Zak had formed and 'booked' himself some very exclusive and extremely expensive weekends with.

"Great. Well, to be honest I think I have only one or two more weekends to attend and I should be the most chilled executive on the planet," replied Zak.

"Oh nothing, it's just that I thought I'd pass something by you. Purely as someone who wants to see you succeed... I hope you know what I mean," said Mike, tentatively.

"Go on," urged Zak, carefully not showing commitment either way.

"Well, it's that recent transfer you asked for... It's an awful lot of money for what seems like an unknown area, Zak. I mean I have no problem with you withdrawing those sorts of funds from the company, you know that, but it's the explanation you give. It's making some of the board kind of nervous."

The difficult discussion was momentarily interrupted by Cheryl's light knock at the office door. She walked carefully in and over to Mike's desk where she placed the tray down.

"That's ok, Cheryl, I'll take it from here," said Mike, with a small smile. Cheryl quickly returned the gesture to both Mike and Zak and walked out. Mike began to pour Zak a coffee from the small pot. Zak waited for him to continue.

"Well, like I said, it's making some of them nervous, Zak. Especially that pie in the sky American ba... well you know. Dave's been making a few waves around the board table. It's not that he can do a great deal, especially as you've been doing this management course with this, Sweeping Hard company but he's been pointing out that within a year you've not only massively increased your private investments but also asked the company to repay some sizeable amounts in the director's loan accounts and..."

Zak gave no impression of his reaction as Mike shifted his weight in his chair uneasily and looked into his own coffee for comfort.

"...Well I think it's a bit of sour grapes that you pay him an enormous amount of money to be Finance Director and yet haven't sought his advice once on your investments... Dave's been talking to legal and says that you haven't even checked out your investments with them! He's making waves, Zak, and says your actions could be seen as a little irresponsible or even sloppy." Mike's eyes nervously went toward the floor in anticipation of outburst. It wasn't long in coming.

"Cheeky git!" retorted Zak.

"No don't go off on one, Zak, it's just that, well I guess he's just concerned," defended Mike, tactfully.

"More like bothered that if I make good choices I'll be ditching him," replied Zak. The thought that Zak might actually be thinking about that took Mike by surprise.

"Is that what you're thinking?" he asked.

"No, not really, but I just like to feel like I have control. I have all this shareholding and yet never make a decision about the firm or the direction it's going in. I'm just experimenting."

"That makes sense, Zak; I can see where you're coming from. Hey, I'll tell you what, I'll sort out something to shut him up. Find him a different project or something, don't worry. OK?" But Mike was clearly worried and Zak admired his tact. Zak liked Mike particularly for his unending support and loyalty to Zak. Whatever happened Zak knew Mike would fight his corner to the end. Mike certainly was more than an employee; he was Zak's eyes, ears and friend.

"But hey, look, if you do need advice, I'm always here, ok?" asked Mike.

Zak smiled. "That'd be a real help, Mike, if you could look after the board for me, I'd be grateful and thanks very much for the offer of advice but no, I'm fine with it."

Mike was true to his word and the Finance Director had been given the unenviable task of setting up International Financial Reporting Standards. Soon the mood and talk in the boardroom was around how grateful they should be that Zachariah had decided that looking out for the company, even if he had a lot to learn, was better than the scandalous sex object that they'd had before. That was the one and only time Mike questioned Zak's investments, particularly when one of the 'investment' companies wrote to him and told him how well the stock was increasing.

The Adviser eventually told him that time was up and no more significant investments could be organised. It advised him to run up debts in the companies and fold them before a date for him to meet once again with The Introducer. Zak's hiding of the bankbooks had been just in case this whole thing was an elaborate scam to remove him of his fortune. His fears were now temporarily allayed as he made a note of the appointment. Zak had rang the banks and checked from time to time that the money placed there was still there, and considered that it couldn't be a scam if it was and if The Introducer was meeting him again… could it? That would be foolhardy.

***

The almost silent action of the doors to the lift opened and Zak walked in. Zak felt the slight surge as his bodyweight gained slightly as the carriage began its ascent towards the coffee lounge. The piped music was a classical remake of an eighties song. 'Perfect' was a hit by Fairground Attraction, and Zak thought the poignant title summed up his life at that time. This was the stage where everything was just that… perfect. The parties had been fun, then, only a few reporters followed him and they were only interested in him if he did anything outrageous. Sometimes he had of course, just to give them something for their efforts. But this was a far cry from the frustration that had led him to where he was now. The lift let out a high-pitched ping as it drew to a stop and the doors opened. Zak stepped out.

Zak made his way across the corridor and into the coffee lounge, the music from the lift faded behind him as the brushed steel doors slowly closed behind him. The music was drowned out by the sound of the doors pushing past the bristles on the top and bottom of the lift door frame. Zak stood in the silence of the lounge and the large window overlooking London. He carefully placed The Adviser in his steel case on the glass coffee table and sat down. The Adviser had been Zak's electronic friend, mentor and confidante for the last year and Zak knew that their relationship, if one ever could be had with a case, was coming to an end. He thought about his previous year and tried to weigh up what he'd done, what he'd achieved, what he'd accomplished and how he'd had to lie and deceive people to get there. His concentrated recollections were sharply interrupted by the chwwuup sound the doors made as they opened behind him. The Introducer, closing the door behind him, walked in as immaculate and confident as ever. He looked slightly older; his

96

hair seemed longer than before, he wore the same suit however, and as Zak rose to his feet to greet him he was reminded of the click-clack sound that his shoes made on the hard wooden floor.

"Good day to you, Mister Sharpe," said The Introducer, with a large smile on his face.

"Hello there," replied Zak, with an equally large smile.

The scene could be compared with a student receiving his honours after a year of hard study.

"I see you have managed to wash quite a bit of laundry this year. I am pleased for you and can assure you, YOU will definitely appreciate your hard work. Your washing is very safe and I am very excited for you. Sit, and I'll explain the next stage of your journey."

What followed was an hour-long conversation about how and why Zak had to prepare well for his journey. It was to start with an ending…. His.

The Death of a Playboy (1994)

Fare well my dear child and pray for me,
and I shall for you and all your friends
that we may merrily meet in H^{e}aven.

Sir Thomas More – 1535

Mike Underhill had prepared well for today. He finally felt like he had achieved something. The last few years had been spent flying from one country to another and in endless meetings with different directors at different sites, each seemingly with their own agenda, and each equally keen to make their own job that bit easier. At thirty-six and happily married to Debbie, Mike was in the prime of his life. From a lower-middle class background, Mike had grown up appreciating the wealth he now enjoyed. As a son to his environmentalist mother, he had always wanted to be a freebie hippie, fighting for the world against the oppressive, capitalist companies for which he now found himself working. He'd longed to make a difference to the environment but as time had gone by and life had presented him with choices, he just hadn't seemed to find the time for it. With hard choices that all of us face from time to time, Mike had opted for the long hours, hard work, well educated route. He had worked on his luck and fortune and success had followed him like a puppy eager for play and attention. Not that his determination had let him rely on this of course, but things just seemed to fall into place and as he rose this morning he felt good. He had graduated with a first at university and had fallen on his feet when he'd met Edwin Sharpe.

The Sharpe Corporation was one of many companies he'd applied to. Mike had found that his handicap of two had opened the door of opportunity just enough to get accepted onto their fast track promotion scheme. The interview with the personnel manager gave him the opportunity to impress and even half jokingly talk of playing some rounds so that Mike could give the interviewer, a keen golfer himself, some 'good games'. Mike understood it for exactly what it was, an offer to teach the personnel manager where he might be going wrong.

The interviewer's obvious interest in Mike's handicap had clearly swung the decision and had given Mike the foothold he desired. Rapid promotion pushed him into the audience of Mr Sharpe, chairman, owner and driving force behind the Sharpe empire. Mike appreciated Edwin's professionalism and had found they had got on really well. Mike was not a man to rest on his laurels and had made sure that Edwin noticed and appreciated his services. Since then, the company had expanded and diversified and Mike had not exactly ridden on the success; more surfed it, and found himself to be the person Edwin wanted at his side. Luckily for Mike, Zak had also grown to like and trust him. This didn't exactly surprise Mike as he knew Zak to be a lot closer to his mother's earthly side, and Mike was also the only director anywhere close to Zak's age. He remembered when Zak arrived at the first of the board meetings following the death of his parents. Zak's nervousness made him look like what he was... clearly out of his depth. It was to turn out that as good a businessman that Edwin was, he was a distant father and not one who'd schooled his son on business management. It was probably a lesson timed in Edwin's head for when Zak had finished university. Mike decided to help Zak navigate through the processes and circumstance of running a now worldwide business. Zak had clearly appreciated this and happily put Mike forward as Managing Director when Sir Alex had resigned.

Mike got out from his bed and walked into the en-suite. The marble tiled floor on his feet sent its usual panged sensation up the back of Mike's legs reminding him that he was now awake. He would be wearing his best suit today. Today was a chance for self-congratulation in the glory that the company had bettered its target by 29%. It was fast becoming the industry standard. This had been achieved under Mike's leadership, and of that he was very proud. Mike had invested enthusiastically in market research on this new line. He had closely monitored public perception of price, quality, desirability and technical specification to ensure that his product remained both aspirational and just about attainable to its market audience. Today, Zak was returning in the company jet from the United States to chair the meeting that would mean celebrations for a good time to come. Mike picked out the head of his electric toothbrush from the chrome rack on the wall and attached it to the handle. After applying the paste he began to brush, happily thinking of what this would do for his reputation. Mike had longed for this sort of success and knew the news would make the front page of all the trade journals and surely a lot of the business magazines. Zak had happily told him the limelight was his for the taking. Zak got enough of that already, although not exactly for the same reasons.

Money had never been a motivating factor in Mike's actions. He wanted pride and achievement and had concentrated heavily on his image, personal skills and reputation to achieve this. The brush buzzed away as he worked the paste up into a lather. The plan for today rolled around his mind as he brushed his teeth.

"You ok, honey?" asked Debbie, as she hugged up behind him.

He looked into the mirror and could see her standing behind him, arms wrapped around his torso. Her lips curved in a welcoming smile before pressing themselves against his shoulder, as she kissed him. Her deep green, inviting eyes looked through the mirror at him. Those eyes were the part of her that he'd fallen in love with. He'd never really told her, but from the moment the lights were bright enough for him to see them in the party he was at, he'd fallen. Not love at first sight, just a certainty that she was the one he was prepared to give up working late for. If she had asked, he would have even given up his golf. He hadn't needed to of course, a blessing really, but he'd been prepared to nevertheless. He smiled back at her reflection.

"Uh huh!" he mumbled through the frothy white substance.

"Good, I was a bit worried about you last night. You seemed to toss and turn for what seemed like ages before you slept. You worried about today?"

Mike lent forward and spat the paste out into the sink.

"No, quite the opposite!"

"Charming!" said Debbie, jokingly, as she walked back into the bedroom. He spat once again, getting the last of the paste out. He turned the cold tap and washed the toothbrush under it. He picked up his glass and filled it and swilled his mouth out carefully, spitting it out into the sink. He smiled and shouted,

"Well, you will talk to me while I'm brushing my teeth!"

Mike took another mouthful of water while Debbie switched the bedroom television on.

"It's gonna be a great opportunity for me!" he called.

"I'm to be congratulated by Zak in front of the board, the press will be there for photographs and I've already got a press interview booked in for later in the day!" Mike gleamed at the prospect.

"So what! That Zak Sharpe is just a playboy and I wouldn't rate his congratulations for a minute," she replied.

Mike carefully put his toothbrush back in its slot on the holder. He wiped his mouth on a soft, pale blue towel and returned it to its ring on the wall and started to the bedroom. Mike was a very particular man and prided himself on neatness.

"Well I know he's had a bit of a time but he's really getting it together now. He's been trying real hard lately to get to know his company, and that's not easy with his parents dying like they did."

As Mike entered the room he looked at Debbie as she draped her baby doll negligee over the back of the bedroom chair. She looked back at him and gave him a look that said she didn't really believe him and started to make her way to the chest of drawers that held her underwear. As the TV chatted away in the background, Mike stood gazing at her beautiful skin, a soft glowing brown, almost flawless were it not for a beauty spot atop of one of her buttocks.

"He's an ok guy!" he exclaimed, trying to get her to see his side, "…and is a lot more realistic than his old man was. Besides he lets me get on with it, which after Edwin is a real break."

Debbie shrugged and gave a look to Mike that said she didn't really believe him but didn't truly care as long as her husband was happy.

"He is!" said Mike, smiling at the thought that she was doing a very handsome job of teasing him.

"Anyway, it's not only that, but this success will let me put

102

forward some of…" Mike's words were cut short as his attention was drawn to the television. The ever-so-familiar television figure of Louise Chapman was looking her usual prim self but had caught Mike's attention when she'd said 'Sharpe'.

"…and as yet there are no clearer details. We do not know the cause or the exact location of the crash site. But what can be confirmed is what we have heard from the US coastal service. They received a mayday distress call at twelve minutes past midnight from the Gulfaire 620 that was carrying Zak Sharpe back from the United States. The twin Pratt and Whitney powered aircraft had been heading from a business conference in the United States back to the United Kingdom. A Mayday request was heard moments before the plane disappeared from radar, and crashed. Coast guards were alerted and the last known position of the plane was given to passing vessels and search teams. This tragic coincidence is only eight years after the accident that claimed the life of both his par…"

Mike had stopped still and in pure amazement had stopped hearing the remainder of the news article. Mike's jaw had dropped and would have stayed there had he not sensed the saliva building up on his bottom lip. He closed it and swallowed as Louise, still looking incredibly professional stood outside a building of some sort.

"Remains were found within two hours and what has been seen in the water suggests that there are no survivors." The picture left her, and switched to a cartoon picture of the American coast. It showed a mark that was labelled New York and a red X gave the approximate location of the crash site. Completely pointless of course, it didn't prove anything except that New York is on the coast, and the plane crashed in the water.

"Establishing exactly what happened is of course difficult,

as coast guards continue to search for survivors in the dark. Fragments of the plane and some personal items have been discovered and these are being kept for a forensic investigation into the cause of this tragedy. It had been suggested by some that this was an act of terrorism. Officials who claim that it appears to have been a terrible accident have denied this. Rescue teams are still searching, but have reported that there is little doubt anyone survived." The picture flicked to a dark haired official from the coastguard.

"All will be done to ascertain what caused this plane to get into difficulty. We have as yet no idea of the cause, but do not suspect foul play. The Gulfaire 620 is fitted with an electronic flight recorder, and it is hoped that we will be able to locate this." The picture flicked back to Louise.

"The coastguard has confirmed that the chances of finding survivors are minimal. Unconfirmed flight records show that Zak and the pilot were the only two people on board, however it is known that Zak liked to make such trips with a companion. We will bring you more information on this tragic breaking story as soon as it comes in."

Mike looked away from the television just as it flicked back to the news reporters who were now going on to mention about the fact that they would keep viewers up to date as often as the story broke, but now they were turning to the other news of the day. His eyes looked into Debbie's; they looked nervous and wanting for an explanation. This staring into each other might have lasted a lot longer had Jessica and David, their seven-year-old daughter and five-year-old son not walked in. Jessica and David often came in first thing in the morning. Jessica was always an early riser and often hassled David until he succumbed to the attention and woke as well. She would then lead him to his parent's room and use him as moral support for invading their space, first thing. Once they were inside their parent's room, David would often stay only long enough to convince himself that he was going to get no more attention than the television offered. David was a bit of a morning television addict, there were just so many cartoons he simply couldn't bear to miss. Jessica would then join Mummy and Daddy in bed or perch herself on the edge of the bed and watch her mother meticulously apply make-up at the dressing table. She seemed to take great pleasure in watching her mother carefully manipulate the make-up tools that made her father wish he'd never have to go to work.

Oblivious to the fact that Mummy was standing there naked at the drawer, unit she happily chirped "Morning," and put on her best new day smile. "Morning," repeated David. Mike and Debbie just stood looking at each other. Mike out of sheer shock, and Debbie trying to read her husband's face. Was it fear, disbelief or plain shock? She couldn't tell and the voices of her children seemed slightly distant. Jessica's face stopped smiling as she realised that Mummy and Daddy weren't really interested in her. Raising her voice, she repeated herself.

"Morning!!" David copied, parrot fashion.

"Wait a minute, honey," was all Debbie could manage to say.

David immediately realised that Mummy and Daddy had better things to do, and walked out, back to his room, to the quickly cooling bed he'd been prized out of. It was a little early for his liking and he was sure that the bed offered much more comfort before the television needed to go on. Jessica stayed where she stood, hoping for some reaction. Mike looked from the television to Jessica and back to the television, before finally settling on Debbie's eyes.

"Go to your room, Jess," Debbie said.

"But Muum," Jessica replied.

"Jessica, I said go back to your room. Daddy and I are busy!" Debbie scowled.

Jessica knew that when her mother used her full name she was on thin ice. Her blonde hair swayed as she turned to go out. She dramatically slumped her shoulders as if the world had just been placed on them and let her arms drag straight down her sides; despondently she plodded slowly out.

"Holy shit," said Mike, staring directly at Debbie. She would have normally scolded him for such language but decided now wasn't the time. Besides the children weren't within earshot. She waited.

"Christ, I'd better get moving!" said Mike, as he turned and made his way to the bedside cabinet. He switched his mobile phone on and quickly found a pair of underpants. The phone beeped twice, he walked over and picked it up. The screen read VOICEMAIL MESSAGE RECEIVED.

Announcement

A lie gets halfway around the world
before the truth has a chance to get its pants on.

Sir Winston Churchill – (1874-1965)

Zachariah decided the air was still a little on the chilly side for his liking and reached into his left pocket. His fingers fumbled through the bits of paper and tissue inside and caught something hard. He cleared the tissue away and made sure he had a good grasp of the white, flimsy metal lid of the Bacardi bottle before lifting it out. Zachariah had always been partial to drink, his high life of old saw to that. Parties where the drinks were free all night long were a common part of his social calendar. Bacardi and a dash of Coke was his favourite tipple, as it rarely gave him a headache, and didn't dry his mouth out like vodka seemed to.

His tastes had hardened over the years and he had become accustomed to the sharp taste it had in his mouth. When he was younger, if he'd mixed too much Bacardi with too little Coke, he'd feel it smack his taste buds. It would work its way up to his nose that then tingled at the fresh, sharp snap. Whilst this was happening he'd never dare to breathe in through his nose. The idea of increasing that sensation and hurting his nose was too worrying. But as time had progressed, and lately as money had dried up, the second sensation Bacardi gave you was ever more

107

inviting. Warmth. For as Bacardi went down you, one thing that could be guaranteed was the way it warmed the very insides of your body as it touched.

Money drying up had been a consequence of that damned place. H°aven. It had sucked him dry and spat him out with nothing but the warmth of the Bacardi for comfort. Rarely nowadays did he have the funds to dilute the Bacardi down with Coke. As he thought about this it occurred to him that rarely nowadays did he have the money to *buy* Bacardi! Most of the drink he'd bought lately was cheap white rum; it tasted harsher but still gave him the same warming sensation. He looked up from his half-empty bottle towards where the Downs girl had been. She was gone and so was her mother.

Zachariah looked around and noticed the reverend. He was a tall, slim man. White hair on the top of his head had long since abandoned him. What he had left was almost ebony and slickly held against his head by copious amounts of Brilcream. Zachariah knew he was no reverend really, but he walked this way most mornings on his way to where Union Street met Prospect Park West. There he would stand with a couple of others to preach to passers by. Zachariah had listened to him a few times but found nothing interested him much. They stood surrounding the preacher for many hours and like followers of the Apostle, nodded, agreed and sympathised with his many proclamations of life. If there had been a shooting or mugging he would talk about penance and seeking God's forgiveness. Other days were spent announcing the end of the world or the damnation of Christ on the non-believers. Often dressed in a pair of simple trousers and brown jumper, his arms would sometimes be clutching The Book in solemn reflection, much like someone at a funeral. Other times he would be waving around in overwhelmed jubilation of the deliverance of his faith.

108

Zachariah thought of this for a moment and recollected the announcement of his demise. Hardly a shock that rocked the world, but he was sure it would've been the cause of many a comment in boardrooms around the world, and probably the butt of many jokes as well.

The Journey

Whenever I prepare for a journey
I prepare as though for death.
Should I never return, all is in order.

Katherine Mansfield – 1927

In the journey of 1994, Zak had been instructed to sack his existing pilot for being black. He was to use an expensive dummy company to defend the case as a method of hiding some more funds. He was also directed to place an advertisement in Plane & Pilot Magazine for an experienced GA620 jet pilot. He was to receive and promptly did so, an application from a South American pilot with excellent credentials. The other applications were binned without so much as a glance at their CV's.

The application arrived in the name of Braulio Gutierrez, who had recently moved (not unsurprisingly for Zak) to the UK to live with his aunt. Zak invited him for an interview and he arrived promptly and with excellent references in hand. An obviously accomplished and well qualified pilot, his log showed that he had over 200 hours flying time in Zak's type of plane. Zak had interviewed people for jobs before but found this experience disconcerting. It was unusual, as both Zak and Braulio both knew they were just playing the game.

With thick, curly black hair Braulio was a quiet man who

kept himself to himself. Zak was to employ him straight away as both his pilot and chauffeur. His first task was to fly Zak to the United States on 11th April for a meeting on the 12th with the executives of one of the dummy companies Zak had dealt with.

Braulio collected Zak from his London home a little after lunch time. The Paparazzi were outside the house as usual.

"This way, Zak," called a photographer. Zak just ignored him and quickly got into the back of his car. Braulio drove him straight to the plane. The rich and famous rarely travel in the same way as the masses. Why should they? Zak often used his own jet and consequently used different terminals to the public at large. This did not stop the press as they always knew which terminals were used by the rich and famous. They also paid well for inside information about who was on the move. Today was like any other, about fifteen photographers in all. Many of them shouting at him to turn their way.

"Where you going, Zak?" asked one photographer.

"Show us your knackers!" shouted another, hoping maybe to get a shocked smile or some reaction from Zak. Zak had heard all the one-liners in the past and had little difficulty keeping his face straight and pointing exactly in the direction of the customs door.

Too many times in the past he had welcomed their attention and had days later seen his picture on magazine covers and the subject of gossip columnists from New York to New Delhi. Zak wondered who had taken a photograph on this, one of the last occasions of an infamously famous life.

Zak passed through the terminal without attracting any real interest and continued his thoughts. As soon as the photographers had realised he was both alone and not playing their game, they drifted away. Zak had tried so hard to be IN the public eye that this new approach of being away from it made him think. An international personality was a most ephemeral of creatures, people wanted to be seen with him, sleep with him, be him. This short saunter, walking alone to use his jet was hardly noteworthy, and yet was to be one of the last occasions this world would have to see Zak Sharpe.

Finances for Customs and Excise didn't always stretch to providing an officer just to check the odd celebrity that came through; and today was no different. They preferred to splurge their budgets and energies on the more understandable targets.

Once safe inside the plane, Zak relaxed and fetched himself a Bacardi and Coke. Putting a number of ice cubes in, Zak then proceeded to half-fill the half-pint glass with Bacardi and opened a small bottle of chilled cola from the fridge. Slumping down in the seat, he put his feet up on the chair opposite and switched the TV on. The turbines in the background began to whir into life and Zak took a large mouthful of his drink. The journey to New York was one of many humdrum flights he had taken during his hectic and busy life. By the time the plane had finished its pre-flight checks, got clearance and taxied onto the runway, Zak was more than halfway down his drink. Braulio was indeed an accomplished pilot and kept himself very much to himself, and Zak used the opportunity to grab himself some sleep, waking shortly before landing.

Braulio then acted as chauffer from the airport and took Zak to the Rockerfella Center and The Hilton Hotel. Zak booked himself into his suite and settled down. Determined not to let this last opportunity slip away from him, Zak decided to go out. He asked Braulio to drive him to Bungalow 8, an exclusive nightclub between 10th and 11th Avenues. It was a mediocre affair, as Zak's enthusiasm was all stored for the next day's meeting rather than the frivolities of the nightclub.

The next day's 'executive' meeting was actually to be with

The Introducer, and Zak spent all morning in the hotel. At 2pm he heard a knock at his suite door. *This is it, no turning back now,* he thought. He opened the door and standing there, looking just as he had when he left from the last time they met, was The Introducer. Quite a familiar sight to Zak by now, The Introducer had, over the last few meetings, begun to develop a slight personality. He even seemed to be opening up to Zak. When talking about whether Zak had managed to find a partner that he would like to take with him, The Introducer had even loosely referred to himself as having a partner. "Hello, Mr Sharpe," said The Introducer, with a large welcoming grin on his face and his hand held out. Zak shook it enthusiastically and smiled back. It was as though he and The Introducer were successful partners in crime and had managed to pull off a very rewarding and famous heist. Zak's excitement had been steadily building ever since he had arrived in the United States, and was now almost unbearable. Zak invited him in and they made their way to the lounge area and sat down.

"Drink?" offered Zak.

"Thank you, but no, Mr Sharpe," replied The Introducer.

"I would suggest that you also do not partake in a drink at the moment," said The Introducer, as he reached into his inside pocket.

What he pulled out shocked Zak, and Zak instinctively sat further back in his chair.

"Do not be worried, Mr Sharpe, I need only about half a pint. It is crucial that the evidence found is convincing. Please, relax, and let me sort this out."

The Introducer had produced a needle that was attached to a petite bag via a tube. Zak had not donated blood before. He had not considered the concept frightening, but his brain had simply found other more pressing engagements to occupy his life. Still, here now with The Introducer, Zak was quite worried. The Introducer walked over. "Please, roll your sleeve up. It is vital we get this done, Mr Sharpe."

Not particularly afraid of needles, Zak put his nervousness of what might be aside and did so. The Introducer took the needle, tube and bag out of the sealed bag and placed it down. He reached into his pocket and pulled out a silver tin and a pair of examination gloves. Putting the tin box down, he put the gloves on and opened the tin box. Inside were some cotton wool, a small bottle of clear liquid and a plaster. He took out a small Velcro bandage and wrapped it around Zak's arm. Using the attached little pump, The Introducer proceeded to pump some pressure into the strap. Zak could feel the pressure, and then noticed he could feel his own pulse throbbing from his elbow and down to the inside of his wrist. His veins rose in his arm. The Introducer put the needle confidently into Zak's vein, in the crux of his elbow. Immediately, the small vessel of the needle filled with rich, dark blood.

The Introducer took out a little bit of surgical tape and secured the needle to Zak's arm, and then connected it to a clear plastic pipe that led to a bag. The thick red blood immediately began to fill the clear plastic tube and make its way down and into the bag. The Introducer sensed Zak's fear. "Just relax, Mr Sharpe, and all will be fine."

The Introducer released the pressure on the Velcro strap, and Zak concentrated his breathing on slowing his pounding heartbeat.

After some time, The Introducer clamped the tube with a small plastic clip, and first removed the tube from the needle and then the needle from his arm. He quickly replaced the tip of the needle with a small ball of cotton wool, and got Zak to clamp it into the inside crux of his elbow. He carried on tidying the items away and placing them carefully back into the tin box and then his jacket pocket. When he had finished he got Zak to open his arm and he removed the cotton wool checking the small hole.

"You may want to keep that on for a little while longer," advised The Introducer. The brilliant white of the cotton wool was only slightly interrupted by a small red blotch; his arm had stopped bleeding.

The Introducer relaxed and sat back down in the chair, taking out his now familiar Cohiba Cuban. He waved it towards Zak in offering; Zak raised his hand of his good arm slightly and shook his head. The Introducer unwrapped it, as he had done on almost all occasions they had met, and began the deliberately methodical process of removing the tip with his small, silver guillotine, and carefully smoking it, and placing the ash into his little silver box. As he did so, Zak studied the man before him. His piercing blue eyes were just as they were when they had first met a year earlier, but the laughter lines, as Zak's mother would have called them, were fractionally more pronounced. Age was indeed threatening to change The Introducer. Unbeknown to Zak, The Introducer would retire two years after this meeting.

"I think we are ready, Mr Sharpe," said The Introducer, finally.

"I think you're right," Zak replied.

"The Adviser has informed me that you have managed to invest £41,684,536 pounds and 27pence." The Introducer said it as though he had memorised a telephone number on the morning bus to work.

"A very fine sum, and one that will help you enormously with your new life," continued The Introducer, raising his eyebrows as he did so.

"How is it that much?" ask Zak.

"We *do* pay you interest, Mr Sharpe. Your investments

115

have been used to good effect and will continue to be invested on your behalf. We take a small fee for organising this of course, but it would be foolhardy to not let the washing earn its powder, so to speak." The Introducer smiled.

"Now onto more pressing engagements. Can you assure me, Mr Sharpe, that no one suspects. I must have complete confidence in this to proceed. Are you absolutely sure nobody knows of either the money OR that you will not be returning from this business trip?" The Introducer did not wait for Zak's reply...

"There have been in the past, people who have hinted at their imminent demise by releasing strangely informative songs or films, with strangely appropriate titles. I think they saw this as an irony, but what it does is fuel suspicion of assassination, or worse still... conspiracy." The Introducer waited for Zak's response.

"No, not at all," replied Zak.

"I take your word in good faith, Mr Sharpe, and that so, I can tell you that your journey home must be piloted by Mr Gutierrez. Mr Gutierrez will advise you en route of any instructions he has, and will tell you clearly what to do. Do not worry, Mr Sharpe, should the plane develop any difficulties, he will be able to cope." The Introducer used the forefinger on each hand to nod imaginary exclamation marks as he said the word, 'difficulties'.

"Mr Gutierrez is a very professional man, your safety is assured, Mr Sharpe, and I have every faith that your quest to find your calling will be achieved. Have you the case?" The Introducer raised his eyebrows in expectation.

"Yes, it's over there," replied Zak.

The Introducer looked across at the silver case that was the home of The Adviser. It was placed near the mushroom-coloured wall, the silver on it was slightly scuffed in places where Zak had taken it from country to country, and such was Zak's reliance on it, sometimes room to room. The Adviser had rarely left Zak's side during the last year, and now showed a few signs that it had travelled well and had been used virtually every day since they had been introduced.

"I'll take The Adviser from you now. I think his work is now done. Remember this, Mr Sharpe, Mr Gutierrez is a very good pilot and knows exactly what to do... you should *always* follow his advice. Do you understand?" emphasized The Introducer

"Yes, I will," replied Zak.

"Do you have any questions?" he asked. Zak thought this over for a moment and suddenly thought of one that had been at the back of his mind for some time.

"You obviously do your homework very well on me, but can I ask you something that has been at the back of my mind for some time?"

"By all means," replied The Introducer.

"What's your name?"

The Introducer looked back at Zak carefully and stubbed out his cigar into his little silver box. Zak immediately knew he wasn't going to be answered. Like an organised, time-honoured and well-rehearsed routine, The Introducer carefully closed the lid and slipped it into his inside jacket pocket. Studying his face and smiling, The Introducer replied,

"I think, Mr Sharpe, that we are unlikely to meet again. H^{e}aven is only possible through people remaining true to their obligations of confidentiality. It is for this reason that I have never met any of 'The Group'. If I ever had met them, knew of their names or their whereabouts, there would always be a possibility that others may come to learn of these things. That,

Mr Sharpe, is a very dangerous prospect. I am advised of my duties by The Co-ordinator, but have seldom met him or wish to do so very often. You will meet other members of The Group on your arrival and will therefore know more than me of The Group and H^{e}aven. It is for this reason, Mr Sharpe, that I beg your forgiveness and ask that you understand why I cannot answer your question."

Zak considered the answer to be a little pre-prepared and considered re-phrasing it to try and glean more. He decided many must have tried this tact in the past, and respecting The Introducer's position, instead smiled and nodded in understanding. At this, The Introducer got up from his chair and held out his hand.

"I wish you well, Mr Sharpe. I leave you in the very capable hands of Mr Gutierrez, and bid you goodbye."

Zak got up and shook his hand for the last time and wondered about the man behind the façade in front of him. The Introducer walked across to the case and picked it up. He looked back at Zak, and with a new-found sincerity said,

"It has been a pleasure knowing you, Mr Sharpe. I am confident that H^{e}aven will suit you and you will find that all your hopes and dreams are met in so many ways."

"Thank you," replied Zak.

He watched as The Introducer made his way towards and out of the door. *You want to go, don't you?* Zak thought. *You have talked so many people into this dream and yet cannot afford the dream yourself.* The Introducer opened and walked out the door without looking back and Zak knew that he would never see him again.

Zak stood there for a few moments and decided that he could now help himself to a small Bacardi and Coke. Zak's idea of a small Bacardi and Coke never was quite that, and before long he was sat chilling in front of the room's television. To his side stood a half-drank bottle of Bacardi and two empty Coke cans. Zak's journey home was to be later that night, in anticipation of a board meeting tomorrow in London. Zak knew he would not be making that meeting and spent the remainder of the afternoon thinking this prospect over.

***

As Zak sat on his balcony waiting for his euthanasic demise, Ron Block drove out of his street. Ron was a portly forty-something flight controller, with too many years under his belt to be interested in anything but keeping the skies safe and his bills paid. Waving his hand lazily to Doug, the airport security guard, he drove into the airport and down the long wide road that led to the control tower. He parked up next to Bill Bate's Impala and, picking up his Newmans Pretzels and Dr Peppers, clambered clumsily out of his silver station wagon.

Bill looked around as Ron entered the control room. Ron's arrival was a relief for Bill as he could be relied upon to make sure things ran smoothly. As Ron walked into the busy control room, he put his ear piece into his left ear. It was a bit long in the tooth now; it had broken some years earlier at a staff party when someone had stood on it. Since then it had been held together by a makeshift yellow plaster modelled from electrical tape. He'd never replaced it; it was his lucky earpiece.

"Hiya Bill. How's it goin?" asked Ron.

"Hey Buddy, not too bad, we gotta small backlog on 4 because of some delayed departures, but they're stacked up nicely in the circuit," replied Bill.

Bill considered Ron's attire. Ron wore black trousers, a white tie and his usual tank top. His mulberry tie with white spots did nothing to compliment his bright red Christmas socks.

"See ya dressed y'self today!" smirked Bill.

"Wus amatter wid you… Like you can talk." Ron motioned towards Bill's brown knitted cardigan and nodded jokingly.

"Yeah, but at least I'm keeping the missus happy," nodded Bill.

"If bein' married means wearing that, I'm happy as I am! Come on, I gotta get a coffee before I start."

***

Zak was finishing his drink as Braulio arrived promptly at 7pm. Zak finished it off as Braulio collected Zak's bags and followed him to the limousine. The airport wasn't far and as they drove to the airport, Zak looked at the dark hair of his new pilot. He wondered how much Braulio knew. Zak also by now knew it would be of no use prying.

They arrived at the airport with the minimum of fuss and, with the necessary formalities over with, Zak walked across the short distance to his plane. Once aboard the twin-engine company jet, Zak went to pour himself a drink.

"Excuse me, Mr Sharpe. Would you be kind enough to not have any more to drink, as we have a lot of things to organise and a clear head is needed?"

It was one of the few times Braulio ever spoke to him, and certainly the first that he had told Zak what to do. Zak's reaction to Braulio was to decide to listen carefully to this conductor of his death.

"Sure, would you like me to do anything?"

"Yes please, Mr Sharpe. In the toilet you will find some clothes to replace those you have on. Could you get out of all your clothes and put them into the plastic bag in the cubicle,

120

please? I will load the remainder of our bags on and get taxi clearance."

As Zak did as he was asked, Braulio went outside and loaded the remainder of their bags onboard. By the time Zak sat down in the lounge area, the airplane turbines had whined into life. The temptation to get another drink was almost too hard to bear, so instead he put the television on. A local news channel came on. "… In sport, USA Gymnastics announced today that the city of Boston has been selected as the site for the 1996 Olympic Gymnastics Trials and National Congress. Boston was awarded the bid over Nashville, San Jose, and Seattle and was considered to have the best overall facilities and plan.…" Zak sat down and let the noise of the day's news wash over him. He looked down at the boiler suit he had been given to wear. It was the same gunmetal grey colour of the T-shirt and boxer shorts he wore underneath. It had a shimmer to it however, and a pair of D-rings in the back that when he sat down reminded him of their presence by the painless but uncomfortable dig they inflicted into his spine. The socks were the same, and the trainers he had been given were black. He turned the sound of the television down a little as he first sensed, then heard Braulio getting clearance for take off from flight control.

The plane moved slowly forwards as it shuttled off the apron and onto the runway. It stopped as Braulio made final pre-flight checks and increased the power. The engines whined into life as their revolutions increased. After a few seconds the plane lurched forwards and the engines began their predictable roar. Moments later they had taken off. It was a little after 11:45pm.

Zak sometimes had difficulty equalising the pressure in airplanes, and immediately and nervously began his ritual of trying to yawn, and flexing his jaw. He needed gum and took some from the waist bag that was kept by the side of his chair.

As they banked left with the airport rapidly leaving their sight, Zak looked forward out of the window and saw the clean line of sea on the horizon. They began to pass through some clouds and Zak caught a glimpse of what looked like a brightly coloured passenger liner, in the bluish, dark, almost ebony waters beneath them.

After some time, the rushing sound of the air being sucked through the turbines was broken by Braulio.

"Meester Sharpe, you must put this on," he said, with a nervous urgency in his voice. Braulio handed a lifejacket to Zak and turned him around. Zak felt a strong pull on the boiler suit, and the crotch and strapping built into it tightened against his skin. Braulio began to take off his clothes. Underneath his uniform he wore a similar boiler suit to the one worn by Zak. Braulio picked up another life jacket and began to put it on. Zak did the same.

"Your watch and necklace too," said Braulio.

"But this was my father's! It's an antique Rolex and worth a lot more to me than the ten thousand pounds it'd cost to buy. I'm keeping it!" retorted Zak, emphatically

"If you wish to remain with it, you will die, as I am not taking you with it. If it stays with you, you stay with the plane."

Braulio looked at Zak with the seriousness of a commander in charge of a military operation. Zak thought for a moment and conceded that now was hardly the time to negotiate his father's watch.

Zak took a distraught last look at the small inscription on the back, 'As timeless as our Son 02/02/1931', and placed it into the plastic bag. Edwin had received it as a 21st birthday present from his parents and Zak had kept it near him ever since his father's death. Still thinking of his heirloom, Zak took his necklace off without a care and added this to the bag. He stood watching Braulio, and waited. Braulio walked over to a bum bag and pulled out the bag of Zak's blood taken only the day before, and began to add the blood to the contents of the plastic bag. Zak's clothes and jewellery immediately turned a dark red colour, and there seemed to be far more in there than needed.

Once fully mixed together, Braulio emptied the contents of the bag onto the rich cream, thick carpet of the lounge area. He folded, and then put the blood-covered plastic bag back into his bum bag and pulled out some small, thick, black plasters. He quickly peeled off a backing tape and stuck these onto the windows. Putting the tape carefully back into a small pouch on his bum bag, he quickly hurried into the cockpit. Zak watched as the glass immediately began to change in colour. The clear around the plasters turned opaque, as it obviously didn't like whatever was on them.

***

Ron's plump frame was sat in front of his monitor, his earpiece crackled into his ear.

"JFK Tower, this is November Delta 2041 we have ATIS information Foxtrot, Gate Bravo 12, requesting IFR Clearance for a traffic Pattern."

Knowing many people heard it, Ron was always conscious of how he sounded and cleared his voice momentarily before pressing his button.

"November Delta 2041, good evening Sir, flight plan is approved; you are cleared to 6000 feet, please squawk 1513, QNH is 1012 Millabars, read back is required."

Ron replied. "Flight Plan Approved, squawking 1513, QHN 1012, November Delta 2041," came the reply from the unknown pilot.

"Read back is correct, contact ground on 121.90 for push and start."

"Read back correct, onto ground now on 121.90 for the push and start, November Delta 2041, good day."

Ron sat back and felt something digging into his stomach and whilst watching the main monitor screen, fumbled with his airport ID badge, attached to his waist. His attention was soon focussed however, as a panic stricken voice shouted at him.

"Mayday, Mayday….this is Golf Foxtrot seven two nine from JFK, we are in difficulty and need to make an emergency landing. We are approximately…" Braulio's voice cut off and Ron jumped out of his chair like an electrified jack in the box.

"Golf Foxtrot seven two nine, this is Phoenix Tower. Please repeat your Mayday message," Ron called back urgently.

Ron normally had the dexterity of a touch typist on the computer system in front of him, but the urgency in his brain caused his fingers to miss the vital keys. Ron urgently watched his fingers, double checking that he was finding the correct symbols. He looked up again at the monitor and saw the small green dot labelled GF729 as it continued on its journey out to sea. Tapping frantically at the keys, he highlighted the plane and saw the altitude of the dot dropping sharply.

"Golf Foxtrot seven two nine, this is Phoenix Tower, JFK. Please report your Mayday condition and position. Over!" Ron's fear and loss of self-control had the other controllers looking at each other.

"Golf Foxtrot seven two nine, this is Phoenix Tower, do you read me? Over!!"

Ron watched the altitude mark drop on the little green dot on his monitor. Desperately looking for a pen, his pretzels were knocked on the floor, his open bottle of Dr Pepper rolled along the desk and lazily glugged out its contents over the edge.

Unaware of this, and the now group of controllers watching him, Ron scribbled the details of the plane's position, direction and speed quickly onto his notepad and looked around for help.

"Nat!"

Natasha was sat almost dumbfounded, looking at Ron.

"NAT! Come over here! Pete, pick up Nat's space. Nat, get this note over to the FAA... NOW!"

***

Oblivious to Ron's situation, Zak stood wondering what was going on. Braulio returned to the lounge as the plane started to descend. Zak looked again at the thick glass windows and as though habited by an unseen spider, small white streaks began to work their way across the glass in a pattern not dissimilar to a spider's web. He looked back at Braulio who was putting a harness on, and parachute onto his back. Clipping his bum bag to the waist of his harness, he pulled two pairs of goggles out and offered a pair to Zak. General fear was slowly being replaced by terror as it worked its way through Zak's body.

"What the hell is going on?" Zak cried, in a shaky voice.

"Do not worry, Meester Sharpe, I will take care of you. Now put the goggles on, please, we must leave... QUICKLY!"

Zak put his goggles on whilst Braulio checked the large wristwatch he wore. He led Zak to the airplane door and turned Zak around. Attaching the two D-rings on the back of Zak's boiler suit to his harness, he motioned to Zak to hold on to the bars by the door. Zak was nearly in a state of pure panic now and instead wrapped his arms up to his elbows around the door handle. Braulio pressed a button on his watch and also held the door hinges. The next ten seconds or so that they stood there waiting seemed like forever. The radio faintly crackled away in

125

the background with Ron's voice calling repeatedly to the plane; the television was onto some advert for the most versatile station wagon in the world, and for a moment, Zak could've sworn that all sounds paused just so he could hear a small pop noise.

The rush of the air into the plane took him by complete surprise, and Zak instinctively tightened his arm hold on the plane door. The windows had finally given way, letting in a seemingly invisible wild animal determined to lift him off his feet and smash him around the lounge of the plane. His ears popped and cheeks buffeted as the roar of the plane's jet furiously competed with the howl of the battering wind. Zak felt Braulio press himself closer to Zak, forcing them against the door, their feet almost leaving the ground as, like the breath of a demon, the air sucked at their bodies, trying to force them towards the windows. This lasted only for a few seconds and then eased as the pressure equalised. Braulio reached down and lifted, twisted and then pulled the emergency release of the door. The door jerked violently away from him, but sheer terror tightened Zak's arm lock, and it brutally dragged them both from the plane. Zak's grip intensified in pure terror as his feet left the comfort and security of the floor of the plane, but finally conceded to the sheer force of the now seemingly ton weight attached to them. The vortex from the plane's engines sent them into a violent spin, as the plane careered off ahead of them.

At the same moment of Zak letting loose his arm lock on the plane door, Braulio was screaming into his ear. Braulio swung his hand into Zak's neck and pinched tightly. Zak had already let go of the door by this point, and his terrorised shock would have lasted a lot longer had his pain senses told him of a more acute problem. A searing pain near his ear shot down his right side and electrified his body into a stiff stance he felt powerless to resist. The flashes of moon and stars, followed by dark ocean as they spun downwards, and the deafening gargle of the wind in his ears began to fade, as Zak slowly passed out.

Confident that Zak was not going to add to his problems of balance, Braulio regained control of their spinning descent and pulled the ripcord to release the parachute. The familiar thump to his crotch now followed, as the parachute opened and rapidly slowed their descent. Braulio in no way wanted an unconscious passenger on impact, and reaching into a calf pocket in his trousers, he pulled out a small bottle of smelling salts. Taking care not to drop it, he undid the small screw cap and placed it underneath Zak's nose. Zak's senses once again rose from their dark, silent world as he regained consciousness. His ears registered the buffeting of the cool night air as it more softly beat his ears and face. Zak tried to work out what he was looking at.

Zak's attention to Braulio's presence was recalled as Braulio threw something away. He was close behind Zak and seemingly relaxed. The shadowy night sky was ahead of them and behind them the flames of the plane lit up their backs. It burst into flames, sending shards of metal and debris into the night sky. Zak turned his head past Braulio's waist to watch the carnage happening almost behind them. Hot fireballs landed in the dark ocean beneath and increasingly behind them as Braulio steered the parachute away from the crash site. Silence fell.

***

A few moments after the small green dot disappeared, Ron slumped back in his chair. Looking desolately at the screen, he loosened his tie. In all the years he'd been an ATC or Air Traffic Controller he had never lost a plane. Ensuring their safety, other controllers read out direction and marker codes for the remaining planes. Ron took a melancholy look at the soggy pretzels that lay strewn in a dark sea of Dr Pepper on the floor. As his shocked vision focussed on a pretzel as it lay there soaking up the moisture he figured that if he were God, he would resemble the small plane he'd just witnessed fall from the sky into the dark sea of the Atlantic.

***

Slowed by the parachute, Zak looked around. Way out to his left, he thought he could see lights. Braulio broke the almost tranquil silence by rapidly talking what seemed like Spanish into a walkie-talkie. A crackled voice responded and Braulio continued to give what must have been directions or co-ordinates. The voice replied with what sounded to Zak like similar words, and culminating with what Zak understood to mean five minutes.

"Are you ok, Meester Sharpe?" asked Braulio.

"Yes, I'm fine, thanks… what the fuck happened there?" shouted Zak.

"We are about to land in the sea, Meester Sharpe, but will be picked up very shortly."

"That's fine, I'm not worried 'bout… JJEEEESSS..." Zak's voice was cut off by surprise as his rate of descent increased tenfold.

Braulio had clearly cut him free and for two seconds of sheer terror, Zak screamed. His screaming stopped as his body realised his face was now under water. He popped back to the surface and took a deep breath just in case the life jacket (the one that had just rapidly brought him back to the surface) failed him and he was to begin sinking. The coldness was intense, and Zak held his breath and teeth tightly together to stop them moving and biting his tongue or lip. Seconds later Braulio surfaced near to him, and instantly began to gather the parachute up into a big

128

wet puffball. Zak watched, and when this was done Braulio began to drag it with him towards Zak.

Cool soft waves lapped into Zak's face as he floated, facing Braulio, who seemed completely at ease with the whole situation. Within minutes a dark boat had made its way towards them. About sixty foot in length, it would have looked like any normal yacht had it not been for the fact that it was a gunmetal grey colour and had blacked out windows. Zak was helped aboard and Braulio followed and brought the parachute with him. As soon as they were aboard, the boat's propellers gurgled into life and the boat began to gain speed. They were both led downstairs into some sleeping quarters. Some towels and dry clothes lay on the bed. They both dried off and changed.

"I am very sorry, Meester Sharpe, for hurting you."

"That was YOU!?" replied Zak.

"Yes, and I am very sorry, but you are a very strong man and I did not know if you were going to hold onto that door. I had slowed the aeroplane down but still did not expect you to try and hold onto the door. I could not control the fall in any other way. This would 'ave meant that the parachute would not work and the fall would have killed us on impact," explained Braulio.

Zak knew he had good upper body strength from his gymnastic days, but the thought of him holding onto a door as they hit the water made Zak realise why Braulio had made sure he didn't hold onto it.

"That's ok Braulio, I understand…"

Zak suddenly felt like a winning prize fighter as the shock and surge of sheer adrenalin overcame him.

"WOW! That was a rush, wasn't it? Bloody hell, that was a ride of a lifetime!"

Zak grinned at Braulio, who gave him a shy smile back as he packed his things away.

"Well I must leeve you now, Meester Sharpe, I hope you weel be very happy. You weel be looked after by theese people. They will make sure you are safe. They will look after you," said Braulio, sincerely.

Braulio held out his hand and Zak shook it gratefully, in the knowledge that this man had completed his task so professionally. Zak didn't know what to say as a goodbye and found that by the time he'd considered it, Braulio had walked out of the door. He heard some momentary talk outside, and the door to his bedroom, lock. A different voice talked to him through the door.

"Do not worry, Mister Sharpe, this is for your own safety. Please enjoy the trip. We will be sailing for the rest of the night. You may want to get some rest. You will have a busy day tomorrow."

"Where are you taking me?" asked Zak.

"You are going to Ye-aven, Mister Sharpe!" exclaimed the man. "If you should need anyting, there is a button by your bed, just press it and I will come," he explained.

Zak heard the sound of footsteps as the man behind the door walked away. He looked around his cabin. He sensed that the boat had speeded up now as the pitch of the engines whining had become higher, and the boat was now thumping harder as it rapidly cut through the waves outside. A large mirror stood behind the built-in double bed, above it was another mirror in a half moon shape, surrounded by decorative lights. On the opposite wall, a small double built-in wardrobe stood next to an equally small dressing table. A door next to this led into an en-suite that Zak had already seen and had dismissed using. Zak had decided the shower was really only for show, figuring no one could possibly fit inside.

To his right, and at the foot of the bed, were more built-in cupboards. He noticed that his foot was getting wet as he had inadvertently put his foot on his wet boiler suit still on the floor. Zak decided to pick it up and place it in the shower tray. He opened up a cupboard opposite the bed to find in one a small cocktail bar and fridge. Zak poured himself a large Bacardi and thinned it down only slightly with half of a small bottle of Coke. He opened up the next cupboard that revealed a TV and video player. He turned it on to see it was tuned in to an old time film channel. On it, Norman Wisdom was stood in a policeman's uniform with his back against a wall, looking around like a nervous criminal. He held a truncheon in his right hand and looked back and forth. Zak noticed the 'Drink Tizer the Appetizer' sign in the window behind him, just before it flicked to some other policemen in a street. Zak smiled at the scene, sat down and drank some more of his favourite tipple. He couldn't think of when it had tasted so good.

Another wave of excitement spilled over his body and sent shivers down his back and arms. Small goose bumps appeared. Shuffling himself further back onto the bed, Zak watched as Norman ran frantically down an empty street, trying to escape from the other policemen. Zak had seen the film before and watched the TV lazily before falling asleep. As Zak dozed off, the boat sped off into the night and the remains of Zak's drink fell almost silently out of his hand, onto the soft carpet below.

The Island – 15th April

I close my eyes and I'm leavin', losin' reality,
I'm in your arms on the beach, the sun and
the sand and the sea,
you're still in love with me, in my dreams every night,
here in fantasy island, I'm living in paradise.

Fantasy Island - John Landry/John Gulley – 1988

Zak eased out of his deep sleep and noticed that the sun was up, and someone had turned Norman off. He turned to face the bedside cabinet and didn't see last night's glass. Noticing it instead on the floor, he got up and walked to the door. He was slightly surprised that it was no longer locked, and opened it and walked out into a galley. At one end of the corridor was a set of stairs leading upwards; the bright morning sun seemed to be pouring down it. Zak made his way along the corridor and up the stairs.

The top opened out into a lounge that last night had completely missed his attention. Windows adorned three out of the four walls, and ahead of him was an open set of patio doors onto a rear balcony.

"Good morning, Mister Sharpe, I hope you slept well." Almost magically appearing from nowhere, like the shop keeper from the Mr Ben cartoons, a small south American looking man appeared, carrying some cutlery. He wore a pair of shorts, a white T-Shirt and a small blue hat.

"Would you like some breakfast? We are nearly there."

"Yes please," replied Zak.

He walked forward and into the lounge area.

"I thought you might like it outside," said the small Spanish man, gesturing Zak towards the rear balcony.

"Ok," replied Zak, not really caring either way.

Zak had been on many yachts in his time, and this seemed in the daylight to be more like a converted, small gunship. Whatever it was, it was certainly quick. Zak noticed the sea was a deep blue colour and very calm, but the wake caused by the yacht's bow was a crisp, constant interjection of white spray.

"Would you like a drink, Mr Sharpe?" asked the short South American man.

"Could I have an orange juice, please?"

"And what would you like for breakfast? Would you like a full English? Continental? Or perhaps you would like something else?" The question reminded Zak of a night in Italy where he'd danced all night with a gorgeous, dusky, Italian girl with olive skin. He had been asked to help the nightclub on its opening night, and had happily made sure the paparazzi in Italy knew he was to attend their opening. Leaving with a dark-haired model did the reputation of the nightclub the world of good, as *the* new place to meet gorgeous young women. She had entertained him all night, and bringing him a cup of morning coffee had cheekily asked the same question, before looking sexily down at his crotch as he lay in bed. Needless to say, he decided on the 'something else'.

"English, please," Zak replied.

"No problem, Mr Sharpe." The little man walked off and Zak sat down.

It was another day before Zak could finally glance in the direction the boat was travelling and notice a small fleck of grey breaking the meeting of two different blues that made up the horizon. After a late breakfast, Zak sat and watched as the island he had been promised to see was finally coming into sight. The grey fleck grew first in size, and then parts of it begun to distinguish themselves. The most notable point was a high cliff point. This was surrounded by an increasing contrast of green as the tree line became more noticeable. Then certain rocky outcrops broke the green up to reveal little sandy coves. A small rock protruded from the water just off shore to the right, and they seemed to be heading straight for the high cliff. Zak could see a small building atop of the cliff top with a considerable number of satellite dishes on it. It looked to Zak like a TV station. It got higher and higher as they neared, and Zak studied it hard. The line of vision showed mainly sandy beaches to the left, and these stretched nearer to the cliff as they rounded it. The sight that met his eyes was one of complete contrast to what he had expected. The coastline curved away from him into a bay of about five miles wide. To the left, the sandy beaches that had so delightfully eased into view suddenly stopped, and were met by a large, unattractive and very functional concrete harbour. In it were a myriad of different boats. A number of medium-sized gun ships and other smaller military vessels were over to the far right. They were next to a small military-looking submarine. Their appearance was a total surprise. They had no markings on them and were all a dark grey colour. None flew any flags and they looked in good order and obviously regularly used.

In the middle of the bay was one large crane that was used to unload cargo from the ship that stood there. The markings on this were not ones that could be read by Zak, and were obviously foreign. About twenty or so small speedboats or small fishing boats were docked near this. There was then a gap of about two hundred metres from this to where lay a barbed wire fence that appeared from the water, and up the beach inland. To the left of that was about another one hundred metres of emptiness before the trees on the land began. The bay was not terribly busy, the main crane lay dormant and there were a number of people milling around or working on boats or trucks. Zak looked at the buildings of the small town and thought how functional the place was. Hardly the paradise he'd expected. The buildings were square, functional and without a thread of charm about them. It reminded him very much of army barracks. The yacht steadily made its way nearer, nestling between the gun ships and the large cargo ship. Few people gave the boat more than a passing glance, and Zak wondered what he had let himself in for.

"We are nearly there, Mr Sharpe," came a voice from behind him. Zak turned to see the small man again. "Please, follow me."

Zak followed, and was led to the balcony below. They stood waiting for the yacht to dock, and Zak watched as a Mini Moke came down between two off-white buildings and parked on the dockside near them. The small man started to un-winch a gangplank that slowly lowered to the quayside. The engines ceased just as it did so, and the small man beckoned Zak off.

"Welcome Meester Sharpe, please go to the car and he will take you to be welcomed."

Zak tentatively walked down the gangplank, ashore. The man sitting in the Mini Moke said nothing, but just waited for Zak to get in. Once he had, the engine was quickly fired up and they set off up a small road. The journey didn't last more than five minutes, but they seemed to twist and turn all ways. Zak swore they had turned left nearly half a dozen times, and with no other traffic in sight, he suspected that the driver was trying to

135

get Zak to lose his sense of direction, or remember where they had gone.

The New Arrival

The kingdom of H^{e}aven is like unto a merchant man, seeking
goodly pearls:
Who, when he had found one pearl of great price,
went and sold all that he had, and bought it.

St. Mathew ch.13, v.45

Zak and his driver pulled up outside some solid oak doors. The doors were very grand and stood proudly in the street. Stern, forceful, dominant and strong. Black stud bolts peppered the outside, and large black hinges looked like they'd served there for centuries. The driver had not spoken to Zak for the whole journey and such was Zak's interest in the building and place, that he didn't realise this until the man beckoned him off the car and to the door. The driver rang the bell, and promptly returned to his car and drove off.

Zak waited as the accelerating drone of the Mini Moke faded, as it made its way down the street. For a full five seconds the street became deathly silent. The door clicked and the hinges moaned in objection as the door opened.

"Good morning, Mister Sharpe. Please, come inside."

Zak stepped in, and the tall thin man closed the door behind them and led him across a large hallway and over a small courtyard. At the other side they went through a door.

137

"This is Mr Sharpe," said the tall man.

"Welcome! Welcome! Welcome!" A white-haired plumpish man who had been reading some papers at his desk, rose and immediately made his way towards Zak. Wearing a white, short jacket suit and holding his arm out straight in front of him, he quickly stepped over to Zak with the widest grin possible. Zak couldn't fail but take a liking to his jolly smiling features and obvious delight to see Zak.

"I have heard SO much about you that I feel I know you already. How was the journey? A bit hectic no doubt, Braulio is one of our best people. I heard his method of landing the parachute was slightly unorthodox, but safety first, wouldn't you agree?" His very English accent and joyous personality made Zak smile.

"But don't worry about that, that's tomorrow's news and by that, I mean exactly that. I've taken the liberty of recording the CNN report of your accident, tragic by all accounts, and it's going to be weeks before they find half the pieces... bloody good news though, I can tell you. Well come on man, take a seat, the journey can't have been all that pleasant and there's lots we need to sort out. Oh, listen to me rabbitting on like an old sea parrot. Let me introduce myself, I'm the welcome committee and customer services all rolled into one. You can call me Mr C."

Sitting down in a large, red leather armchair, Zak couldn't fail to be impressed with the man's likeable enthusiasm. He smiled at the mysterious use of pass-names. No one ever seemed to tell you their name. Zak's consideration of whether that really mattered was interrupted by Mr C.

"Would you like a drink? Of course you would, who wouldn't after being killed, kidnapped, taken miles from the rest of civilisation and reinventing himself all within 48 hours! What would you like? Don't tell me... a Bacardi and Coke!"

Zak smiled and accepted this warm invitation, whilst wondering whether this man possibly used air to breathe or just to talk.

Hunching up his shoulders and moving his arms back and forth like a runner from Chariots of Fire, Mr C grinned excitedly, and did an exaggerated small run towards the small bar against the wall. Zak looked at him in amusement. About 60 years old, he looked very well for his age and wore small silver-rimmed glasses that as he moved, bobbed dangerously up and down on the end of his nose. Zak looked around the room and waited whilst his drink was being made.

"I don't know about you, Mr Sharpe, but I am *so* excited. You are going to truly love it here. Let me fill you in on a small number of rules, and get the formalities out of the way. We do need to cover this, and then we can get to the fun part."

Mr C walked over with two drinks, handed Zak his, and placed his own on the small round table between Zak's seat and his own.

"OK, rules is rules as they say, and we have some... but not too many, mind, and none I think you'll have a problem with. Firstly... Contact. Come what may, your presence here is strictly confidential. I mean you are officially dead after all. So to let anyone know you are alive or to even hint as to your whereabouts is strictly prohibited. Now I know you might be thinking that's obvious, but I can't stress it enough. If The Group ever learns of you trying to make contact with the outside world, you are unlikely to see this one for much longer."

Zak looked at him, hoping he might clarify.

"...And no, I don't mean he would send you home! Anyway, that being that, you are allowed to watch just about any TV channel available to the island. That said, that's just about most of them from around the world! You're also allowed to

139

own and use a computer and browse the Internet. Now we control and monitor all incoming and outgoing data, and firewalls stop anyone knowing exactly who or where we are. So any attempt to email someone will be treated as the same thing. If you want to view a site that needs paying for, you must first email me. I will arrange access. The system will not allow you to enter any details without access... even false ones! Now, Mister Sharpe, let me make myself clear on one point. I am *very* broad minded. If you want to log onto a site that allows you to watch live sex shows between a man and his pet poodle, that really is no concern of mine. I will simply allow you access, pay your bill and invoice you accordingly. Is that understood?"

Zak thought that Mr C could've easily used a cruder example, but was grateful he didn't.

"Is the point of no contact clear, Mr Sharpe, because if it isn't, then it needs to be."

"No, that's fine. I'm here 'cause I'm avoiding people, not trying to get in touch with them," Zak replied.

Mr C simply nodded, grinned enthusiastically and took another gulp of his drink.

"Now, rule number two. Religion. Sorry, not allowed..."

Zak looked at him, confused that such a thing was so high on Mr C's agenda. As if recognising his confusion, Mr C continued.

"...I am hoping this was covered by The Introducer, Zak. But in essence, it is has been used by people to control others for longer than people can record. It has rarely in that time achieved anything, and has separated mothers from sons, brothers from sisters and turned friends into enemies. It tells you what to eat, what to drink, what to wear, what to do, what NOT to do and who you can or can't do those things with! H^{e}aven does not believe in religion as it is used by people to enrage the population into war! And H^{e}aven will not have conflict on the island."

Zak looked at the man and grinned at his salesmanship over a concept that had seemed thus far to Zak, to be an unworthy pitch.

"You win... No religion. What else?" asked Zak.

"Well that's very nearly it. I will say this though; there is an expectation that you are going to be a good citizen. I mean there are no double parking laws, there are no late night curfews, no planning departments or driving regulations... well I mean we *drive* on the left, but apart from that there's nothing.... You don't need a licence or anything. What I do mean though, is that we do expect you to be a good citizen. By that I mean that we would not be impressed if you raped, murdered or stole from others on the island. That, I am afraid, will bring you in front of The Controller, and as you can imagine, Mister Sharpe..."

"Please, call me Zak," interrupted Zak.

"...As you may imagine, Zak, we do not have a prison on the island and nor do we want one. Punishments are only decided by The Controller for non-compliance and he only has two. The first is penance to the person or people you have offended. The second is death."

Zak looked at the now very solemn face of Mr C. Once Mr C was sure Zak had heard him correctly, his face brightened immediately back up.

"...But that said, we expect others to live in the same harmony that you do. Punishment may be harsh and swift, Mister... sorry... Zak, but it is rarely needed. If you have a problem with another person, you can sort it out between yourselves or call the IRS. That's me! The Island Relations Service!" He said smiling. "And I will try and replace the previous harmony. For example, we have a couple live on the

141

island that adore dogs. One of the dogs managed to get out of their grounds and bite a Mister Lennon living next door. Thankfully, Mister Lennon did not see it as being too serious. But as a sign of good citizenship we asked them to ensure that their dogs could not possibly escape again. If Mister Lennon had requested it then the animal may have had to be put down. Good citizenship, Zak, that's all we ask for."

Zak's mind raced back to earlier. The words, 'like the man sung about', began buzzing around his head. The name, so casually thrown his way. Lennon. Surely not *the* Lennon.

"Okay Zak, let's get things organised. We have a small town on the island and it has many cafés and bars. It has all the amenities you'd expect from a modern town. A school, park, library, hospital… it's all there. If you need anything, *anything* that the town does not seem to offer, do not despair. Call me or contact me, I spend a lot of my time in and around the town. I will arrange it for you. Cars, motorbikes, boats, whatever it is, can be bought. But there is a price. You see, if you ask for a red sports car we cannot simply order one for you."

Zak frowned at him in confusion.

"You don't exist!!" Mr C laid his hands out in front of him as though carrying an invisible platter.

"See! If you don't exist, and the island doesn't exist, we can hardly buy you your sports car!"

Zak sat bemused at Mr C's obvious enjoyment of explaining this concept.

"What we have to do, Zak, is *steal it* for you! Our operatives are able to get just about anything, given a price. What I'm going to do today is take you there, and help you settle into, *The Welcome House*. It is such a fine place; you are going to love it. Then over the next few days, I am going to help you make a life for yourself here on the island. Choose some land,

142

build a house, get your new life organised... Excited? Well you should be. Now come on, finish that drink of yours, and let's go and have some fun!"

The Welcome House

Welcome to the House of Fun, Now I've come of age.
Welcome to the House of Fun.
Welcome to the lion's den, Temptation's on his way,
Welcome to the House of...

Madness – 1982

The drive to The Welcome House was to be the last time Zak saw that side of the island. They got into what Mr C very proudly told him was a cream and black 1939 Silver Ripple Cabriolet. He had made a point of telling Zak it was one of its kind, particularly as it had a very un-standard bonnet badge on the bonnet. Instead of traditional, 'The Spirit of Ecstasy' that was modelled on Eleanor Velsco Thornton, and had adorned Rolls Royce bonnets all over the world since 1911, Zak noticed that she had been joined by a man behind her, who seemed to be enjoying her charms whilst holding onto her hips. They drove slowly through the narrow streets until they left the small village. The village had been eerily quiet, and Zak's unease with this was apparent.

"Are you wondering where everyone is, Zak?" asked Mr C.

"Yes, I guess I am. I expected people, but have only seen a handful," replied Zak.

"Don't worry, most of the islanders on this side of the

144

island only work until noon. It becomes uncomfortable to work all afternoon."

As they drove on, they broke out of the streets and onto an empty country road, and travelled along this for about ten minutes. Weaving their way past hedges and trees, Zak could make out the crop fields beyond. Once or twice he saw someone tending crops or driving a tractor. Zak had never been to many struggling countries or ever seen the harsher side of life, so to him, country life the world over seemed to be pretty much about the same.

Mr C talked cheerfully the whole time, telling Zak about himself and how he had been in the British army as a lieutenant colonel, and been posted in many countries around the world.

"It was an amazing place, walking down the street it seemed like every balcony had two or more buxom fillies beckoning us to come up and join them. Such a place is a wonderful…"

Zak's attention wandered as they had to sharply pull over to the side of the road. The white walled tyres of the Rolls Royce gnarled with annoyance as they had to contend with the dusty, stoned edge. A large, dusty, tan, American personnel carrier passed them. The driver did not take his eyes off the road, and simply raised his hand to signify thanks. Mr C's conversation did not wane for one moment. The road here was not terribly wide and they were in the wrong vehicle to argue with such a large truck.

Not long after, the glistening blue sea on both sides became visible as the island narrowed. Zak looked from side to side and could see nothing but the vast expanse of water. They arrived at what looked remarkably like a 1950's tollbooth or border guardhouse in the road. The island at this point was barely half a mile wide. For about four hundred metres before and aft of it was completely barren, not a plant, tree or bush. A man stepped out of the little hut as the car drew near. He looked of Mexican descent, and was dressed in military slacks and was wearing dark sunglasses. He walked towards the car smiling, and carrying his clipboard in hand. Zak could see he was happy to see Mr C and wondered how many people this man saw in a day. The border guard reached up and took off his glasses.

"Good day, Mr C, and how are you today?" he asked, with a strong Spanish accent.

"I'm fine, Dario, how are you today?"

"Well, Mr C, I think it is like this. I sit here all the days and sometimes I feel good, sometimes not. And when I am thinking I am alone, I say to myself, Dario, you have a wonderful life, with a wonderful family, and you have all of this time in the day to rest so you can play with your children. What more could you want? And do you know what answer I find?"

"No?" said Mr C, smiling.

"I think if only my wife had a job like this, she would maybe have more energy for me when I get home... do you know what I mean?" laughed the guard.

Zak smiled, as Mr C laughed heartily with the guard.

"I can see exactly what you mean, Dario."

Dario's eyes fell onto Zak, and his expression became slightly more functionary.

"Okay, Mr C, I have your car booked in here, and I will need only your signature and you will be free to enter." The guard passed the clipboard to Mr C and reached into his chest pocket to take out a biro. He handed it to Mr C, and waited while Mr C signed.

"There you go!"

"Thank you, Mr C," replied Dario. He walked happily back to the gatehouse and lifted the border gate. Mr C drove slowly under.

"And you say hello for me, to Consuela," said Mr C.

"Of course, Mr C, of course," replied Dario, with a wide grin on his face. Zak had never met anyone so joyous before, and so relaxed when carrying a gun on their hip.

Almost like an east, west divide in Germany, the road quality improved the minute they passed through the gate. The previous one had been quite narrow and bumpy. The Rolls had made easy work of the bumps, but now as the road was smooth, she glided along as if on air. The rumble of the tyres had now given way to the soft purr of the engine.

Once in a while they passed an entrance to an estate. Some were what Zak imagined must have been ranches; wooden fences with large wooden arches over gates propped open by bits of wood. Others were in true Hollywood style, where large white pillars supported ostentatious gold mascots. Between them, dark black, ornate gates with gold gilt details hinted of the opulence inside, but would only open should the called have the magic code on the electronic panel.

***

After some time, Mr C brought the car to a halt, and turned the engine off.

"This is the site of your new home," he said delightedly. Zak looked to his right, where Mr C had pointed. The entrance was neither completely rural nor opulent Americanesque. Clearly built some years ago but was still in very good condition, the rather wide and thick wooden arch sat on short granite pillars. Zak could just make out the faded letters r and c across the top, but couldn't make out any more. Underneath the arch and showing only mild wear, were two almost black wooden gates. Birds and crickets sung in the sun as they sat there.

"Don't worry about the look of it, Zak, the men will help you make it into whatever you like… unless you want to do what Mister Lee did, and do most of it yourself?" Zak looked at Mr C quizzically, whilst analysing his words. There it was again, name-dropping.

"Is that who I think you mean it is?" asked Zak.

"Mister Lee? Perhaps. I am talking about the son, Brandon. He arrived a little over a year ago, you know, to be with his father!" Mr C looked forwards, smiling. He had a knowing smile on his face, and a twinkle in his eye that Zak read as, 'You think *that* was surprising!' An excited and warm glow came to Zak and a smile grew on his own face. Brandon Lee, son of the famous Bruce Lee, had died tragically in the March of the previous year. It had been a mysterious tragedy whereby what had apparently shot Brandon should have been a gun loaded with blanks, during the filming of 'The Crow'.

Zak recalled that he had not long opened up his bank accounts in the Cayman Islands when he heard on the news that the film star had died. He remembered wondering whether there was any coincidence in his own situation at the time. He had passed it off as quickly as it arrived at the time, but now… bloody hell, this is bigger than I thought!

Not long after passing what was to be his new home, they approached a town. A sign simply reading, 'Town', signified that they were indeed in a place which was to be the life of the island. The houses were neo-traditionalist in their design, and typically reminiscent of the colloquial British Empire of earlier Americas. With pastel colours and large front verandas, they were set back neatly from the road. Their tidy lawns surrounded clapboard exteriors and were encircled by little white picket fences. Almost all the balconies housed benches or rocking chairs, where owners obviously spent a good deal of their time chatting over life. The town reminded Zak of a typical Midwestern American street at the end of the nineteenth century. Images of, The Waltons, and, Little House on the Prairie, soon came to mind. Zak grinned at this delightful timescape. People milling around, carelessly chatting their time away, not a scrap of paper nor a coke can in sight.

They weaved their way through the streets without so much as a glance off anyone, yet clearly their car stood out. Cars parked on the drives of these houses were not as opulent, nor as old as Mr C's fine example of automobile engineering. They turned right, and then finally left into a busy but not overly bustling market square. Mr C slowed the car to walking pace and drew up outside a fine looking building, facing the square.

"This is the centre of the town, here in the square, there's a market every Sunday. People from all round the island bring their wares and goods to sell them. Mostly its fruit, vegetables and small handicrafts, but there's a fine fish market here that sells an assortment of fresh fish that will simply melt your taste buds. Well, this is your home, for as long as you need to get yours sorted out, this is... The Welcome House!"

His hand gestured to the large building, as though he were opening a show to an audience. Mr C had made clear on the way that, 'The Welcome House', was what could only be described as the most exclusive and possibly smallest of hotels in the world. It was a very grand place, but only ever had two guests at any one time. Owned by The Group, it was the only building outside of 'Southside' that wasn't owned by islanders. It was designed and placed to do exactly what it said, welcome people. He could live here and they would help him get settled onto the island and decide what he wanted to do with his land. They would build his home using local craftsmen, and it would be built to whatever standards and in whatever design and using

149

whatever materials he wanted. What's more, if he didn't like it he could simply tear it down and start all over again. He told Zak about a couple on the island, whose standards were rather bizarre. He seemed to think that this was mainly the woman's influence as she seemed to have a 'larger character'. Her somewhat hen-pecked partner was talked into submission, and very often did things for a quiet life.

Very old in style, The Welcome House was indeed a beautiful place. Zak was, through his wealth, very used to opulence, and this was no exception. The tinted half glass entrance doors were opened by a porter dressed in a cream uniform with mulberry collars and cuffs that matched his hat. The reception area was not too big, but very well presented, with light oak floors and walls. They walked across the reception to a 1930's style lift.

What Zak was not quite prepared for, was where the lift took them. The doors opened to a large lobby. Opposite, were two doors leading to a lounge area.

"Let me show you around your accommodation," said Mr C, smiling.

He led Zak off to his left and showed him round a small, but well equipped gymnasium area with its own shower area, sauna and steam room. Through the patio doors, Zak could see a jacuzzi big enough for eight people, let alone one. The centre section of the suite was Zak's bedroom, this shared the balcony with the gym, and Zak looked out across the sea. The walk in wardrobe and cupboards already held a set of clothes for all occasions, that were in his size. They walked further round to an open plan lounge and dining area with a kitchen beyond. Once again, patio doors led out onto a balcony that overlooked the town, and part of the market square. Mr C could clearly see that Zak Sharpe felt at home.

Settling Down

Is it any better in H^{e}aven my friend...?

William Carlos Williams – 1944

Over the next few days, Zak settled in, and was introduced by either Mr C or the hotel concierge, who was more like a lifestyle manager, to the local shops, and encouraged to start building himself an individualised wardrobe. Very used to luxury, Zak was still surprised to find that every morning his underwear had been laid out for him and his slippers were waiting. If he ventured downstairs for breakfast, by the time he had eaten and walked back to his room, his clothes had been straightened, his bed made, and his sunglasses cleaned for the day. It seems they had done their homework on Zak Sharpe, as the Gucci glasses were the same as his favourite back in the real world.

The café's and ice cream parlours in the town were interspersed with shops that were all well stocked, and offered a complete array of differing local casual styles, and more formal attire for those important parties.

The streets were often busy with people milling around and getting on with their daily chores. Zak simply loved the fact that no one recognised him nor hassled either him, or what was obviously an important figure on the island, if he was accompanied by Mr C. Not exactly famous for anything other than being a rich playboy, Zak had still seen more than his fair share of attention from autograph hunters, girls wanting him to sign various parts of their anatomy, or photographers pathetically following him to see whom he was meeting for lunch. This was a refreshing change.

Mr C introduced Zak to a designer with whom he was to discuss and explain what sort of house he wanted. Zak had, until now, lived in two types of properties. The first was typical of the home he was born in. Richly English and opulent in the extreme, it was a large building with many windows and old enough to warrant planning protection, and be considered to be a classic example of its era. Generally full of antique furniture and pictures, it was chintzy, with lots of dark wood and colourful drapes of rich reds, beige and gilt edge.

The second kind of home Zak had experienced was quite the opposite. The very simplistic décor found in halls of residence or Mediterranean villas. With lots of magnolia, at the time these plain walls and simple lines were a breath of fresh air to a young man who'd known only extravagant chintz. Now, this style merely reminded him of places in the sun where the hot lifestyle made you too lazy to decorate. In places like these, plain was good. Instead, for his own home, Zak chose a very modern look. He had seen a house once in a film where everything was ultra modern. Simple, but colourful and stylish. He wanted the interior to look modern but stylish, timeless, yet it had to have that 'Wow' factor.

The builders were all local people from the island. It initially appeared that they were all almost obviously out of work, but Zak later found out that the pay he was offering was obviously higher than local jobs, and so they heartily left current jobs to start his. Zak had decided on lots of glass and grey steel framework. He was particularly self-impressed with his idea to have a staircase up a wall made out of glass steps without a rail, so they looked almost as though people climbing them were simply walking uphill on air. His first meeting with anyone not native to the island after his initial meeting with Mr C was a most bizarre event.

Elvis – 8th Jan 1935 to ..oops!

How I pray, h^eaven answered my prayer
when I reach out for you, you'll be there.

Elvis Presley – 1965

The sun streamed between the high rise buildings at the far end of Prospect Park. The haze of the city made the bright colours of yellow and tangerine appear to swirl together behind a frosted glass window in the sky. Every pore on Zachariah's face accepted the colours and, despite the cold air, the increasing warmth. It reminded him of his first morning at H^eaven, where a very similar warmth was felt as the sun shone through the mock Georgian window of his bedroom.

***

Zak's eyes had winced as the bright glow became an intense light with piercing insistence that he woke up. He could feel the warmth of the sun growing and although he enjoyed it; his eyes were now flinching in annoyance. He turned over and faced towards the small beech table on the opposite wall. On the right of it stood a large fern in a clay pot with its chrome lip, his pen and notepad strewn messily nearby. Zak had sat in the beech canvas chair next to it for much of last night, writing down what ideas he had for his house. Some of his ideas were now crumpled up bits of notepaper on the floor near the chair. Some things had started off in his head sounding fine, but had deteriorated into flawed idealism as the night had worn on. He began to consider whether his idea of a glass staircase was a momentary flash of brilliance, or just plain stupid. Other similarly novel ideas were becoming hard to find. Still, it wasn't his job to think of them, and any he did have were to complement and add to the thoughts of others.

His eyes flickered into life and settled on the gold-framed print of a seaside resort. He studied it carefully, too lazy to move. The print showed a house, very typical of the island, perched on the top of an outcrop. Its windows looked across a smooth sandy beach and gently lapping waves. Zak thought it looked very picturesque and quite idyllic, but then casually dismissed it as a design for his house, as he was opting for a modern design. He lay there.

The peaceful, early morning sound of birds slowly gave way to the distant hum of people and cars. The sun was now warming the back of his neck, and Zak thought he'd venture out and see a bit more of this town. He eased his body from his bed and sat on the edge. The sun was indeed quite warm as it touched his arms and legs, and he closed his eyes whilst he bathed in its heat. Feeling soothed, he rose and took a shower in the adjoining en-suite. He rang the receptionist and ordered some fresh orange juice, bread and cheese. As he dressed, the door knocked and in walked a slender young woman, pushing a trolley. On it was a selection of sliced cheeses and hams, and some soft white bread. He ate heartily, and was grateful for a side dish of sliced melon that had accompanied his order. He walked down the single flight of stairs to the reception and out into the street.

155

Zak had been given a credit card and some cash, and had previously been escorted round most of the small town by Mr C. He had bought a few clothes and other furniture items that caught his eye, but had resisted the temptation to buy much, wanting instead to wait until he knew he had the full concept of what he wanted from his home in his mind. Today was a market day, and Zak decided to wander around to see what was on offer. He walked off the pavement and across the road and onto the market square that fronted The Welcome House. People were hustling and bustling by with varying degrees of urgency. Zak watched as a small, elderly lady with grey hair and a crooked nose tapped the behind of her mule. It lazily ignored her as it carried what looked to Zak like an impossible load of melons, in four large string sacks. He walked across the square and to the entrance of the small street almost opposite the hotel. Here began the market and many people pushed and dodged their way up and down the small road between the stalls. Zak meandered through. He decided to look left only as this would mean that he would not miss stalls, as his return journey would take care of those now on his right.

The first stall sold rugs, and was operated by a man whose face was as hard as buck leather. Zak's interest in them was very short lived; rugs he would leave until he had a floor to put them on. The next sold ladies' clothing. A young girl was serving, whilst an older lady sat at the back watching Zak walk by. His courteous smile to her was returned with a brief disinterested smile. The next stall had a multitude of assortments on it. It resembled a stall from a jumble sale, and had everything on it from books and records to wooden ornaments and jewellery. A dark tanned man in his fifties sat there peeling a slice from his apple with a bone-handled penknife. Zak stopped and began to look through the different ornaments.

"Yes, ma'am, two please." The voice he heard was clear and confident and of a deep south American accent. Unmistakeable. Zak looked to his right, and was amazed by what he saw. He could have sworn the voice he'd heard was that of Elvis Presley and yet the man and lady stood at the next stall were hardly what he'd expected. The man he saw was a grey-haired slim man of just under six foot tall. He wore a pair of brown suede shoes, khaki coloured trousers and a white short sleeved shirt. His hair was grey and neatly brushed back off his face.

"Wadda ya think, honey? Shall we have some?" He motioned towards some bananas. The younger Hawaiian lady with him, possibly a native, smiled and nodded. She could have passed for someone a lot younger and Zak thought she must have been stunning in her time. She was about forty and equally slim with long dark hair. Zak could not believe his eyes. Here was Elvis Presley in the flesh, and buying melons and bananas at a market! Zak wondered if he really had seen what he thought he had. This man was trim and grey and nothing like the dark haired, obese, glitzy Elvis that had wooed crowds in Las Vegas. He stood, fixed to the floor by wonderment; he studied this man's features carefully. He was now certain it was him. The facial features had changed little in the last... how many years had it been?

Zak watched as they bundled first the two melons and then bananas into a bag and paid. They began to walk towards him, and in embarrassment that he'd been staring, Zak looked away.

"Well hello there." Zak quickly looked back at the man before him.

"I guess you're the new arrival?" The sweet south American accent poured out of the man's lips like warm custard. He smiled and held out his hand to Zak. Completely in awe, Zak

157

responded in an almost automatic way.

"...Er yes, I am, I arrived only a few days ago," he stammered.

"Well hell then, you're barely findin your way round here. I'm Elvis, and this is my lovely wife, Kaike. Pleased to make your acquaintance." Still the words rolled off his tongue, silky smooth.

"I'm Zak, Zak Sharpe... from England."

"See, I told ya, honey, I knew he'd be here!" Elvis exclaimed. Zak was amazed that he could possibly be known to the great man.

"Knew!?" he asked. "Well hey yeah, we saw it on the news the other day and I said to Kaike here, 'he looks like he's on his way here, didn't I honey?"

Zak looked towards the woman by his side. She smiled sweetly and didn't attempt to respond, as Elvis continued.

"Well say look, whenever you wanna come on over just head up the north road, and we're the last estate at the end. You'd be mighty welcome." Zak couldn't contain his obvious look of immense pleasure at being invited.

"I'd love to," he replied.

Elvis sensed Zak's excitement, and smiling, began to warm to Zak's childish glee.

"Anytime... okay honey, we'd better be on our way. It's a pleasure to meet you..."

"Zak... Zak Sharpe," interrupted Zak.

"Okay Zak, like I say, anytime." Elvis nodded his head and smiled to reveal glisteningly white teeth and facial features unmistakeably Elvis.

As Elvis and Kaike walked away, Zak watched after them. Kaike only reached to his shoulder and her dark long hair was in contrast to his almost white short hair. Zak stood dumbfounded until they were out of sight in the crowd. He turned and looked at the stall holder. The apple was now nearly half finished, and the man looked back at Zak, disinterested at Zak's amazement. Realising Zak didn't want anything from his stall he turned his attention once again to his mid morning snack. Much else in the market barely raised Zak's curiosity past mildly interested. The idea of shopping now was a distant memory, thrown to the wind by a chance meeting with one of the planet's most famous ex-celebrities.

After a small snack on the front terrace of a café, Zak ambled back to The Welcome House. In the foyer, an excited Mr C was waiting for him.

"Zak, come here, my fellow. Come, have a drink. I've got some great news. Waiter! My usual please, and a Bacardi and Coke for Mr Sharpe."

He led Zak to some wicker chairs and coffee table in the corner of the reception area.

"Zak, I've got it sorted! Things are progressing wonderfully…" For the next few hours, Mr C slowly pulled Zak's attention back into the task of getting his house built. Zak's surprise and delight of the day's events would never be equalled in his lifetime but simply built upon like one builds a house of dreams… slowly, and one brick on top of the last.

Daily Pickings

*You took my freedom away a long time ago
and you can't give it back
because you haven't got it yourself.*

Solzhenitsyn – The First Circle

May 2000

Zachariah had sat for far too long watching the people walk through the park. Of the hundreds that passed him, barely more than a few ever put anything into his cap on the floor. This wasn't a tourist spot and for that Zachariah was glad. The last thing he wanted was being recognised by The Group, and taken care of. So albeit these were small takings, Zachariah was happy enough.

Zachariah wasn't old but he *felt* old, he leant forward and picked up his cap from the sidewalk, as Americans called it. The tarmacadam had warmed during the day and this made a welcome change to earlier in the month, when it had been really cold. Zachariah forced his aches to dispel as he got up and began his seemingly daily homage to the bread shop in 3rd street. He ambled along Prospect Park West and turned right into 3rd Street. The small bread shop was a little over halfway down on the right hand side. Zachariah slowly made his way along the sidewalk, taking care to blend into the surroundings as much as possible, and looking carefully for any dropped coins. Just before he reached the shop he turned right into the alleyway that separated 3rd Street from 2nd Street. Turning left, he came to the large waste bin that held the bread that was made at 4am, but was now too old to be as fresh.

The MacNamaras were very fussy about their bread, and this attention to detail and focus on providing the best they could worked out very well for Zachariah; for he would arrive at 2pm and it was an almost certainty that some bread would be discarded in the bin. If the bins were empty, the youngest son would often place the staling bread next to the bin, knowing full well that local down and outs would make use of it. Today was no exception and Zachariah found a large, once soft centred loaf on the broken old fridge that lay next to the large red bin. Taking a look around, he picked it up and made his way back down the alleyway to the main street. Cutting straight across Prospect Park West he went into the park through a gap in the fencing. Pushing his way through the bushes he arrived at his small but quite tranquil spot on the grass he liked to think of as his, and sat down. Satisfied with his day so far, he looked around. The wind often picked up around this part of the park. The breeze kneaded the blades of grass with an invisible hand sweeping it too and fro, folding it this way and that as the grass succumbed to its force.

Taking out the large loaf he examined it. One time he'd started to eat a loaf and discovered far too late that a bird had managed to direct its daily excretion perfectly onto his lunch. A scruffy boy walked past; Zachariah immediately pushed his loaf inside his coat to protect it. He'd experienced how youths can cruelly steal things from you, even if they clearly didn't want them. He had tried to fight once, but it had cost him more than the bottle of drink was worth. He'd hoped he could defend himself against the small groups of lads, but they had overpowered him and left him worse than if he'd have just ignored them and walked on. The boy carried on past, reading a small book. Zachariah checked his loaf again. No bird shit on this one, he thought to himself; mind you, it's a far cry from the food that was laid on for his Welcome Party. That seemed many moons ago and not long after the arrival of one, Ayrton Senna…

Moving House

*Longevity has its place. But I'm not concerned with that now…
I may not get there with you. But I want you to know tonight,
That we, as a people will get to the promised land.
And I'm not fearing any man.*

Martin Luther King – 3ʳᵈ April 1968

Zak sat in the rear lobby of The Welcome House talking over the finer details of his house with the chief builder. It's May 3ʳᵈ 1994 and although they only physically started building the house a week ago, Zak is confident that it will be finished by July. The sheer numbers of people available to work is in sharp contrast to the level of focus and customer service offered by builders Zak knew in Leicestershire. Zak had once struggled to get quotes for his indoor pool extension. After weeks of searching, the builder he had chosen was more concerned about the next job than about meeting his obligations for Zak. This was different. Outside, he heard a light squeal of brakes as Mr C arrived in his Rolls Royce. Zak listened to hear his usual enthusiastic chatter as he entered the lobby area.

"Come, come, come, Mr Senna, I will show you around our Welcome House." Zak watched the now familiar figure of Mr C and the only slightly shorter figure of Ayrton Senna. Zak was not entirely surprised to see him as he had heard of his death two days ago, and had been tipped off that Ayrton hadn't wanted the home country pressure and international pressure of press covering his obvious rivalry with Alain Prost. Mr C led Ayrton up the wide sweeping stairs still chatting merrily away. Some time later, and with the chief builder now gone, they both returned.

"Zak!" said a bright and ever so cheerful, Mr C.

"Zak, I'd like you to meet your temporary neighbour. This is Ayrton Senna da Silva. Ayrton, Zachariah Sharpe."

"Just call me, Zak. Pleased to meet you."

Zak held out his hand, and shaking his hand, straight away noticed how cool and soft the driver's hands were.

"Sit! Sit! Let's get something to drink. Zak here used to be in the textile and electronics business."

"I have read a lot about you, Zak. You seem to have been in many gossip columns around the world."

"Not always for the right reasons though."

"Maybe not, but who are we to judge?"

Zak looked at the tanned face and into the dark eyes of Ayrton. The racing driver everyone admired gave a knowing smile back. He and Ayrton both knew what they had been through; Mr C, who was now ordering drinks, couldn't possibly understand what had brought them to H^{e}aven.

Just as Zak had witnessed first hand, the next few days saw Ayrton surrounded by people with drawings and pictures of different types of bricks, wood and all manner of materials. A multitude of out of place and contemporary designs of house, barn, shack, bungalow and mansion were given. Ayrton had opted for a roaming and very casually styled bungalow, very reminiscent of his home country.

July had nearly arrived and Zak was nearing the end of his stay at The Welcome House.

Over the next week, Zak saw a lot of the person who

164

occupied the floor above. Ayrton told him how he'd started racing at twenty four and had been forced to work hard for his success. His obvious determination to succeed was still firing inside and Zak asked him why.

"I had achieved all I wanted to. Formula 1 racing is getting faster and faster and more dangerous day by day. It's not the racing that scares me… it's the public. I love the win, I HAVE to win, but with the victory comes the accolade and fame. It is those that I am not comfortable with."

"How long did you plan it?" asked Zak.

"I knew for about a year. I lost the ninety three season to Alain and received many criticisms for my driving. I am thirty four, Zak. I love the sport; ever since the day I won my first karting race age thirteen I have been hooked. Now, nearly twenty one years later, I don't need the press fuelled rivalry or the fame that makes it nearly impossible for me to step out from my own front door."

"I've had none of the successes you have but I know where you're coming from on that one. So how did you 'die'?" asked Zak.

"I am told that my death was a very difficult problem for The Group. Many things had to be put into place as my death was so obviously in the public eye. First the steering column had to be weakened so as to create controversy away from myself. It was then arranged that no forensic examination would be performed, and any telling footage of the driver or crash would be lost. I've heard that it had been done before for a presidential arrival. They even filmed footage for him! But the most difficult problem for me was the driver."

Zak had been too busy of late with his house to give the details of Ayrton's death a great deal of thought. If Ayrton wasn't driving the car, who was?

"You see I am quite a religious man and would never

normally contemplate allowing this to go ahead, and for a long time just said no. However, I met the driver and knew that it was the right thing to do."

Ayrton lifted the tall glass of ice-chilled water and gulped it down eagerly. Zak watched him and wondered if he really had come to terms with it.

"You see, everything fitted. He was my height, weight and build; he was a fan, was penniless and had AIDS. I knew all this even before meeting him, but when I did, I knew that he had nothing to lose and his family had everything to gain. There were people on earth that would've happily given their lives for the honour of saving mine or being able to be me, if only for one race. He knew of the plan and was going to fulfil a dream before his short life would've ended anyway. His sacrifice made his wife and three children in south Brazil richer beyond belief, and provided a better future for them. His price was to cut his own life short by about a year. THAT is what I hope I can live with."

Zak looked at Ayrton and saw the pain and anguish in his face. The torment of thinking that he'd done the right thing, and the realisation that if he hadn't it was now too late, and he would have to live with it forever.

Ayrton looked at Zak with small tears forming in his eyes, as he broke into a slightly hysterical laugh.

"He had lessons you know," he exclaimed, through a faltering fake smile.

"He'd never had a decent car and had only really driven a tractor before they chose him! Yet they somehow managed to get him good enough to pull it off...!" Ayrton's voice trailed off as he took another gulp from his glass.

"All I had to do was to sort out any loose ends. I didn't want to let anyone down you see, so I made sure I'd done those stupid little things that you promise people you'd do... it cost me though. But like they say, money talks, and if you've got enough anyone can live here."

"Anyone?" Zak queried.

"I thought that you were almost selected, that your character on the island had to be right?"

Ayrton looked at Zak like he had been sold a fridge in Alaska.

"Money talks, Zak, believe me. They don't sel.... I even know that the, 'old German guy', that lives down the track, wedged between the lake plot and Jan's place, is Hitler!" said Ayrton, in a manner that left Zak's mouth wide open.

Zak mouthed the word, no, silently, and looked at Ayrton with the astonishment and realisation one gets in only a few occasions in one's life. Zak had heard of Jan, and that he'd arrived two years earlier than Zak, but had never thought anything of the German accented man next to him. "Well... think about it. He's the right age, looks not unlike him, he'd raped the Jews of millions, and then disappeared with only a set of teeth to show he ever existed! If you were Hitler and over half the world wanted you dead, where would you go?!" The island was indeed the most strangest of places: no rules to speak of, no religion, no politics, no prying, no problems. Zak had indeed landed in a strange place.

***

Zak rose lazily from his bed. The morning sunshine peered through the bedroom window of The Welcome House and greeted him like an old friend. After taking a shower and putting on some loose beige shorts and white polo shirt, Zak made his way downstairs. The rear of The Welcome House housed the bar and eating area. Zak made his way out onto the wooden decking

167

that backed into a courtyard. The dark wooden chair groaned slightly as he eased himself into it, and closed his eyes in an effort to relax. The sun had just risen over some houses behind the courtyard and the early morning warm glow of the sun was a like being massaged with some hot towels whose softness tingled the skin.

"Zak! Good morning!" Zak opened his eyes and looked around towards the now all too familiar voice. Mr C was walking towards him with his slightly reddish face carrying his usual glasses and mile-wide grin. He grabbed a chair and dragged it to the side of Zak's. His paunchy figure fell into it, making it creak and groan in protestation at this early morning intrusion.

"You look well! ...I've been thinking, Zak, it's a rather large tradition here on the island where new arrivals throw a salutation party, and so I have arranged for you to have such an event in the very near future!" Mr C smiled at him with obvious glee at his cheek and forethought, his eyes sparkled behind his silver-rimmed glasses.

"I have sorted out the food, wine AND entertainment and have invited not only the people that have helped you build the house, like Valdermiro and Odorico, but also one or two *special guests*," gleamed Mr C.

"Special?" replied Zak.

"Well sure! I mean I know you've spoken to Ayrton and Elvis, but there are many more people on the island, and this is an ideal opportunity to get to know some of them!" Mr 'C' leaned forward, and was now excitedly waving his hands in the air.

"And what better way or time to do it!" he said, with obvious glee.

Zak looked at him quizzically, not really fully

168

understanding what he was on about. To Zak, it sounded like a house warming.

"Why, July fourth, dear man! It's an excellent opportunity for a party, an introduction and a celebration of the date itself. Why, it's bound to attract some of H^{e}aven's American guests... Elvis included!" Mr C clearly anticipated that his final point would cement the idea.

"But I'm not American!" Zak exclaimed, in explanation. By now Zak wasn't entirely sure this was going to be a good idea.

"Besides, isn't the fourth of July celebrating the Americans beating the English?" Zak asked.

"Why, that doesn't matter, my dear fellow, nor is anyone here perturbed by the details. Besides, if this place doesn't exist, we don't exist. So it doesn't matter who won a war in another world, does it? It is however a great opportunity for a party!" Mr C smiled as though his proposition was simply unquestionable.

Zak thought on this for a moment and decided to take advantage of Mr C's obvious enthusiasm.

"Where exactly are we, anyway?" asked Zak.

Mr C stopped smiling and began to frown whilst he thought about Zak's question. He looked up at the canopy over the veranda and sighed as if seeking moral guidance or countenance from above. He looked back at Zak as if calculating the likely effect of the answer.

"Uuh come, no... Where shall I start?" Mr C sighed again and looked around to check no one was eavesdropping. He sighed. Zak knew he had Mr C on the run and was now determined to get the answers he wanted. Mr C finally continued.

"Let me tell you a little bit of the history of H^{e}aven," said Mr C, as he positioned his chair opposite Zak. Mr C let out a half smile and took a swig from his drink before setting it on the

169

small table. For privacy he leant forward to begin.

"H^{e}aven is a small, tropical island, about 30 miles in length. It is divided into two halves. The northern half, that is where you are now, is about twice the size of the southern half. Both paying guests and local families that have been here for generations occupy the north side of H^{e}aven. It includes the exclusive and sometimes reclusive properties, some of which we passed on the way to the town. The southern half of the island is where all the real work is done. There we have all the necessary equipment to protect your identity. We have a military post, a small airport, a communications centre that not only constantly controls outgoing data, but also listens in for stray ships, planes and submarines that may venture too close to the island."

Thoughts raced through Zak's head and as eager as he was to ask thousands of questions, he dared not stop Mr C from talking.

"Anyway, that's where The Group now lives. Well, when I say group I mean the sons and daughter of the original group. Anyway, that's also where any imports arrive. You're not allowed on that side of H^{e}aven, Zak, it is out of bounds. Anyway, why would you want to? All the fun is here on the north side. Well anyway, you can't. The south side was originally developed many years ago by Cuba. Cuban forces for many years occupied the island, you see. Being such a small island in a vast ocean, H^{e}aven is the least well-known island on planet Earth. Cuba wanted to utilise this obscurity and use the island as a military springboard if you will, for any attack it wanted to launch against America. With nobody seemingly knowing that the island existed, it was a very natural Area 51." Mr C raised his first and second fingers of each hand and drew inverted commas with them in the air on the words Area 51.

"So, many years ago, Cuba decided to turn the island into a

170

fortress. The airstrip was built on the southern half of the island together with the military port, communication tower and military buildings. Then, a huge way out to sea, an electronic perimeter fence was set up. Invented by the great minds of the day, it was far in advance of anything that any other country had. This was the island's early warning system." Mr C reached for his drink and after taking a small sip, continued.

"Have you heard of Horatio Rubens?" Zak shook his head.

"Rubens was a lawyer and heavily into the race of arms and guns towards the end of the last century. This is going back some time you understand. But not only did Rubens watch over the invention of the Dynamite Gun, he also had rather a lot of secretive input into the construction of the early warning system still in place and protecting the island. It's still called by its codename from the time La CSS or Cubierta Secreta Seis. It apparently took Rubens six attempts to perfect." Mr C shrugged at this minor fact.

"Ever since its introduction the military have known about ANYONE getting near the island. They've known if any boat, submarine or airplane is within nearly one hundred miles. Now, if ANY of those came near, the military would send out planes or small gun ships to make sure the island's identity was not compromised." Mr C was making sure Zak understood each point before he continued.

The morning had begun warm and today the temperature on the veranda was obviously getting to Mr C. He lent back and took a small, white handkerchief from his inside pocket and dabbed his brow. Eager to continue his story telling, he lent forward once again…

"Now, they were *so good* at this that the area surrounding the island began to get itself a reputation. You know, for people and things going missing, and so people started to avoid the area

171

altogether making the island even easier to care for. The island began to be protected by the very fear of mankind to come any where near it."

Zak thought this over and looked at Mr C expectantly. Mr C simply looked back, waiting for Zak to realise what he was talking about. The idea was not too long in coming.

"THE BERMUDA TRIANGLE!" exclaimed Zak.

A wide grin spread across the face of Mr C as he bathed in Zak's excited enlightenment.

"You mean to say that we're in the *Bermuda Triangle*!?" asked Zak.

"My friend, without this island and the military protection of it, there wouldn't *be* a Bermuda Triangle! People have only ever gone missing in the triangle because they've come too close to the island and therefore compromised its secrecy."

"Wow!" said Zak, astonished. Mr C leaned forward once more.

"However, its purpose as a military springboard never came to be. In 1895 to 1898 the Cuban War of Independence saw to that. You see, the files on the island were only for the eyes of a privileged few. They had to be! To maintain its secrecy! So, during the war, the files got lost and the only people who knew of the island were killed. The island was lost for a few years but then re-discovered and taken over by a handful of people who developed it into what it is today. The most secret getaway in-the-world! A haven for people who want the world to leave them alone, a place where you can do what you like and be who you've always dreamed you'd like to be… in short for those who choose to live here, this is Heaven." The smile returned to Mr C's face as he delighted in his own storytelling.

"I didn't think you'd tell me," Zak said quizzically, pushing for more information.

172

"I don't mind telling you anything, Zak. The truth is you'll never leave the island to tell anyone to whom it would matter. So it's information that doesn't really count for a lot, isn't it?" Mr C looked at him as if he was waiting for Zak to realise.

"I guess not," replied Zak.

But Zak's mind was still racing, like a football player in possession of the finest ball in the world and running with it as hard as it would go. Zak had heard many stories about the Bermuda Triangle but had always considered it fireside storytelling or simply tragic coincidence.

"Of course, since the perimeter fence was installed there have been numerous additions to the island's defences. The biggest contribution was made by JFK," said Mr C.

"JFK?" repeated an astonished and confused Zak.

"Yes. Our friend, Mister John Fitzgerald Kennedy, arranged that future space satellites were not to look at certain areas of our planet... To protect the public interest, you understand?" said Mr C, in a condescending tone and a wry smile on his face.

"He kindly made sure that the island, and the water surrounding it, was considered one of those areas. This was in the months before his arrival..."

"He's HERE!" shouted Zak.

Two waiters who were stood at the bar, both stopped their conversation and looked across, one mindlessly carried on rubbing a small white tea towel around the inside of a glass, waiting for any more outbursts. Mr C looked across at them and constructed a nervous smile before facing Zak again. He lowered his voice and lent toward Zak to restore a bit of privacy.

"Zak, you would be amazed at who is on the island. I do not know if you recall, or whether this is the case with yourself, but The Introducer is known to sell the island by telling people that whoever you could think of that died before their time, who was

173

rich, and who had a vested interest in becoming unknown, was probably on the island... he was not kidding! He is only guessing of course, but there are film stars, pop stars, royalty and political figures from all around the world. All of these are in the same situation; all have found the world just a little to congested for their lives." Mr C sat back.

"Now!! if you would like to meet some of the people on the island, have a house warming party!" Mr C nodded the last three words at Zak in what was to be a successful attempt to get his way. Zak's eyes lit up at this news and from that moment onwards there was never any question about whether, more only about when.

Zak became quite glad that he had decided to have a party. The concept of a party for Mr C was the vehicle for many conversations regarding the build, decoration and finally, furnishing of Zak's house. Mr C appeared resolute in his desire to get the house finished and ready. July 4th 1994 arrived and Zak stood in his glass reception hall nervously awaiting the first of the guests, whilst Mr C busily discussed the final preparations with servants and catering staff.

The Party! July 4th 1994

One's prime is elusive…
Be on the alert to recognise your prime
At whatever time of your life it may occur.
You must then live it to the full.

Muriel Spark – The Prime of Miss Jean Brodie.

As Katarina sat in front of her dark wood, kidney dressing table carefully applying her lip-gloss with a brush, she pondered the arrival of this new celebrity. Zak Sharpe, the playboy from England. She had read about his die-hard party lifestyle, and was intrigued about the night ahead. She wanted that man. He appeared handsome from the press photographs she had seen, and understood he hadn't a partner at the moment, and that made him a prime target. She carefully studied the gloss of her light-coloured lip-gloss and pouted her lips. Perfect. She was ready.

She stood up and looked herself over in the mirror. The white designer dress was one of only a few she possessed. Special occasions only, and to her, Zak was a special prize. She turned to go, and turned back to make a final adjustment to the wisp of blonde hair that always seemed to fall out in front of her left ear. She slipped it back into place, turned her bedroom light off and walked carefully down the wooden stairs. Checking around the hallway, she strolled out of the front door and into the street. The night, sea breeze was faintly blowing her along the street as she made her way towards the edge of town. Katarina didn't drive; Elian had made sure she never had to learn. Bastard as he was, he had ruined her life. But now she had Zak in her sights, her ticket to a better life.

Even with Zak's notoriety for the good life this would hardly be the kind of party she had been used to in Amsterdam. Art History at the UVA gave her plenty of time for socialising around her degree, and being eighteen and living life to the full, she had found university life to her liking. Exercising at the USC and drinking at the Atrium were great ways of learning about life.

As she slowly wandered past the last of the town houses she pictured Zak, and made comparisons with Elian. No resemblance really. The thick-set features of Elian were at the time dashingly attractive, but in hindsight, perhaps that was more his money that had attracted her. She didn't know. But, for whatever reason she now preferred to believe, his frequent visits from Cuba to Amsterdam brought with them heady days of drugs, laughs and parties. The Atrium was then replaced by The Bells Club, where things seemed just perfect. She found solace in the opinion that this was the motivation behind her attraction to him.

Elian's desire for rough sex had been their downfall, but that was all in the past. Katarina had learned the hard way to take the rough with the smooth. Gifts, apartment, money, servants, now with all that gone she had very little left; but she did have her dignity and she didn't have to take the beatings any longer. Tonight was an opportunity to find herself a new life, a rich one, with all the luxuries wealth brings. Katarina walked confidently along the small road that led out of town. There were no streetlights on the island and were it not for the silver sheen of the full moon, it would have been quite dark. A large car drove past, and shortly after doing so turned left into Zak's driveway. Katarina strolled on and followed it to the house.

***

One by one they arrived. Most of the people invited were involved in the design or construction of his house. However, like the head of a groom on his wedding day, Zak's head soon swooned with more information and more delights and experiences than his alcohol-infused mind could cope with. The names of famous and infamous alike swirled round his head like a psychological washing machine. John Lennon was there, someone else called Jim, Zak couldn't quite recall, and women! Zak had been introduced to so many people he had difficulty remembering anyone, let alone who was with who.

Lee Hsiao Lung, or Bruce Lee as he became known, was there looking as though little had changed since his arrival in 1973. Still a very slim man, greyer certainly, and he had developed many laughter lines over the years. But his eyes were the same and when he did smile, Zak immediately saw the years fall away. He was still recognisable as the man who had changed the Asian film industry and brought kung fu to the western world. Bruce's son, Brandon, looked exactly as Zak had seen him in, The Crow.

Brandon's cool, dark hair and perfect white teeth complimented a charm that Zak envied. As predicted by Mr C, Elvis Presley also made an appearance with his wife, Kaike. All the guests introduced themselves to Zak as though he was one of them, one of their group. It almost seemed like a meeting of the Masons, a clan, a tribe based on an understanding of the personal and costly decision made in order to arrive there.

***

In the morning, Zak, just like many people after their big day, was awash with smudged memories of the revelry itself. Zak remembered Mr C had helped himself to rather too much of whatever his favourite tipple was, and had comically sat on a chair in the hallway, laughing heartily at his own reflection. Zak could also recall being amazed at how well Bruce Lee looked, and was equally surprised to find out that his father was an opera singer!

Zak lay in his bed thinking of the night's events. The reasons Brandon gave for leaving just before a planned wedding, the problems Elvis had with the organisation of his death. Zak tried to recall what song Elvis had done on the karaoke, a song he'd never heard before. Mirage, was it called? The train of thought trying to recall the name of the song, yet knowing it mentioned H^{e}aven, was ripped from sight and replaced with the amazing recollection of John Lennon's comment that his song, Imagine, was based upon the island. John had joined the island back in 1980, well before the electronic adviser given to Zak. His adviser (apparently a West Indian man) acted as introducer and adviser and had let out more information than he should have. John thought he might be on a bonus system that was dependant upon John's decision to come and how much money was laundered, and this made him give out more information than he should, as enticement. John said that this became the inspiration behind the song and was the basis and spark of genius that he had become so famous for.

Zak finally got up in the early part of the afternoon; Mr C had come to visit and had been shown into the lounge. Unbeknown to Zak, he was there by way of an apology. Another party on the island had meant that some of the island's more

178

colourful guests had not shown and Mr C was worried.

"Zak, how are you, old fellow? A wonderful night wasn't it?" Mr C beamed, as he tried to read Zak's mood.

Zak rolled his eyes and smiled.

"I am amazed. I had no idea who was on the island and can't even now remember all the people I was introduced to," replied Zak, smiling.

Relieved at Zak's response, Mr C rubbed his chin with his hand thoughtfully, then theatrically threw his arms in the air.

"Well I'll be honest with you Zak, that's why I'm here. To say sorry."

"Sorry?" Zak asked.

"Yes, well I should really have organised your party better, but you see I just didn't know that another party had been organised. I don't get to hear about them all you see and I honestly didn't know about the other party. If I had I would certainly have advised you to have it on a different night."

"Why, what went wrong? I thought everything went well!" revealed Zak.

Mr C sighed.

"Well it did, and I thank you for your kind words, but I really did expect more people," conceded Mr C.

"Well the only person I noticed not here was Ayrton," commented Zak.

"Oh, sorry Zak, it is not good policy to introduce two people at the same time to the island. It always means that one person takes more than their fair share of the limelight and so we keep people pretty much under wraps until their first party," explained Mr C. He looked at Zak, trying to read Zak's mind, and to see if Zak's understanding of the situation was genuine. Zak clearly either didn't realise or appeared to truly not be concerned. A maid arrived with some refreshments and to Mr

179

C's gratification, broke the topic of conversation.

Mr C popped back to see Zak later in the week but only to drop in a visitor book. In it were the telephone numbers of the people who had attended his party and a description of where they were on the island. No one had addresses on the island as everyone simply learned where they were. It turned out that Elvis lived on the very most northern tip of the island and had bought quite a considerable piece of land. He'd apparently found it difficult to conceive that he wouldn't be hounded and so had chosen a plot far away. Between his and the outskirts of the town was Bruce Lee's property. That took care of most of the very northern tip and the right hand part of the island from the town upwards. North of the town, on the left, was mainly undeveloped and part of this land had its own lagoon. Zak had not seen it but it sounded simply gorgeous. Zak had heard the builders commenting upon it and speculating about its use. South of the town and down the coast, before you reached Zak's property and the reef, was mainly undeveloped but Zak had seen that the town was expanding into this area.

The remainder of the week saw Zak's welcome on the island slowly cementing into something more than the ephemeral relationship he'd so far had with islanders. His time on the island was spent developing relationships with celebrities and natives alike, one of which caused Zak to wonder as to the reason for her presence. He recalled being introduced to her at the party but with so many people pushed before him, he had scarcely remembered her. Since then Zak had noticed her a number of times in town. Her blonde, almost white hair and fair skin were in stark contrast to most islanders, and Zak knew she had taken an interest in him.

Of all the celebrities, Zak found himself getting on best with Brandon who, at only two years older, had the most in common with a still young, Zak Sharpe. He found Brandon to be very approachable, funny and easy to relate to. Brandon introduced Zak to one of his favourite games of Backgammon, and it was during an early evening game that Zak found out about Brandon's motives for his arrival.

"Why did you come?" asked Zak.

"Here?" asked Brandon.

"Mmm!" hummed Zak, as he took a sip from his glass of Bacardi and Coke.

"Well my arrival wasn't really planned like a lot of others here," replied Brandon.

"I didn't have to go through the process of hiding money like most people. I met a man who said he was The Introducer, and could put me back in touch with my father. I thought at first he was some sort of wacko, but he could tell me things about my father that no one would ever know outside our family."

Brandon placed his backgammon chip down.

"Well, what happened then?" Zak enquired.

"To be honest my father sort of sent for me. He's great friends with Elvis, you know, they train together... or rather should I say, he trains Elvis. Elvis is very keen on the martial arts and had many lessons from other stars during his life, before coming here."

"He does look slim!" exclaimed Zak.

"Nothing like how I imagined him to be. I'd have expected to meet a man with a jet black quiff and still wearing his white diamond suit!" Brandon smiled back.

"It's funny how the island changes people, and your image is one that comes straight from the magazines and papers. We expected you to be eyeing up every female on the island, and we'd have to lock our wives away!" Zak laughed.

"Very true. The papers do love to print a good story... but

181

the bad ones sell better!" Zak conceded.

They laughed in unison. Zak had found a friend in Brandon, and they understood each other well.

"My father also trains a number of islanders. Now Elvis and my father have quite an influence on the island and when Elvis heard that my father wanted his son with him at H^{e}aven, he supported the request to The Group. After conducting some research, they decided that I could be approached... and here I am! I decided to join him and within two weeks I was here."

"Two weeks!" said Zak, astonished.

"Yes! They decided I might change my mind if I was left to think about it too much, and by then they'd shown themselves to me," explained Brandon.

Brandon's explanation would, in future years, when Zak researched his death on the internet, seem quite plausible for a man who seemed very happy with his life and very keen to marry his fiancée, Eliza. Brandon's enthusiasm for following in his father's teachings would in later years become Zak's saviour. Lee's, Wing Chun style of Wushu, would later teach Zak to build upon his personal strengths. Many people have followed this well known, Jeet Koon Doe, style of self defence.

***

Zachariah had pondered the food at his welcome party, as he took the bread left by the MacNamara boy, and snapped off the tip. He carefully laid it upon his lap and stuck his fingers into the slightly-staling soft, white bread inside, eagerly digging his hard and grime-entrenched fingers into the bread before he put some in his mouth. He picked out some more and squashed some between his thumb and forefinger. It stuck just momentarily before separating again.

Zachariah's dry encrusted lips parted to reveal plaque-covered and yellowed teeth that once shone brilliantly bright on the cover of newspapers around the world. Zachariah had, over the years, spent many thousands of pounds on getting his smile perfect. Now with a loose tooth and a further two crowns missing, his once laser-white and contoured teeth were now a yellowed, crooked fraction of their former selves. As Zachariah sat smiling he thought of the bread in his hand, this is good bread he thought. Zachariah knew cheap bread and this wasn't it. Cheap bread when squashed would stick and form itself back into the emulsified dough from where it came. The Macnamaras knew their bread and how to make it and Zachariah knew he'd enjoy this. He leant back and let his mind wander as he ate…

***

Since Ayrton had now moved in, Zak had asked for Ayrton's address and Mr C was prompt in visiting Zak with a small mag. Presenting it to Zak, Mr C was happy to see that Zak had every opportunity to settle in.

"Thank you," said Zak,

"You're very welcome. Ayrton said he's not seen you much since your leaving of The Welcome House," said Mr C.

"I don't seem to have had much time, to be honest," Zak retorted.

"I've been sorting out the last of the problems with the hot water system that's not worked properly since I moved in."

Zak felt a little under pressure for his absence from keeping in touch with Ayrton. Zak knew that Ayrton couldn't easily get around the island and felt that he had failed to make him welcome as much as he could've.

"Don't worry, old chap, Ayrton has been very busy too!

I've helped him organise a welcome party much like you own," explained Mr C, in an attempt to contain Zak's frustration.

"Look, he wants you to come, it's the 14th October, you will won't you?" he pleaded.

"Of course I will!" Zak replied, grinning.

"I just felt a little like I'd left him there."

"Well you sort of did, but that's hardly a reason to worry, old chap. Right, I'll tell him you'll be there, it'll be a great celebration, believe me!" And with that, Mr C turned from Zak's door and holding his right arm above his head, waved at Zak.

"Cheerio!" he yelled. Ayrton's party soon arrived.

***

Ayrton's house didn't loom on you like Zak's did. Zak had heard that Ayrton was a frugal man and had happily done a number of things to the house himself in the effort to save some money and personalise his house. Much smaller than Zak's, Brandon's and even John's, who Zak had gone to visit a week or so earlier, Ayrton's bungalow was set amongst a group of luscious green trees.

Concrete pillars and posts gave the house a feel of permanency and this contrasted with the large, open, redwood beams. The furniture was made of the same wood and it looked like a millionaire's camping shelter. As Zak approached, the sheer number of cars already there surprised him. Zak had arrived only fifteen or so minutes after the 8:30p.m start time, and already there were a number of cars there. Ayrton had not apparently wanted a late night and had resisted Mr C's enthusiasm for holding a house warming party, until the last minute. He had preferred to sleep early and concentrate on maintaining his health. He'd apparently likened the island to a

184

lazy holiday resort that offered little in the way of either exercise opportunities nor the fulfilment of spiritual or cultural needs.

By now Zak had become very good friends with Brandon who altogether seemed far more relaxed to Zak than Ayrton. Ayrton's party did indeed bring out a lot of guests, the most notable of whom was the grand-daddy himself. A man who had been on the island a massive thirty-nine years... James Dean. A small, gaunt 63-year-old veteran of the island, Mr Dean had bought a large patch of land many years ago when prices were much less. He'd loved a race and had bought enough to build himself a racetrack. Now he mainly watched, but often reminisced whilst giving guided tours of his car collection. He had amassed quite a variety of Porsche, Ferrari and Maserati. His most treasured were however those that reminded him of his youth: a Triumph 500, the Porsche Super Spyder and his first racing car, an MG TA. These, Jim showed off with pride, and the memories of times past shone in his eyes brightly as he recalled driving them.

A very welcoming man, Jimmy Dean was the equivalent of a walking, talking billboard for the virtues of H^{e}aven life. To him, H^{e}aven was a world of its own and the TV sets and radio were simply ways of keeping in tune with what was going on in that other world he had now so happily left behind. Zak thought Jimmy had gained a somewhat twisted version of the other world. He had seen many news articles on the hurt, pain and suffering of people around the world and saw none of that where he was... and he was thankful for that.

Island Life

My advice to you is get married:
if you find a good wife you'll be happy;
if not, you'll become a philosopher.

Socrates – (470-399 B.C.)

Zachariah slowly rose to his feet and began his daily walk back down Prospect Park Drive and over to Flatbush Avenue. Here, he could try again to get some money together. Zachariah knew he was a weak terrified man. He had often sat for hour after hour begging for money, dreaming of getting enough cash together to fund an air ticket back to England, not even considering that to do so he might just need a passport. He could visualise arriving back in Leicestershire and knocking on the door of his parent's home or strolling into a board meeting. Watching Mike Underwood's jaw drop as their eyes met and he realised Zachariah Sharpe was still alive. He would walk up to Nicola, embrace her like only family could and live happily ever after. This dreamlike fantasy was intensely satisfying and sometimes at least, gave Zachariah hope in the future. Zachariah sometimes even fantasized about returning home to find that his parents were also no longer dead, and his mother's 'broth of a boy' had finally returned to her.

It was normally after ideas of return or fantasies of parents no longer dead, that Zak would sickeningly turn back to a bottle of alcohol for solace. This sad, unsatisfying affair normally involved him walking over to 6th Street and seeing the grey, wiry-haired Jake Jordan in the off licence, to negotiate a bottle of rum. White rum was nicer but he often only had money for the dark. When money wasn't around he'd even scavenged for methanol from other down and outs. His pain seemed to be in direct correlation to how much he'd punished himself in his thoughts. Zak's mind was also schizophrenically paranoid of The Group, and their control. Such was his fear of being caught before he could go public, that he'd kept a diary, and even thrown money away that looked or felt like it was an elaborate secret bug.

But today he was more determined than ever to plead for money, and this time make it work for him. The bread the Macnamara boy had left had given him a good start. He stopped to get a drink from the park, water fountain. The crisp, clear, cold water touched his lips and tongue, wakening his senses. He sucked at the short flow of water and swallowed. Pausing momentarily for a breath, he gulped some more water down eagerly and swilled it around his mouth. A shooting pain pierced the front of his mouth. The tooth between his front and pincher tooth screamed at him in pain. Yelling out, he threw his head back from the fountain as though some unseen ferret had bitten his bottom lip. The water flew out of his open mouth and fell to the path below. Zachariah winced.

"Aah, bugger," he yelled, and he began shaking his head from side to side in a futile effort to stop the pain. His tooth had been getting worse ever since last December in Charleston, where a run in with three teenagers had left him with a loose tooth and eighty four dollars lighter.

Zak had always had a knack of settling into places quickly. He never was one of those children who go on camp with their school and cry themselves to sleep. As much as he enjoyed home life, neither university nor the Winston Stanley School for Boys had fazed him. He had managed to find friends and colleagues quite easily and island life proved no different. Invitations to various parties followed. Either organising or hosting parties turned out to be one of Mr C's favourite past times, and Zak was grateful for this in the Christmas of '94. One of Zak's main worries since the October when he'd attended Ayrton's Welcome party, was whether he would be spending Christmas alone. As things turned out, it was a very pleasant event and one that reminded Zak a lot of a traditional family get-together, a little like he'd imagined Thanksgiving would be in America. Zak also managed to notice Katarina was there. His attention in her was growing.

1995 arrived and Zak continued to build a group of friends on the island, not least of which was Brandon. This relationship developed to the stage where Zak even helped Brandon organise a birthday bash for Bruce's 55th Birthday. This was to prove one of the most interesting and enjoyable memories Zak would ever have.

***

One balmy evening in the November of 1995 was to be a turning point for Zak. For at Bruce Lee's 55th birthday, he was to meet a person who was to make island life far more pleasurable…

***

As a soft breeze was blowing off the sea, Zak stood on the veranda talking to Ayrton about how they had found Heaven life so far. Katarina was talking to one of the townsfolk who secure invitations to parties through their service. Silhouetted against the backdrop of a dusky grey, night sky, Zak watched as Katarina talked to Oswardo and another young lady whom he had never seen before. Ayrton's voice had faded quietly into the background as Zak watched Katarina cheerfully talking to the fisherman from the town who offers a delivery service. She occasionally looked his way and smiled.

As Zak watches the distant conversation, the hint of salsa music behind him and the noisy chatter of partygoers seems to develop into the main sound in his head. Zak decides to excuse himself and fetch a drink for himself at the table next to Katarina.

"Hi, Oswardo isn't it?" Zak feebly enquires from the fisherman.

"Yes, Mister Sharpe," replies the fisherman. Zak thanks his lucky stars that he was good at remembering names.

"I wondered if I could talk to you at some time to arrange for you to deliver some fresh fish? Would that be ok?"

"Of course, Mister Sharpe, it's no problem!"

"I see you are managing to captivate two lovely ladies, would you care to introduce me?"

"Well, this is my niece, Yelina, she lives in the town and teaches the children at the school... in the kindergarten."

Zak turned to face the first of the two ladies.

"Well I don't really teach, I help out, but I am very pleased to meet you, Mister Sharpe." Yelina holds out her hand.

"Please, call me Zak, everybody does," replies Zak, as he shakes her hand.

"..and this is Kat, she also lives in the town."

"Hello!" says Katarina. As Zak takes her hand, Katarina leans forward and kisses him on the cheek.

"Hi, I've met you before, haven't I?" asks Zak.

"Yes, we met at your party last July, and I have seen you a few times since," said Katarina, smiling.

"Yes, I think we have," said Zak knowingly going along with this polite conversation, that seems destined to be so much more.

This introduction was enough to ensure that the night was a complete success. To Zak's delight, the conversation was easy, and covered a variety of different topics. Zak was not tempted, as had been the case in the past, by the bar, and instead preferred this new lady's company. She was certainly beautiful, but her charm and laugh were intoxicating. Zak had a moment of caution, uncertain of her motives, but he decided these fears were of a previous world and a previous life.

So when Yelina and Oswardo excused themselves, Zak decided to find out more about Katarina.

"So I guess you haven't lived here all your life?" enquired Zak.

"Hardly, but that's a very long story."

"Oh," replied Zak, disheartened.

"But if you would like a coffee, I could tell you!" said Katarina, smiling. Zak's eye's lit up with hers and at that, Katarina led Zak out of the party.

***

The wind had picked up ever so slightly and Katarina's soft shiny hair delicately floated as they walked the short journey to her modest but immaculate house.

Zak and Katarina walked back into town, the cooling night air made them both feel quite drunk. Katarina led Zak inside the wooden front door and Zak followed through to a very busy lounge. He had not imagined from the prim and neat exterior that a room inside could be so busy. The whole room was a mass of colour. Elaborate throws adorned chairs and tables. The thinly striped blue and pink wallpaper was almost hidden behind a myriad of different sized pictures and paintings. Every inch of table and mantle was covered in ornaments, pictures or books. As Zak followed her through the room he clumsily knocked a book off the coffee table. As he picked it back up his drink, infused head swooned a little. He placed the book, 'Casa Columbiana', back on the table and followed Katarina through towards the rear, to what Zak thought would be a bright, airy room by day. Two easels stood in the room; one faced the back yard, the other a wall. Against the wall a small chair faced the easel. In the corner was a small sideboard with countless pots of paint on it. Leaning against it were about forty frames and paintings, all different sizes and of many different things. Katarina picked out one, of a portrait of a family. Clearly, from the hair and skin colour, these were natives of the island. The father on the left sat large, proud and smiling. In between himself and his wife was their eight or ten-year-old daughter with large, dark eyes and beautifully tanned skin colour. The wife was also smiling broadly and wasn't much bigger than the daughter. Zak looked at it admiringly. "That's very good!"

Katarina smiled and told him about the people in the picture. She left him to wander around the room whilst she fetched some more drinks.

"So, come on then... I've told you about how I got here, how did you?" asked Zak. Katarina had pondered this tricky

191

dilemma and very nearly decided honesty was the best policy. She instead decided to miss out some of the more gruesome points and as she handed Zak his drink, she motioned for them to sit down on a small bench on her veranda. This man is now or never, she thought.

"Well, I guess it all started when I met Elian in Amsterdam, I was there doing my degree, you see. This would be in about eighty-three. I met Elian and fell in love. He treated me very well and took me to all the finest nightclubs like the Bells Club… and restaurants that were out of this world!!" Katarina's eye's lit up as she spoke. "So when he asked me to, I went back to Cuba with him. I lived there for some years and we would have a wonderful time. Parties, cool nights on the veranda, hot, passionate nights in the bedroom…" Katarina looked Zak straight in the eye to gauge Zak's reaction as she talked.

"We decided to take a vacation in our yacht, to Italy. Elian had a wonderful yacht. We were sailing not too far from here and he had an accident. The boat had developed a leak and Elian went to take a look at it, but whilst he was doing that he had a massive heart attack. I was petrified. You see, whilst I was his true love, I wasn't Elian's wife. He was married to a very religious family, fanatical in fact. So if we were found together, it would be curtains for me and disgrace for him." Katarina kept looking but Zak's face seemed quite happy with this explanation.

"As you can imagine, I didn't know what to do. I couldn't contact home for fear of what would happen and I couldn't fix the yacht. I tried my best to revive him and when I did call for help I got no response. Elian died, and after a day or two the boat was listing to one side." Katarina took another anxious look at Zak to see if her story was holding true. Zak was listening intently and seemingly unaware of this only slightly plausible report.

"…So with a sinking yacht that I couldn't repair, a radio that seemingly didn't get anyone's attention and the thought that I might be killed if found with my dead lover, I gathered as much as I could and got aboard the life raft."

"My God! What happened?" asked Zak.

"Well, I used the motor for as long as it lasted and then drifted for another day. I was panic stricken, no radio, only a little water. I tried paddling… it's pointless though when you don't know where you're paddling to! By the third day I had eaten all my food and drank all but the last litre of water. On the night of day four I ran aground. I was heavily blistered, I hadn't packed any sun cream and as you can see I'm not exactly well prepared for sunlight." Katarina gazed into Zak's eyes before glancing down at her chest, encouraging his eyes to follow hers. She looked back up to see they had.

"I woke up in the morning and scrambled ashore, shouting as best as I could for help. A man and his wife came to help me and they took me into their house. Well, they didn't, a servant of theirs picked me up and carried me in. They gave me some food and water but shortly afterwards a furious-looking large-muscled man dressed in khaki uniform turned up. I didn't know where I was and thought I must be back in Cuba. He said he was the security chief and thinking I was back in Cuba I just pleaded with him for my life! Well he was having none of it and put me in handcuffs and takes me to Southside. I think, he is determined to kill me so I say I'll do anything and, I've got money! Well, at that he gets on his radio and asks someone to look in the dinghy. I am scared witless. Well, I'm taken to a room and sit there for what seems like ages, I am so terrified. Then finally someone comes in and says, The Group wants to see me. I go to this building and into a room with six men inside. All the things from my dinghy are on the floor in the room. I told them my story and they explained that I was on a private island and that I couldn't stay without paying my way. I said they could have anything they wanted as long as I didn't have to return to Cuba. Well, I traded in most of the items I had brought with me to buy my life and a house, and this is where I've been ever since! The medical treatment here is excellent. I had blisters all over my skin and was really frightened I would have skin cancer again. I had it as a child, you know. Squamous cell carcinoma the doctors had called it. Luckily, I didn't get it again."

"Wow!" Zak exclaimed. "That is such an awful story!"

"Well, I'm not like anyone else on the island… I'm a pure accident. My dinghy was too small, apparently, to be noticed by the grid and if I hadn't have landed here AND had valuables on me, I think I'd be dead by now. They say money talks and it certainly does here!" Katrina finished her drink and with the drinks she'd had at the party, was feeling a little tipsy.

"So what do you do now then?" asked Zak.

"I paint! I paint landscapes or portraits and sell them to the guests. I have a small stall on the market and get by on what I had left from the house and what I earn, painting. It's not that expensive to live here as long as you don't want too much from the mainland."

After showing him some pictures, Katrina led Zak back into the lounge where they sat next to each other on the hippie style settee. They talked about pictures, boats and people. To Katarina's delight Zak did not hesitate when she asked him if he wanted to stay with her that night. It was to be the first of many and the first time that Zak had dated anyone without fearing cameras and photographers.

***

The following week Zak made a special trip to the school where Yelina worked. He had talked over with Oswardo how he might find a housekeeper. Oswardo had put his niece forward as an obvious choice, and had explained how Yelina had to work at the school to help fund her son's education. Zak's job would pay a lot more than that and enable Yelina to pay for her son's education and still have money left to improve their standard of living. Zak thought it was a great idea and decided to approach Yelina about it.

An unseen brass bell rang out to tell staff and children that it was home time. This was followed by a flurry of activity and noise. The angry growl of the chair legs from inside the classrooms preceded a wave of children who came bursting through the classroom doors, and into the corridor. Running, laughing and squealing at each other, they darted this way and that to gather their things and make their way out of the door and off home. They didn't seem to notice Zak's presence and ran round him like he was part of the furniture. A couple of minutes passed and the crowd lessened, just as Yelina came out of the classroom. She didn't notice him at first but offered a glowing smile to Zak when she did. Zak's confidence in his decision lifted. He walked over to her, and just as he reached her bumped flatly into a small boy who had been running to make his way home. The boy bounced off Zak's right leg and fell backwards onto the floor.

"Oh, sorry!" Zak exclaimed, shocked.

The boy looked up to see what he'd run into, smiled and got to his feet. Zak looked at Yelina who was laughing at the incident. Picking up his bag and a book the boy yelled, "Sorry mister," and ran off once more. Zak turned to watch him dash further down the corridor and on turning back to face Yelina, noticed her smiling at him.

"You poor man! You look terrified! Don't worry, he's fine." Zak smiled at Yelina.

"I have come to ask you something." Yelina's smile brightened.

"Yes?"

"I was talking to Oswardo about a job I have for a housemaid." Zak noticed Yelina's smile falter momentarily and then reappear. "Well, I was wondering if you would be interested in the position? I have found out what the normal rate is and would be happy to pay that, if you were interested?"

Not knowing of Zak's new found interest in Katarina, Yelina's hopes of being asked out for a date were dashed. She tried to hide her disappointment and instead graciously accepted his offer.

"Great!" said Zak. "That would be really good. You can start as soon as you like, and maybe you could teach me how to scuba dive?"

"Oswardo told you, did he?" asked Yelina, with a smirk on her face.

"Well I did say at the party that I'd love to learn, and he said you were an expert!" smiled Zak.

"Not exactly an expert, but I'm sure I could teach you." And so it was agreed that Yelina would work for Zak.

Between the November and the January of 1996, much to Yelina's disappointment, Zak became ever closer to Katarina. The grand-daddy's big birthday bash, the 8th of February, was Jimmy Dean's 75th birthday party. Zak, along with most of the island, got an invitation. His birthday party was held on a large patch of grass in the centre of his race track. The area had been decked, and a small stage added to one end. Different coloured floodlights changed in sequence, creating a metamorphosis atmosphere that added a sense of style to the whole occasion.

Distant trees were adorned with the same effect making most of what the eye could see very impressive. Jimmy had bought a huge plot of land north of the connecting road, and halfway between the town and the border to the military south side of the island. With nearly eight miles of sandy beach and part of the seabed as a reef, he had indeed by far and away the grandest of plots. Taking up a good two thirds of it was his race track, complete with lap timer and well equipped pit sheds. It was on this track that whoever had organised the event had placed a firework display that would have put most town displays to shame. A number of famous artists did one or two live songs including a very slim, gaunt-looking and grey-haired, Buddy Holly. When he was being introduced, Zak expected him to do traditional tracks from his heydays, but Buddy instead sang some soft melodies, sat in front of a piano. His dark-rimmed glasses he was so famous for had gone, and been replaced by silver ones. After he had completed his short repertoire Buddy rejoined the crowd and mingled. As Elvis did a few songs from his heyday, Zak made a point of talking to this favourite of his childhood icons. Buddy was a very gentle man, quietly spoken as Zak had thought he would. Bob Marley came on just as Buddy told Zak about his break into England back in '58. "Something out of the London Palladium," was apparently Buddy's big break. The greatest cheer of the night came from the crowd when Lennon began to sing Imagine. The crowd simply erupted. They seemed mesmerized by the fact that a song had been written about their island, their paradise, their world. It was akin to a national anthem.

Zak sat with Katarina and enjoyed the night at the party. Yelina stopped and chatted a few times as she mingled with many of the guests. Zak suspected that he'd seen Martin Luther King and would spend at least an hour later that night lying in bed next to Katarina as she slept, thinking about the possibility that it was him.

***

Most of 1996 offered Zak an increasing amount of security in his life. He and Katarina got on great, she moved into his house and continued to produce her paintings and decorate his house with, 'a woman's touch', as she called it. Zak decided to work his land and grow some fruit and vegetables for themselves. By the time Zak was twenty nine he thought he was finally in H^{e}aven.

By Royal Assent

I was very close to Diana and I know many things from her that show this was no accident.

Mr Al Fayed

Nearly a year of blissful happiness passed and Zak and Katarina became ever closer. Casual meetings at bars for a chance to talk became regular meals out. Zak found, for the first time in his life, that someone accepted him for exactly who he was. When he and Katarina made love he knew it was because they both wanted to, not because he wanted to simply fulfil his desires and not so she could brag to friends, or even worse, the press.

Zak kept his acquaintances with islanders, both natives and ex-pats. His awareness of Yelina grew, as she turned out to be a wonderful housekeeper and friend. He found he enjoyed the peace and serenity of activities that some years earlier he would have balked at. Zak was slowly growing unknowingly into an old, young man. With his younger and former life well behind him and his aspirations for conquering the world (or at least every attractive lady on it) were now distant memories. Zak happily let such financial and self-gratifying obsessions blur silently into a past part of his brain only used for party conversations. Mending his hedges, gardening or fishing slowly took precedence over late night parties and mornings after. Zak became quite close with Oswardo and learnt a lot from him about how and when to catch the best the sea could offer. One of the few things Zak still found a passion for was driving. His friendship with Ayrton also blossomed and Zak spent many an hour studying engines and how to get the best from them. Driving was certainly the younger side of Zak, and Ayrton, who had taken advantage of the idea that the island can import anything, had bought a small collection of very exclusive cars. Ayrton's favourite had a 65 painted down the side of it. Apparently this was his favourite number as it was the number of pole positions he'd achieved in his previous life. The thought that Zak might have enjoyed working with a spanner is not one that his father would have approved of, and even though the cars needed very little maintenance Zak learned a lot about engines, and loved it nevertheless.

Brandon also continued to be a source of friendship for Zak. When Katarina was visiting other friends on the island, Zak often called in to play backgammon or to talk about islanders and island life. With such a diverse range of famous people, the conversations often ran far into the night. Like the irony that Marylyn Monroe's last film was called, 'Something's got to give', before she came to the island or the paradox of Brandon's own father, whose first film had been called, 'The Birth of Mankind', and last, 'Game of Death', which again was left unfinished. Few new arrivals to the island remained unknown. Island gossip and Mr C's parties often saw to that. He had once said to Zak that he did not want an island of natives and recluses, but a haven of communal living where everyone benefits. Despite this, Zak couldn't help but imagine that Hitler must have been a recluse on the island, as he rarely saw the ex-German dictator. That was the amazing thing about The Group, and the way they ran the island. It didn't matter what you had done in a previous life, what counted was your money. The island stripped previous politicians of any status and made clear to them to leave previous beliefs and ideologies in their past, lost life. The Group realised how people may wish to hold onto their values and beliefs, but made it clear to all comers of the dire and permanent solution they had as a response.

***

Faced with a single balloon, a child is often captivated by its bright colour, shape, texture and movement. Give that child a second, third and fourth balloon and their allure and fascination weakens. As time passed, Zak found himself becoming less captivated by the thought that famous 'dead' movie stars, singers and politicians had, or were living on the island. Often, hearing about how they came to be on the island was enough conversation and as much interest as was necessary. The memory of the awe and fascination of first meeting Elvis in the market now seemed a distant one. September of 1997 saw the arrival of not the first, but to Zak, the most famous of royals.

***

Princess Diana and Dodi arrived shortly after their official death, a few days earlier. Zak knew of their arrival but didn't actually get to see them until their house party shortly, before Christmas 1997. Next door to Ayrton's plot of land, they had purchased a piece of land that was quite unique, insomuch as it had the island's only lagoon. Actually, Zak wasn't sure if it was a lagoon, as he'd never seen it first hand, but when he'd looked at available land on the map of the island for himself, it was certainly the most expensive.

Dodi & Di's house warming party was attended by just about everyone on the island. Zak expected it to be lots of pomp and circumstance and was gobsmacked to find it to be far from it. Diana looked taller and slimmer than Zak had expected. Martin Luther King made another appearance, as did the now eighty-year-old JFK with his 71-year-old wife, Marylyn. With an air of informality about it, Zak couldn't help but be in awe at the class and sophistication. Everyone seemed to be on their best behaviour. Yelina managed to get an invitation through Zak and spent a good deal of the night with him and Katarina. Katarina had drunk probably a little too much wine than was wise.

"Can't she just clear off sometimes?" whispered Katarina to Zak.

"Who!?"

"Yelina! I mean she's at our door in the morning, she is there all day nearly every day, and we hardly get a moment's peace. Then when WE get invited out there she is! Again!"

"Hang on, Kat, she's at our house 'cause she works for us," explained Zak.

"Yes, I know she works for us, Zak, but it's getting tiring. I mean, she comes with us when we go out on the yacht. Ok, so she drives the boat and cooks the food but when that's done she takes off her bikini top and wanders around half-naked like she owns the bloody thing! She's there in the day and sometimes she's still with us late into the night. It's just a bit much. Why can't we employ Mrs Pena?" asked Katarina, as she gulped some more red wine.

"Mrs Pena! Why the hell would we want Mrs Pena? She must be seventy if she's a day!" replied Zak. Two guests looked around as they'd clearly overheard his excited tones.

"She's not! She's fifty four. Anyway she's not likely to muscle in on our days out."

"Muscle in!" replied Zak. "Yelina comes with us because YOU can't be bothered to cook, clean or even get me a drink!

You sit there in the lounge reading your precious novels and don't wanna move! What's the point in a day out? If it wasn't for Yelina enjoying the sun and liking a swim or scuba diving or jet skiing it wouldn't be worth me having a yacht! ...And ok, so when she's done she relaxes with us. The boat isn't big enough to need two hands so what is she supposed to do? Sit below decks until we ring for her?"

"I don't do anything? I pay you all the attention you need! I fuck you like a top payer at the Yimyam and you put her above me!"

"Well, I'm sorry love, but unless you can find a reason why not and a better replacement than Mrs Pena, she stays."

"Urgghh!!" Katarina squealed and walked off.

Zak let her go. Katarina always was a little over-protective of Zak and apart from the fact that he did like diving and swimming with Yelina, he actually enjoyed her bouts of jealousy. She'd sleep it off and things would soon return to normal.

Zak figured it must be Katarina's menstrual cycle and went back to mingling at the party. Zak had never been to an English royal function before and he wasn't going to let a small disagreement with Katarina stop his enjoyment of this one.

***

It would be months later that Zak would hear about Diana's pregnancy and the hardship and turmoil of leaving two sons behind and a family suspecting but not knowing the truth. It seemed that just like American society had not accepted that JFK might actually want to be with Marylyn Monroe, English aristocracy, with its elitist critique, did not also want their princess marrying the son of a Muslim who they wouldn't even give a British passport to.

Over time, Zak learned of each person's reasons for obscurity. Sometimes it was fear, with some it was sanctuary and others, love. But with most it was hope. Hope for a life of normality where peer or public pressure did not damage and destroy the basic need to live for the sake of living. Zak had asked Mr C (a man whom, Zak realised, knew a lot more than he ever told) about JFK.

"Zak, I asked that very question of the man himself. He is, or was, a great leader of his time, a wonderful speaker with a vision that is almost unprecedented. I will never forget his reply. He said, 'Whoever said, one man's will can move a mountain, was wrong. One man's will in a sea of mistrust and apathy is but a dream. One needs not the will of the people or of the nation to achieve great things, but of those who sit down with you as your friend at dinner. I had a nation's dream in my hands but I have only two hands, and there were many more hands around those dinner tables that were pulling in other directions'. John added that had he not orchestrated his own demise, he feared others would have done it for him."

Zak watched as Mr C stood proudly recapturing this previous conversation with JFK.

"The how started off as a simple overdose for Marylyn and a faked assassination for JFK. But it became our biggest problem. If any death is to uncover the truth about H^{e}aven, that is it. We had to make and doctor tapes, provide witnesses, sub plots, intrigue. Quite frankly, I'm amazed we pulled it off."

Taking Care of Business

'Fickle Fate'
is a vicious goddess who brings no
permanent good to anyone.

George S Clason – 1955

The day was warming up now so, reaching into his jumper he pulled out his sheet of newspaper. He kept a sheet on his chest to stop himself getting cold. It worked too. Zak had seen cyclists' early races like the Tour de France, stuffing paper down their tops when they rode over the tops of mountains. His father had told him that it was for warmth. He folded it carefully and put it in his inside pocket. Zachariah, still reeling in the pain of earlier, continued his slow walk to Flatbush Avenue. Walking slowly, he kept a watchful eye on the tarmacadam paving. A small wooden lollipop stick with a joke imprinted on it, a small piece of silver foil wrapping from a stick of chewing gum, a cigarette packet, all lay discarded on the pavement. Zak continued to look as he walked slowly along, as he was often successful at finding one cent pieces or nickels. Nobody seemed to bother with them much anymore. Ten cents, or dimes, as Americans called them, were harder to find, as they were smaller.

Zak watched as the blackness of the pavement as it passed under him was interspersed with white spots of old chewing gum. His concentration for money was interrupted.

"Say Zak, how's it goin', man?"

Zachariah looked up from his feet to see Judah. Judah was a kid not more than about ten years younger than Zachariah. A street kid, there was very little he didn't know about what was 'goin' down' in the neighbourhood. He was part of a slowly dispersing Brooklyn graffiti crew known as the Crazy Ghetto Bastards. Judah had told Zachariah that he used to spray his tag in and near the B line, or ride on top of the trains for kicks.

"Uh... fuckin toothf!" Zak slurred, pointing at the offending tooth. Judah smiled.

"I thought you were headin back to Englund! Last you told me was you had them MILLIONS waiting there! Wassup, chauffer not turn up for ya!" Judah laughed heartily and walked on.

"Fuckin' eejit!" Zachariah murmured to himself.

He continued his search for small change and walked on towards Flatbush. He didn't find any money today but he did pick up a perfectly good piece of tissue paper from a fast food outlet. Zak had learned some time before that good tissue paper was rare and felt a lot better than newspaper. He sat down at his normal spot. Reaching into his pocket he pulled out his handkerchief and placed it in front of him as he had done that morning. Placing his lucky quarter on top, Zak hoped to encourage passers by to be generous in their charity.

And the Walls
Come Tumbling Down

I hate and I love:
Why I do so you may well ask,
I do not know but I feel it happen and am in agony.

Catullus No. 85 – c84-c54bc

Zak had decided to take a snorkelling trip with Katarina and as was usual had asked Yelina to accompany them. They weren't allowed too far from the island but there were plenty of nice coves that they could moor in. The Group always kept a thin strip between properties and these often gave natives and islanders somewhere to go and still not end up on private property. They decided to visit a dive site not too far down the coast. Yelina, the ever loyal helper went below and began preparing lunch. Katarina sat comfortably in the main lounge reading a novel. Zak had begun to resent her novel reading. To him the books took precedence. She always took one to bed with her and sometimes had two on the go at once. Zak lay out in the sunshine.

"You coming out?" he called to Katarina.

"Do I ever?" she replied.

"Just thought I'd ask!"

"Well, come on, Zak. You know I can't come out too much.

I've had more than my fair share of SCC, thank you!" called Katarina, with as much sarcasm in her tone as she could muster. Confident of its effect, she promptly put her head back into her book.

"Please yourself," Zak muttered to himself.

Yelina appeared a few minutes later with some pieces of melon and a large iced glass of Bacardi and Coke. Zak saw her walking towards him and a large satisfied grin spread across his face. This was more like it.

"You're a star! Hey do you fancy a dip?" he asked.

"Sure! That'd be nice. I'll go and get changed," she replied, and put the small tray down next to Zak, then disappeared down the steps. She did have a gorgeous tanned body. Certainly curvier than Katarina, with bigger hips and generously proportioned breasts and full, dark nipples that Zak couldn't help but be attracted to. Yelina was a Raquel Welsh to Katarina's Goldie Hawn figure.

Zak took a gulp of his drink and ran straight off the side of the yacht and into the clear water below. The cool, fresh water awakened his senses. He surfaced and swam around for a short time waiting for Yelina. He watched as she appeared in a red and yellow bikini and dived in towards him. They had swum around for a while and Katarina appeared on deck.

"Are you coming back!?" she shouted. Zak felt mischievous.

"Not yet! We're just gonna go ashore for a bit of a sunbathe… it's nicer on the beach!"

Without waiting for a response Zak motioned to Yelina to swim ashore with him. This cove and reef on the south side of the island was quite a popular unowned section of the island. Zak had been there before and had noticed fencing stopping people going too far up the path or beach. He and Yelina walked ashore and sat down in the sand.

"She doesn't like me, does she?" asked Yelina.

"Sure! She just gets a little cranky sometimes. You know how women get when... well, you know," said Zak, slightly sheepishly. Yelina looked at him with unbelieving eyes.

"She's never like that with anyone else."

"Ah, that's women for ya! I mean us men can be just the same. Her husband used to be as nice as pie sometimes and beat her other times, so men can be just as changeable."

"Husband?" Yelina asked.

"Yes, before she came here!"

"She wasn't ever married to him," Yelina said.

"No," Zak conceded, "but they were really in love and even with all that love they had, he still treated her badly when the mood took him. So men can be changeable."

"You're not," said Yelina.

"No, well some people are, I guess," remarked Zak.

"Well I think he got what he deserved."

Zak considered what Yelina had just said. The thought of slowly dying, not being able to get help didn't really seem to be justice to him, particularly as Katarina had told him only a little of the way Elian treated her.

"What do you mean?" he asked.

"He deserved it. He deserved to be killed." Yelina looked at him as though she were talking about a fictional character in a soap opera, not a real life human being.

"Killed?" quizzed Zak.

Yelina realised Zak didn't know the full truth about Katarina and saw a questioning glint in his eyes.

"You have not heard, have you?" she asked.

"No."

Yelina spent the next forty five minutes or so filling in the gaps left out of Katarina's explanation of how she came to the island. Yelina knew, as most of the island did, about how she had arrived at the island. She did not know about the rape and beatings and had adopted the now well-known belief that it was money that had been her greatest motivation. This belief had spread across the island and made most men avoid Katarina, the killer. Zak listened intently and found himself questioning many of her little characteristic traits. There was the time when they were in the spare bedroom. Katarina was her usual self and receptive to his advances until he playfully suggested they play tie me up and rape me. He thought about the conversation.

"Who gets to play being tied up?" asked Katarina.

"Well, I was thinking I could blindfold you and undress you, use these to tie you to the bedpost and have my wicked way with you!" replied Zak, smiling and teasing her with some of her silk stockings in his hands.

"You see, that's just my point! It's all you, you, you, isn't it? Why the hell can't I tie YOU up and have MY way with you!" she retorted.

"Hey! Easy. I was just suggesting it, that's all. You can if you like!" replied Zak, tentatively.

"No, I can't be bothered."

Katarina walked out of the door waving her hands at him, and started down the stairs.

"Well, what the hell are you on about then!?" shouted Zak.

"Nothing! Just leave it. I'm not in the mood," replied the voice from the staircase.

Zak considered this event and began to find other examples where she had refused his advances… and here was her saying she fucked him like a Yimyam whore! Not all true at all. Zak felt that he had been trapped once more and lured into a relationship on a bed of lies and deceit. Their sex life wasn't perfect. She had lied to him a number of times, sure they were normally small ones, but they were still lies.

***

Their swim back to the yacht that day was a sombre affair, with little to laugh or joke about. This was to be the beginning of the end for the Zak and Kat relationship that had started out so well. Over the next few weeks rows and arguments became stronger and more embittered, as Zak resented the fact that she hadn't told him that she had murdered her lover. She never did, and Katarina was finally asked to move out.

Throughout this time, Yelina continued to reliably turn up at Zak's house, cook and clean for him and offer a friendly ear for his troubles. After Katarina had moved out, Zak's interest in Yelina grew. He felt that she was foremost a friend. It wasn't many weeks later when they became lovers.

What Light? What Tunnel?

The simple solution for disappointment depression:
Get up and get moving.
Physically move.
Do.
Act.
Get going.

Peter McWilliams – Life 101

Zak sat comfortably on his sun-lounger. It was about half past ten in the morning and the sun shone brightly, just to his left. The shade caused by the large round umbrella on the terrace would soon be working its way slowly down his chest as the sun rose. Zak loved the sun, its warmth, its energy. With a Bacardi and Coke with ice and a slice next to him, and without a care in the world, this was beachside bliss. Zak's life hadn't looked happier. Yelina had stole his heart and with over a year of dating behind them, Zak was very much in love. He loved her smile, her laugh and the way the quiet girl he'd met back in '95 had now grown and blossomed into the vibrant, sexy woman he knew now. His house, not the grandest on the island, was plenty big enough for them. Yelina had many reasons for resisting moving in with him. Less hassle from her parents, a stable environment for her son, her parents acting as good babysitters.

212

Zak had increasingly thought about asking Yelina to marry him. Zak knew Yelina's excuses were just that and living together out of marriage was not the done thing with natives. To Zak, the native's beliefs were a unique combination of sexual freedom and repressive tradition. Zak found that whilst islanders welcomed and enjoyed an active sex life, they frowned upon people living together without formal commitment. He would change this situation soon though, he was sure of that. He knew he loved her and at times felt that the only reason he hadn't asked her to marry him yet was because... in fact Zak had forgotten why he hadn't asked her. At thirty (got to be 1997) he really should be thinking of settling down. Zak pondered.

Zak felt cosseted on the terrace that he now sat on. The bedroom that overlooked it, with its large windows facing the sea, had been a delightful den of passion where he and Yelina had made sweet love in the evening. The house's dome-shaped top and large white pillars made it a complete contrast of designs, but it was Zak's style, and he knew no one else on earth had one like it. He closed his eyes and, listening to the soft breaking of the water on the beach, imagined an aging sea god with a long white beard waving gently in an underwater world. The soft rumbles of small pebbles and swoosh of water landing rhythmically on the soft sand, sounded comically to Zak like the old sea God had smoked one too many Cigar Wrasse. Yelina interrupted his solitary mind wandering.

"Morning," she called. The picture of a sea god on some sort of nautical ventilator vanished and Zak sat up with a start.

"Hi!" he said, smiling brightly. His best good morning smile was met with a half hearted and at best, consolatory grin. Something was wrong. In an attempt to pretend that he'd read the signs incorrectly, Zak asked brightly, "You ok?"

"We need to talk," replied Yelina.

213

What followed that bright morning was to bring Zak's world crashing down once more. It seemed that the fishing trips, the lovemaking, the nights in and parties out, the closeness that Zak had come to count on meant nothing. Zak was being dumped. He'd never pleaded or begged before, but that morning he did both to try and hold on to the woman he'd fallen in love with. She left later that day, with a sorrowful last look that would be imprinted on Zak's mind for most of the rest of his life.

She had not even fallen for someone new. A childhood school friend was taking her heart back and had everything that Zak couldn't compete with… Memories. Yelina had spent a lot of her childhood with a boy. Played, sung songs, danced, held hands… they had grown up together, and had a bond which made Zak's love for her look ephemeral and shallow.

***

1998 turned out to be a year of suffering for many people. Whilst Hurricane Mitch devastated Honduras and its central American neighbours, when economic problems affected Russia, North Korea, China and Latin America causing massive food shortages, Zak suffered in his own private world. Whilst Sudan experienced civil war and crop failures, Bangladesh its worst floods ever and in Kosovo and Albania, war displaced tens of thousands, Zak sat in his own haven, oblivious to it all. He was in his own hell on earth. To him these events meant nothing. He had lost the closest thing to love that he'd had since his mother died. In 1998 even H^{e}aven was a world of hurt. Zak turned eagerly to the bottle for solace and gave up any hope of having a family.

The Discovery

Discovery consists of seeing what everyone has seen
and thinking what nobody has thought.

Albert von Szentgyörgyi – 1962

Zachariah sat watching the neon lights glitter away their advertisements of fantasy. They all promised you better health, more wealth or happiness. The big screen at the junction of Plaza Street East and Plaza Street West flickered its message of what to buy next. Zachariah could easily see the pixels of lights that made up the complete image. It reminded him of a computer screen. He looked carefully, analysing the screen for small cameras. Government surveillance. He reached into his pad and finding an empty space scribbled,

Why do they insist on expecting us not to notice??? Why doesn't anyone STOP THEM LOOKING?? Well mark my words, Mr Bill Clinton... I will, when I return!!!

***

Zak had once met a boy, a youth really, called Earl. Zak thought Earl to be a bit of a geek. He was a scrawny lad with one too many zits and a crooked smile. His ruffled chocolate-brown hair was never in the right place. However, Zak found him funny and very likeable. Earl had a strange and overly keen enthusiasm for the scouts and had possessed a surfeit of badges. One thing that Earl did know about however was computers. Zak became impressed with Earl's knowledge of computers and secondly, curious about them himself. When Earl showed him how easy it had been to get the word 'Hello' to bounce around the screen on a BBC B, Zak was intrigued. Not only did Earl know how to do that, but he also knew how to lock the keyboard of the Commodore 64 that also took pride of place in the classroom. To a schoolboy, these were feats worth knowing!

Zachariah's early introduction to computers had forced him into taking note of how they worked. This was a good head start and bode him well for later in his education, when students' use of a BBC for educational purposes became hot educative fashion. A few years later and the 'big boxy one' in the corner of the classroom slowly began to multiply, and the Commodores and BBC computers finally disappeared. The Personal Computer made by IBM was born and Zak finally ditched his own computer and gave into its charms. Zak never did bother to learn how to make 'Hello' bounce round the screen on this computer, but he did recognise it was ideal for writing his homework on.

Whilst in H^eaven, Zak had purchased and installed a very up to date computer system. It allowed him to record pictures from his digital camera or camcorder and save the images directly to a DVD. Marylyn had been very impressed. Zak was even allowed to surf the web. Rules on the island regarding this use of a PC were very strict. The computers actions were all noted and recorded by the island's security system. Zak could visit most sites, but the system would not allow him to buy anything online or even place bids for items. It would not allow e-mails, and any attempt to contact the outside world in any way would result in the confiscation of the computer.

The rule of H^{e}aven was that any information or data was allowed onto the island but not allowed off. Obvious attempts to do this were severely punished and Zak was strenuously advised against trying. Zak was happy with this. He could visit just about any site in the world and look up anything he liked. If the 'big brother' island system didn't want him to look at a site, it would alert island security who would check out the site before sending Zak an e-mail telling him he was now allowed to visit the site until further checks were made, or would not ever be. Online subscriptions to web sites were made on Zak's behalf. Zak wondered if the island actually paid for access or simply hacked into it. Either way he would be invoiced and receive a log on ID and password. Zak knew that his Internet browsing was monitored closely. He once went to a site that allowed him to log in and give personal details; his connection was speedily terminated. No online chatting was allowed and web searches relating to some subjects were disconnected. If Zak had ever attempted to buy anything his connection would immediately be severed. Religious sites faced the same veto, connections were terminated and the resulting shortcuts led nowhere, apart from to such sites as positiveatheism.com, that was a site supporting non-belief in any religion.

H^{e}aven's communication systems were extremely hi-tech and his online speed was phenomenal. The television signals were inputted directly via a single cable from the dish on top of the lighthouse on the south side of the island. The information it received was then distributed to the homes on the island, always by cable. No aerials were allowed anywhere, by anyone. Even cars were not allowed radio aerials and had to rely upon CD's or tape for music.

Such was the command of H^{e}aven's controllers. Zak had once spoken to Ayrton about religion being practised at H^{e}aven, and had found Ayrton to be very unsure about divulging the answer. Apparently, according to Marylyn (herself a reformed religionist), Ayrton had once been caught by H^{e}aven controllers trying to organise a meeting based on prayer and had been warned in no uncertain terms about the consequences of being caught again. Prayer, it seemed, was fine in one's own house, but any form of congregation or sharing of ideas was heavily frowned upon.

"It's where it leads to, honey," Marylyn had said one day.

"That's the problem with it. They say that too much religion is dangerous. What is it they said darlin? Oh... that's it, the last place had just enough of each religion to make us love ourselves, and too many religions to make people happy with their neighbour. Now that confused the bejesus outa me I can tell ya, but Jack here, he knew what they meant by it, didn't you honey?" Without looking up, JFK had nodded in affirmation and continued to read his book.

"Well the upshot of what they meant was, what you do behind your own doors is ok... just don't go invitin' anyone."

Zak had held no intention of practising himself anyway, his interest in religion had waned ever since his mother had let him know that she never really believed in the religion into which he was being nurtured. Zak had been raised as a Christian and had one day talked to his mother about beliefs. She mentioned that some people think that way, but others, including her, believed in Mary. The 'Holy Mary, the Mother of God', was more important.

So it came to pass that Zak had a more than transitory interest in computers and the Internet. He had also amassed quite a collection of recordings of films and series from the television. 1999 was a year of discovery for Zachariah Sharpe; a newspaper item a little over a week old caught his eye...

218

WASHINGTON, D.C., September 14, 1999 – *Solar Photovoltaic (PV) energy can be made cost-competitive now with conventional fossil-fuel and nuclear electricity, by significantly increasing PV production, according to a report released today by business and accounting firm KPMG. The report, commissioned by international environmental support agencies went on to say that diversification by companies like The Sharpe Corporation, who earlier this year expanded into solar energy and wind turbine power by buying up the Progress Corporation, was a welcome re-emphasis towards environmental protection. New, young corporation president, Nicola Jameson stated, "The Progress Corporation was a company specialising in green energy. The takeover by The Sharpe Corporation is a recognition that environmental issues matter. We believe in the future of our planet and will invest in its long-term prosperity. The purchase of The Progress Corporation is our commitment to the belief that regardless of squabbles over Kyoto agreements, where 38 industrial nations in the treaty promise to cut their emissions of greenhouse gases by 5.2% – environmental protection, sustenance and development will be the biggest market of the 21st century."*

The words rode over Zak's eyes like a kaleidoscope of colour dissolving into a sea of questions. He went to his computer and logged in. The anticipation of answers made his hands moist on the keypad. He typed in 'SEARCH: The Sharpe Corporation Nicola Jameson'. The cursor blinking boldly back at him whilst he waited for a response, seconds seemed like minutes to him. The computer finally responded.

The Sharpe Corporation

MARCH 8, 1998 3:12 PM FOR IMMEDIATE RELEASE

CONTACT: The Sharpe Corporation England Michael-Underwood, Media Centre, 201-329-2135. New Owner becomes CEO
Www.sharpecorporation.org/pressreleases/march98/030898c.ht m - 10k - Cached - Similar pages

Zak clicked on the result of the search. The resulting page was a white screen background with a news release about how the new owner of The Sharpe Corporation had decided to take the position, CEO of worldwide affairs and how a management shake up had meant Mike Underwood was promoted to Corporate President. Zak read and searched some more and was about to make an amazing discovery that would transform Zak's outlook on life, and would be destined to lead him into unknown waters.

A Learning Experience

Maybe this world
is another planet's Hell.

Aldous Huxley – (1894-1963)

In the strange combined scent of swimming pool water and pine needles, Brandon sat. He didn't mind the barren rocky surface that made up his back yard. The hard limestone, almost Mexican landscaping suited his irregular windows and almost cave-like abode. The clatter of pots, pans and tinkle of glasswear being tidied up inside, was interrupted by the crackle and rumble of the wide rubber tyres as they noisily rode over the rough ground outside. He looked up from his book in anticipation, his ears straining to catch aural clues as to who it might be. The faint click of the door opening gave him his first indication. Most car doors opened with an almost silent click, followed by a sucking noise as the door's seal broke and it sucked air into the car. This was slightly different and had a much louder click. No creak meant it wasn't a van. Besides, the engine would have given that one away.

Having opened his door with the internal button, Zak pushed the cream leather on the inside of his door to his TVR and got out. Proud that he'd bought British, Zak loved the uniqueness his car had on the island. It often got people's head turning, regardless of whatever else was on the island. The

221

unashamed roar of power his engine pushed through his exhaust was better than many a music system. As he got out and pushed the door closed, a hummingbird flew quickly past him. The door made a healthy clunk sound as the catch grasped the hook on the bodywork. The bird flew even quicker, darting through the bushes. Zak followed the path round the house past the mini cacti, Joshua tree and small rocks that made up this desert-like landscaping. Brandon was sitting in a lounger in the shade, a book in hand. Brandon smiled.

"Hello Zak! How's things?"

"Brilliant!" replied Zak. "Can we talk?"

Zak's eyes looked nervously and momentarily towards the house, where the sound of the housekeeper continued.

"Sure, it's ok. Why, what's the news?" asked Brandon.

"Well, I think I need your help." Zak's voice became hushed and secretive, his eyes became nervous and focussed on the smallest of movements. Brandon put his book on the small table and lifted his legs either side of the lounger so that he could close the distance between himself and Zak. Zak was nervously excited and that got Brandon's attention.

"I've discovered the most amazing thing! Almost by accident. But Brandon, it's changed my outlook and my life… and I want it back," said Zak.

"Want what back?" asked Brandon, confused and bewildered at Zak's disposition.

"My *life*!" Zak looked away and back at Brandon, urging him to understand what he meant. A clatter inside dragged Zak's eyes away from Brandon. "Let's go for a walk."

Brandon got up and placed a bookmark in a page of his book, 'The Sailor who fell from grace with the sea', and gently laid it onto the table. He put on some sandals and they began to walk. Zak explained the whole process of how he had stumbled

222

upon the discovery that he had a half sister. The Internet was a wonderful thing, and Zak had managed to discover that his mother had given birth to a baby girl at what could have been only about seventeen. Zak had searched the Internet thoroughly and discovered that his mother had gone to a private school in Ireland. There, it seems she'd met her sweetheart, and in 1964 had become pregnant. Zak couldn't find any mention of the boyfriend after this date, but knowing what influence religion and Irish culture of the 1960's had on pregnant single women, he figured that she might have been advised to let her relative adopt the child. Rather than be shunned by them or terminate, this option seemed to be the best. Besides, high society available females were NEVER with child. Zak knew that his parents had met at the 1966 New Year's party, and also knew that Edwin would've never looked at his mother if she had had a baby.

The daughter, Nicola Jameson, was apparently like her mother… feisty. She hadn't the privilege her mother had enjoyed and had instead attended a local school. She had apparently excelled at mathematics and was told at eighteen that her parents weren't hers. It seems that she had done nothing about this for quite some years. Zak assumed it was because she obviously loved her adopted parents. In 1997, and with a child of her own and both adopted parents dead, she had decided to search for grandparents for her child to know. The discovery in 1998 that her real mother and step-father had owned The Sharpe Corporation, came as a real shock. She was apparently mortified to discover that she had a half brother who had also died only four years earlier. The Sharpe Corporation website had provided much of this information, and other searches of school records and public records had filled in any gaps. It had taken a simple DNA test to prove her entitlement to a multi-million pound inheritance. The Sharpe Corporation had a new owner.

"I want out! ...I want out of here! I have a SISTER! I have family! It's the first time for what seems like an eternity that I have someone on this god-forsaken planet that is related to me!" explained Zak.

"But we're not on that god-forsaken planet and neither can we get there!" pleaded Brandon, hoping his friend hadn't gone mad.

"If I got off the island and told the world that this is here they would never believe me anyway! I'm not interested in letting the world know it's here I just want out and... and just because the world doesn't know it exists, it doesn't mean it doesn't, and it doesn't mean I can't get home! Nothing is impossible!" Zak looked at Brandon, searching for acceptance of his thoughts.

Brandon finally conceded. He knew what Zak meant, part of him longed to go back to Eliza, and his eyes reflected back an understanding that Zak welcomed. It seemed that Zak's enthusiasm was catching Brandon's attention.

"Do you know what that feels like?" asked Zak. Brandon smiled and nodded. As a man who had lived in the shadow of his father's greatness but had never really got to know him, he didn't hesitate to be reunited with him.

"But how do you possibly hope to get off the island? You can't get anywhere near the south side of the island without an appointment either with The Group or Mr C. Then even if you get there, you'll need to be able to highjack a boat or plane and escape without detection. No. It's impossible," said Brandon, despondently.

"Now I KNOW that if there's a way to get here then there's got to be a way to get back. But I need your help. I was thinking, the ships that bring the goods in that we order, they must go back somewhere!" said Zak.

Brandon thought for a moment.

"I think they use a small port on the American coast. It's all pretty hush hush, but I do know that the port is owned and run by The Group and they give preferential secrecy to the boats that arrive here. That is the only way they control any customs investigations."

"There you are then!" Zak said.

"But nothing's ever taken off the island!" remarked Brandon.

"Oh but it is! Waste! This place produces waste like you wouldn't believe and they don't burn it because it might show up on some monitor somewhere. They recycle it. They package it up and put it back on the same boats that bring stuff. I noticed that the ships are full arriving and departing! They couldn't keep it here! There are far too many millionaires who simply wouldn't want it near them."

Brandon thought for a moment and wondered whether this excited Englishman might be on to something.

"I've heard that even big things, like boats they've captured, are taken thousands of miles away before being dumped. Now, if I could get on board one of them undetected, I could sail back to the nearest bit of land and make my way home."

"You're forgetting one thing aren't you?" asked Brandon.

"What?" answered Zak.

"THEY won't let you. THEY would kill you the moment they knew... and that might be before you've even landed. The Group would hunt you down at all costs," Brandon explained.

"I don't care," Zak retorted.

"Where there's a will there's a way, and there's no way I'm staying here without trying. I have no choice. I'm going, it's as simple as that."

The Freedom Plan

It's kind of fun
to do the impossible.

Walt Disney – (1901-1966)

Oswardo's face was softening as the years rolled by. In his youth he'd been a very handsome man. Rugged, healthy and full of life. But as the years progressed, the sun and sea had taken their toll on his skin. He had developed course, hard lines, and skin so leathery you could strike a match from it.

Now, as he grew older still and did less fishing, his skin had relaxed, and whilst it was still as wrinkly as ever, the wrinkles had taken on an oak-like quality, tanned and rich from years of life that were now etched like a contour map on his face. He had seen the relationship between Yelina and Zak grow over the last couple of years, and had equally recognised that his niece did not hold the same flame for Zak as Zak appeared to hold for her. He had however, grown fond of Zak. Here was a man who seemed to excel and delight in enjoying life. Many of the islander's arrivals carried the pretentious character flaws they'd developed whilst in the public eye. Here, some seemed to expect that the island owed them something. Not all perhaps, Elvis was certainly a man who'd surpassed many islander's expectations of settlement. Zak was, in many ways, quite similar to him and

226

seemed to delight in accepting life as it was.

Oswardo had learned through time, and Yelina, that Zak's parent's had died at what was obviously a part of Zak's life when he would have really needed them, and might have just been getting to know them. Oswardo thought that children are conditioned and shaped into believing and experiencing their parents as supernatural idols whose words, whilst not always agreeable, were voiced from centuries of experience and knowledge that made it pre-eminent. As children surpassed adolescence and grew into adults, they often found logistical flaws that questioned these previously held presumptions. It was often at this stage, when with greater knowledge and worldliness, that they would mature and exhort psychologically greater respect from their parents. It would've been at about this time that Zak lost his parents, and due to the private school upbringing that he'd endured, it was obvious why Zak had gone off the rails like he had. But Oswardo considered him a good kid at heart. He wondered how Zak might have taken the final rejection by Yelina. He knew Yelina had feelings for Zak, that much was obvious, but her heart had never really left a boy from her childhood and the father of her child. Zak thrived on settlement and the sense that he had people with whom he could relate so well or be so close to as to call family. Yelina had shattered that dream.

Zak had approached Oswardo only a week earlier and had asked Oswardo for something that he knew he couldn't provide. The unfortunate dilemma for Oswardo was that he knew who could. The dilemma was whether he should tell Zak. Oswardo had gained himself, a good reputation on the island, and was a trusted member of the community by The Group. Getting even marginally involved in what Zak was trying would result in death for himself and disgrace for his family. The goods boats.

Goods were brought onto the island, and trash taken off, often using the same ocean vessels. These were often large boats with carrying capabilities for cars, building materials, even small yachts. They went to and from the mainland or other parts of the world, and imported anything the island or its handsomely paying guests wanted. Owned and operated by The Group, he had learned that the death penalty awaited anyone trying to stow away in them. Despite this very real threat, he had heard of escape attempts. The difficulty was that no one had ever escaped, or if they had, they had never let on to islanders that it was possible. Many of the islanders lived in fear. Fear of The Group. They also lived on what was obviously a pittance compared to members of The Group, or the islanders paying guests. The Group often reinforced the belief that without anonymity, the islanders wouldn't come and without them most natives would starve. So whilst the television and Internet tempted, abject anxiety kept most inhabitants from even considering excursions abroad.

Oswardo's quandary needed resolution, and fast. Zak would be there any moment now and he would be expecting an answer. The easy one was No. However, Oswardo couldn't help but feel a kindred empathy for this man and an understanding of his desire to leave. Oswardo was fuelled by a knowledge that it had been his niece who had provided the gasoline to ignite the necessity.

Jamie Keys

I never travel without my Diary.
One should always have something
Sensational to read in the train.

Oscar Wilde
The Importance of being Earnest II

Jamie Keys casually brushed back his blonde, wavy hair. The centre parting fell naturally for him and was disguised only by the incessant manner in which it constantly fell in front of his ice-blue eyes. It was his main attraction and he knew it. It gave him an edge over other boys his age, and at fourteen he'd worked out that any advantage was worth keeping. Girls seemed to half expect him to be a skater boy or even into surfing.

This laid-back, nonchalant image was one that Jamie was happy to encourage. A bright boy but inherently lazy, Jamie cared more about looking good and being popular than succeeding at anything as dull as academia. A repeatedly convicted school truant, he'd often kissed his mother, well more accurately step-mother, goodbye and bunked off. This morning at the gates to his school, dressed in his baggy jeans and pale blue designer-label top, he'd carefully delayed walking anywhere. Whilst he surreptitiously fumbled in his bag, she'd driven out of sight. It was easy. Simply walking away from the

229

school in the opposite direction was then a piece of cake, and if anyone questioned him (which nobody ever had), then he was going home to collect his homework.

This day seemed to bore him though. None of his friends had bunked that day and so he was left to entertain himself. He wandered down to the benches and flower planters that stood outside the shopping mall and waited to see anyone he knew. Then he'd spent a good two hours in the shopping mall, walking aimlessly round from store to store. Listening to the latest tracks with the earphones in the music store, watching the television screens in the shop windows of local TV stores or bumming around Century 21 or Macy's, he'd done it all. Now as he passed Harris' department store he ambled along, staring mainly at his sneakers. The lace on his left foot was virtually undone, but it added to his image and would take far more effort to tie than it would be to leave. As he took each step along the paving, he noticed how the lace on the outside of his left foot swung over to the top of his trainer and bounced back to the ground. Like a pianist's metronome, it swayed rhythmically over and back, over and back. His indifference was interrupted by a small notepad. He stopped, gazed at it for a moment, looked around and picked it up.

Picking it up, he became aware of the cover.

"MY DIARY – PRIVATE AND CONFIDENTIAL" was written neatly on the outside. He opened it up. The plain blue cover camouflaged a convoluted world of observations, interpretations and statements. Statements made by an intelligent yet confused individual, who plainly saw the world through glasses that were far from rose-coloured. Jamie started, as people often did when they were right handed and just browsing, at the back. The last page read:

Now that the revolution has collapsed and tranquillity has returned, what is the object of the exercise?

Puzzled, he continued to walk and investigate his find further.

Too much Alcoholic Liquor can be risky - But mixing one's drinks can be LETHAL! Be kind to your innards!

Continuing from the back forwards, the pages prior to that contained a list of numbers; Jamie read some of them:

7) My suggestion to this god-forsaken country is - Has nobody anything to offer a penniless prodigal son?

8) CAUTION! There IS a magical camera in the ~~sky~~ sKy - Believe it or not - and THE WHOLE WORLD is watching you!

9) The fact that I know (8) and that I'm shrewd and suspicious DOES NOT mean that I have a criminal record, and something to hide! It means I have already been subject to Victimisation! My record is quite spotless in fact... It was my money, after all!!

10) If I may presume to remark - All work and no play may make Zak a dull boy – But all play and No work do much more damage to Jill!

11) I should like to point out that although I was born more intelligent than most (it's what got me out!!), I was not born intelligent, stuffed full of information and ideas - I had to go out and find it!

Jamie was intrigued. He turned to the first page to decipher the contents of his find more carefully.

I don't know how they managed it, but they gave me a real knock out slug last night - Could they have found their way into the Rice Pudding Factory?

The next page read,

An awful lot of people have been relying on tinned rice pudding for a safe supper!! And NOW the TAP WATER has been

231

poisoned again - My morning cup of coffee submerged me once more!

Houdini, would you believe it!
BLOODY MASONS!
BLOODY MASONS!
BLOODY MASONS!

Goodbye
Ari Verdecee
Auf Weidersehen
Au Revoir
Sorry,- But I feel as though I am Target number ONE!

Like a shire horse might pull a barge further and further down a towpath, Jamie's attention was drawn along its journey of discovery into this strange new world. He walked aimlessly along, not having any regard to where he was going nor who was watching him. He laughed at some pages and openly puzzled over others. The notepad seemed to have been written by a person, obviously intelligent but desperately critical of the world and the way it treated people. The person writing the book seemed almost schizophrenic, but had an insight into the news of the day that captivated the young boy. After about ten pages, Jamie stopped walking and looked around for a place to sit. He was at the entrance to Prospect Park and so he decided to find a place to sit there. He walked along the path and read some more. From the corner of his eye he noticed someone. He looked up and saw a tired, dirty and vulnerable tramp half hiding a loaf of bread in his jacket. The tramp's skin looked a dirty brown colour, hard and cold. Yet the man's eyes looked nervously towards him. Jamie continued his way towards the park bench, and the tramp turned his attention back to his bread.

Jamie reached the dark wooden bench; he sat at the end furthest away from the bin, as it smelt like some late night reveller had been sick in it. The page that had made him want to read this interesting account read,

NO, I DO NOT ENJOY BEING ME! (I do not know which is worse - Blatant harassment by mindless camera wielding morons, or secret subterfuge by clever agents of a distant dreamland).

Jamie wondered who would write such a thing? Who were the morons? And who were the agents? He turned the page again,

It may seem obvious but - There are two main methods of corruption, Namely - Intimidation and Seduction. (A third, less efficient way is to mislead the stupid but well-intentioned down the wrong path).

I can't believe they believe that man! When they said the world's a stage they didn't realise the acting was going to be so bloody awful!

Jamie heard something and instinctively looked up from the notebook, half expecting to see someone watching him read. A lady in her fifties with a haircut not dissimilar to Marge Simpson walked passed with her poodle. No one seemed to be paying any attention to him whatsoever. He relaxed some and continued to read.

If you actually read American magazines, journals and newspapers, you would realise that their burdens of anxiety and responsibility do not include the $^{(noxious?)}$ influence of the British monarchy in world affairs. Are they trying to make Britain a Republic?

Today is voting day - You must all come along and put your cross by the side you want to support! (Rather you than me!) (Who really rules this country anyway?)

233

I don't know about other parts of this HUGE country, but pollution of the mains water supply in this area is rife. I can tell by the taste.

Note – I wonder if that's why the Rice pudding is also affected?

Jottings:

In case you're new around here. I've been here for some months and tried to become associated with people. I won't bore with the details of how I know, but I've become embroiled in a damned chimney sweep, spy hole, sabotage etc etc kind of war that THEY are determined to win. I try to make contact to establish some credibility and THEY stop it!

1.   In case you are still watching - Q) Did I see anyone I recognised this morning? Anyone I had become better acquainted with? A) Not a soul!

2.   Some people resort to being treated as experimental animals in a big game. I'm not one of them but have little choice ["professor,- does the animal suffer at all?" "Oh nothing worth worrying about… they don't feel a thing!"]

Today's note to remember.

Because THEY stole my cash and THEY stole my identity I have found it increasingly difficult to get some damn RECOGNITION. It has however taught me to keep my head down and not let them track me. They know I'm hereabouts (that sounds like an American word to me) and have employed many secretive methods such as tap water tampering. I have managed to sustain myself (being broke) on bottles of milk from doorsteps (not that there's that many – what's wrong with these people!?) and the odd donation of other foodstuffs.

Wednesday

I have begun to fear that the milk was spiced with

something, something to make me need hospital help - but I'm
not some pleb of a man.. I am not going to succumb to such
blatant methods by these mysterious and anonymous poisoners.

The crisis in our world is more ugly than it looks,

It's not the politics that plagues us, but the bunch of
scheming crooks,

They're holding all our loot, they accumulated when,

We were living in their homeland, in a most exclusive den!

They're running out of victims, and targets to exploit,

I'm sure they've planned their exit, with precautions most
adroit,

And being blessed with English, as a kind of second tongue,

It'll be the bloody English, that they'll happily settle among,

They dragged them in and pampered them, let them run
amok,

Whilst they robbed all their money, this rich and famous
stock,

Masters of disguises and performers of finesse,

They do not just rely on oppression and duress,

So versatile and skilful, you just would not believe,

How these diplomatic monsters, are able to deceive.

For they can be quite charming and generous at times,

If that's what suits their purpose and their ultimate designs.

And their predatory targets, are rich and famous folk,

Who're always so susceptible, and never see the joke!

But cross them and they'll get you, lay you out to die,

Rob you of identity, like some caught and punished spy,

So beware my friend, be cautious, do not fall into their trap,

Cause H^{e}aven is a fraudster with a most exclusive rap.

Note to oneself - With so many dangerous characters,
armed to the teeth in this bloody country! I'll make a point of

235

shopping for milk earlier and sleeping down by the petroleum plant (I don't think they like the smell☺)

Tuesday
I am afraid all your tricks, manoeuvres, strategies and devices are so glaringly OBVIOUS, and the reasoning behind them so moronic that you must think the whole world is yours to play with like some pack of cards. Well I'm the joker in the pack and I'm gonna bring your house of cards down!

The Escape

The bleat, the bark bellow and roar
are waves that beat on H^{e}aven's shore
Auguries of Innocence.

William Blake

Zak sat in a small upright chair in the corner of the parlour. The walls were painted like a digestive biscuit, both in colour and texture. The room was clean and smelt of the wood that slowly burnt in the stove next to him. "I have been giving your question a lot of thought, Zak, and if I can say so, you are mad. It has rarely been tried before and even when people have tried, they have failed. And yet I am willing to help you."

Zak found Oswardo's reaction to his idea both inspiring and exciting.

"So that's a Yes!?" Zak exclaimed.

"Zak, if I am to help you, you must promise to do this my way. I do know of a way to get off the island but it will mean a lot of money. These people do not like to take these sort of risks Zak, and if there is a doubt in their minds, they will not help you and you will not see them again. This is very serious."

Oswardo looked at Zak to try and gauge whether Zak had understood. Oswardo did indeed know such men, he also knew that they were ruthless and untrustworthy. Zak seemed

237

determined however and Oswardo knew that it was them or not at all. Zak immediately put his plan of escape into action.

EMAIL MESSAGE
To: Mr C
Cc:
Subject: Import Order
Date: 17/09/1999

Dear Mr C

I have often wondered about the works of art that I have seen in some of the guests' houses.

I would like to be able to appreciate some of these works of art myself. However, not being an art 'buff', I have asked some of my friends. I have decided that (as I don't know many artists) that I would like to start with a portrait. I have been told by a friend that Guercino has painted some pictures like these?

I have done a little studying and have decided to purchase 'The Holy Family' as it is beautifully simplistic, and feel it would complement my study wonderfully. I would be very grateful if you could investigate if this, or other works similar to this are available, and advise me of the cost.

Regards

Zak Sharpe.

By placing an order for a work of art Zak knew that Mr C would not suspect anything. Many of the island's guests were collectors of stolen art. Of course everything on the island had to be stolen from somewhere around the world because none of the islanders could pay for anything – neither they nor their money existed. The money they paid for 'imports' was always to the black market dealers who stole to order. That way the money the island handed over for any item was always handed to a person who had a vested interest in 'cleaning' it.

Following this e-mail, the next few months were spent in secretive preparation for the escape. Zak put all his faith in Oswardo and never questioned the considerable sums needed to bribe co-conspirators. Like his arrival to H^{e}aven, his departure from it placed great faith in men unknown to him. Money was needed to whet the attention and bribe crooked shipping workers, dock workers and different people in whom Zak would be putting his life. Oswardo had told him to order many things, but warned these would never arrive. The money handed over (less The Group's standard cut from all imports) would stay as bribery. But Zak knew that whoever helped him would face the same fate if caught. Nothing could be laid to chance. Oswardo and Brandon were both people in whom he could trust his life, and was doing so with what at times seemed like a kamikaze mission to certain death.

The fountain, once alive and vibrant now stood dead as Zak sat at the rear of his house. He looked down at the yellowed-green grass nearby and pondered his actions and convictions. The more he did so, the more worried he became about the escape. The more lonely he felt about his future. Who could influence his success? Who could cost him his life? Zak thought about any evidence he'd left. Zak had always kept a diary but now began to question its use. Zak had remembered hearing about Gary Glitter, whose trip to a computer store at Cribbs Causeway in Bristol had cost him dearly. A simple computer error had caught him. Zak had often asked for repairs to his machine. Now these men who had seemed so likeable, so pleasant, kind and warm developed a sinister foreignism. He tried to recall their faces, their body language, and their voices. Their smile no longer gave Zak the impression of sincerity, moreover they were wryly devious. Zak decided he didn't trust them as far as he could see them. He began to think about whether he could trust other paying guests. Zak decided he couldn't and was grateful for the unmet temptation he'd had a few days earlier with Ayrton. Zak decided that too many people knowing was dangerous.

So, with these thoughts milling around his head, what started out as worry became fear and finally panic. The resulting wave of sheer terror welled up inside him. He seemed powerless to stop it and his body, like rocks in a hurricane shook him violently. His back stiffened and he became anxiously aware of this panic attack as the fear rushed from his centre towards his skin in a desperate attempt to escape. Jumping up from his couch he hadn't a moment to lose. He pushed anxiously at the round power button on the front of his PC. Moments seemed like forever as finally, up flashed the familiar logo. It hung on the screen for nigh on an eternity and was finally replaced by the turquoise screen of his PC desktop. Where should he look first? He quickly calculated that most, if not all evidence, would be in his diary or Jotting document. He opened both and systematically went through each daily entry with a fine toothcomb. Down each paragraph, page after page he meticulously read each daily entry. He altered visits to Oswardo's and Brandon's with private moments, meals, chats and time wasting activities with other islanders. He fleetingly considered removing the diary from his PC completely, but wouldn't that create suspicion? He didn't know. All he did know was that should he alter any part of his normal island lifestyle, he would probably be rumbled. That night, for Zak Sharpe, was ten hours of sheer hell, broken only when he'd finished at dawn.

***

The evening finally arrived and Zak was ready. All preparations had been made, he had managed to stash some American Dollars away and save them for his trip. He didn't figure that he needed a great deal. Enough to see him from port to New York should be plenty. There he could make his presence known and enjoy life once more. He'd have a sister, a niece... and a brother in law! He hadn't imagined what he would be like. He hadn't also realised how much space used notes actually took up. He had seen programs and films on television where burglars had made off with a heist of millions. When he started to collect his funds, it seemed that ten thousand dollars was almost more than he could carry. Oswardo had told him to be at the water's edge just up the coast from James Dean's property. The land near here had been sold and was being levelled prior to a new arrival.

Zak left his house after making final preparations. He had installed some timers to his light switches, curtains and sound system. He had set these to act exactly as though he was at home and busy living island life. The curtains were to open at 8:00am and close at 9:00pm. The lights were to go on at 9.00pm and switch off at 00:30am, the television on at 8:30pm and off at 00:15am, and had scheduled his PC to email Mr C.

To: Mr 'C'
Cc:
Subject: Import Order
Date: 14/10/1999

Dear Mr 'C'

I understand that it is not necessarily easy to source works of art. But you told me to expect the painting soon, as a copy was being made.

I must say that I am most disappointed about the response. Many of the islanders have informed me that works of art of this nature rarely take more than a couple of months to deliver. I know Guercino is a famous artist, but other islanders have Monet's and Rembrandt's and they seem not to have taken as long to source. I chose The Holy Family as many of his pieces are too bright and religious in context. I do hope that the next time we speak it will be because you have very good news for me.

Regards

Zak Sharpe.

Zak hoped that the complaining attitude would keep Mr C happy that Zak was still around but would discourage Mr C from visiting until the painting was ready. Meanwhile Zak considered he would be well into America and probably in New York.

Zak stood looking at his reflection in the mirror, drinking a strong Bacardi and Coke. He figured that if he looked like a labourer, he'd have more chance fitting into the crowds in the docks. He'd worn some black boots and trousers, a dark blue woollen polar neck and a black hat. He looked like a dock worker alright; he'd deliberately bought everyday attire rather than designer gear. No one worked near docks and wore designer gear. He checked his small rucksack. Inside were some essentials. His money, sunglasses, a spare pair of trousers and top, some sun-in solution for his hair and some curling tongs. Zak was determined not to get recognised by the people bound to be hired by The Group to find him. He'd already spent a good part of his wealth on the hiring of the boat and crew willing to risk their lives to return him to the mainland. He tightened the bag, just in case. Underneath his trousers, and strapped to one of his legs, was a scuba diving knife. Zak figured he needed all the protection he could get. He'd hired what he could, but knew that The Group would stop at nothing to kill him before he got to tell the world who he was.

Zak took one last look at his lounge and set off into the night. The night sky was crystal clear and a full moon shone brightly in the darkness. Zak looked at the moon and surrounding stars as he walked along his driveway and to the main road. It was quiet. The silence was both comforting and eerie. He checked both ways carefully before stepping out of the shadows and across the road. The whitewashed wall of the empty property opposite his was easy to climb over. Zak scrambled over and landed on the limestone rocks the other side. They gargled as his feet pushed them aside. He looked around nervously, then confident no one was around, he started on down the dusty disused driveway.

The moon lit the route well and all that could be heard was the relentless sound of the crickets, and they seemed to be out in force tonight. Zak nervously glanced left and into the darkness of the bushes each side of the driveway as he made his way north, towards the sea. Bats flew in the space above him, circling and swooping down. The total journey lasted about an hour as the island was about 5 miles across at this point. The one main road in the middle of the island afforded the paying guests plenty of privacy. The driveways finally opened out into a courtyard area and half demolished building. The Group always cleared each site ready for the new occupants. This, Zak thought, enabled them to charge each new guest for building a new house. It also ensured that native workers were rarely without work.

Zak made his way past the site and finally reached the beach. The house's hard patio area finally gave way to damp sand that gave way under his feet. He had been told to clear any sign of his presence and so dragged a small branch behind him to disguise the footprints. He turned right and began looking for the bucket. He walked for a further five minutes before he noticed what he thought to be a bucket, slightly further up the beach. He walked on towards it.

Upon reaching the bucket he looked at the rope it was tied to. Hidden half under sand, it led both out to the broad expanse of calm sea, and also back inland. The rope leading back up the beach should lead him to a small inflatable boat; the other should lead him out to sea. He followed the rope inland and the rope led him to some large leaves. He lifted them off and saw his craft. A small inflatable dingy lay waiting for him. It looked comically like an oversized action man toy as it was crudely painted with gloss paint to camouflage it. The rope that led to the bucket had been threaded through one of the oar loops of the boat and tied at the back. He picked it up and carried it back to the bucket. There he gathered the excess rope and bundled it into the dingy. He put the bucket inside as directed and carried the dingy towards and into the sea. He barely noticed the temperature of the water, such was his excitement. He waded out until he was up to waist height, and jumped in. Sitting at the back of the dingy, he began to pull himself out to sea with the rope.

"Bugger!" Zak whispered to himself. The bucket had a tendency to fill up with water and this seemed to slow his progress. He emptied it and lifted it into the dingy and put his left foot between the wall and floor of the dinghy so as to keep it inside the boat. He began pulling himself further and further out to sea. After about ten minutes he heard the thump of metal against plastic. He looked at the rope. A small half-kilogram body building weight had been tied onto the rope. The rope would pull through no more... he'd made it. He tied off the rope to secure its position, and waited.

Zak sat like a lonely figure, white and motionless, lifeless, hopeless in the dark. As he sat in the moonlight smelling the salt of the seawater around him, he looked back at the island. Further up the coast to his left would be the new plot, now occupied by Dodi and Di and their young daughter. Not far to his right would be the massive estate owned by James Dean. Zak thought it a waste now that James so rarely drove his sports cars. Age and sensibility had caught up with him, and the plot was far bigger than James really needed. Zak was not sure how long he'd waited, but some time later a small container boat sailed nearby. It had, as Zak had expected, an ice-blue lantern on its nose. It pulled slowly up beside him. Relived and excited, Zak climbed aboard the boat. Saying nothing to him, two men helped him drag the dingy onboard, and lift the anchor to which it was attached. Once this had been done, he was led down into a small musty cabin. Inside the smell of salt, fish, whiskey and sweat mingled together in a strangely comforting, homely way. Zak was told to rest, as the journey to the mainland would be a long one. Zak did as he was told.

Land Ahoy

I've had a wonderful time,
but this wasn't it.

Groucho Marx – *(1895-1977)*

Mr C rose at his usual time of 5am. After many years in the army his body time clock had become accustomed to waking very early, and keeping all aspects of daily life organised.

One of his main ideas was being available to the paying guests. He made sure his face was available for as much of the day as possible. He was often rewarded handsomely for his efforts, by them. Getting business out of the way was always his first priority. Afterwards, his day was free to make house calls and sort out the day's problems. His computer, this morning, had an email from Zak Sharpe, chasing his order. Mr C checked his file on Zak. The Guercino was ordered less than a month ago! 'Did this new arrival think one could just walk into a shop and purchase the item?' Mr C considered to himself. Never mind, Guercino wasn't like a Da Vinci, so it shouldn't take too long. He sipped his orange juice and moved onto the next e-mail.

***

As Mr C, Zak tried and did eventually sleep on the journey back

246

to the mainland. He was awoken with a start as a man shook him by the shoulder. "You must get ready!"

The crew of the boat had not said more than a few words to him for the entire journey. Zak checked his moneybag was still secured around his waist, and collected his things together. He looked out of the small porthole to discover that it was dark outside. "Come quickly!" urged the crewman. Zak followed him as they made their way through the ship. Zak was led to the main cargo hold. The crewman pointed to a crate and motioned for Zak to get inside.

"You must hide in here."

Zak didn't much fancy the idea, but could see little option. He gingerly climbed up and into the crate. Cooking oil drums had been placed around the outside of the crate and stacked two high, thus creating a small space in the middle. On the floor were four round crate bases. Zak sat down on them and the crewman placed a lid on top. On the inside were four more drum lids. To the outside the crate would look full of cooking oil drums. The crewman nailed the crate shut and walked out of the hold, turning the light out as he went. Zak waited uncomfortably in the darkness. After some time, the boat slowed and eventually docked. Zak could hear people talking and working in the background. He looked through the small 2-inch gap formed by the curvature of the drum lids above him, and watched through it as the top of the boat opened up, and the lights of the dock flooded in. Zak could hear as one by one different crates were lifted out of the hold and ashore. Finally it was his turn.

Zak listened as a crewman shouted to the crane operator to begin. The crate shook violently as it lifted up and out of the hold. Zak watched as the ship, between small gap in the floor, shrunk away from under him. Water. Then the concrete of the dockside. It swung dangerously high above the dock for a

247

moment or two and then down to the back of a truck. It landed with a thump. Here two men undid the four chains that connected it to the crane, got into the pickup truck's cabin, and drove off.

Zak could see nothing from between the drums. It travelled only a short distance along the dockside. Above, Zak could see the yellow hue of the streetlamps by the dockside pass as they drove under them. They turned right into what must have been a container shed, as the night sky was replaced with a high, corrugated roof. The pickup stopped. Out got the two men. One walked away, and Zak heard him closing the big doors behind them. The second of the men pulled down the small lip at the back of the pickup and climbed on. He began to use a crow bar to lift the slats off the lid of the crate. As he did this, Zak heard a door open, not one of the big doors, but what must have been a side door. Quick footsteps were followed by two quiet, but punctuated, chhoop noises. The man with the claw hammer stopped and his breathing became harsh and laboured. He waited for a moment, gurgling help from his accomplice. The clang of the crowbar on the floor of the back of the pickup was the last sound the man heard. He fell to his knees, before toppling off the pickup and onto the floor. The crack, crack, crack of a pistol was followed by the now barely audible whooshing noises of the silenced pistol of the intruder. Groans, running footsteps and Zak's own breathing seemed to silence it even more. Zak's head switched and his eyes darted from gap to gap between the drums. Crack, crack, crack, more shots from the pistol. Zak had seen plenty of movies where heroes or villains used automatic pistols to maim or kill their opponents, and felt sure this was what he was hearing. He sat still, frightened. The second of the men ran to the far side of the warehouse and took cover there. The intruders ran up to the side of the pickup and sought shelter from the opponent's automatic weapon. Crack, crack… crack, crack, crack, went the pistol its noise loud and echoing around the inside of this half-corrugated warehouse. Speaking in hushed voices, the intruders clearly wanted this whole mess tidied up as quietly as possible. The whispered chhoop sound their guns made was now only about a metre away from Zak. He sat, frozen to the spot. Watching, waiting, his heart beating loudly in his chest. The man made a run from his shelter, cracking his automatic pistol towards the pickup as he went. Clearly not a good shot, all his bullets hit either the wall behind them or the door they had just driven through. The pickup tilted violently forward and to the right, as a stray bullet hit one of the tyres.

Choop, choop went the gun near him, and Zak heard a scream of pain before a thud, and the clatter of a dropped gun. One of the men to Zak's side ran out in the direction of the final man, and Zak heard a final punctuated chhoop, signalling the end of the man's life. Zak heard voices, and was now terrified. Sweat formed quickly on his forehead, and he fast developed severe claustrophobia of his position. As much as he wanted out of the crate, Zak hoped that in some wild fantasy that the intruders were not there for him. He sat as still as he could. He tried in vain to slow his breath down, but could only manage to quieten it by breathing in less deeply. Try as he might he could not get it to slow down, and yet that seemed so important right now. Carefully, slowly, he wiped his brow. He wondered what was going on. More voices near the side door. As if the world was listening out for him, he turned his head excruciatingly slowly to look through a half centimetre gap between two drums. Nothing nearby was recognisable. He slowly, painfully slowly, moved his head nearer the drum to secure a better view. In the distance he caught a glimpse of a man he'd only seen once before… and it turned his skin grey.

Many months earlier, Zak had been at an island party and had seen a giant of a man in the distance. Wearing dark trousers and a Hawaiian shirt that just about held his muscles in, he was obviously not a native. Zak asked who he was. It turned out that he was not a paying guest either, but a member of The Group. He looked after the island's security. He was the man whose responsibility it was to make sure the island never got discovered, both physically through discovery by a passing plane or boat, and also electronically. He was affectionately known as The Bodyguard. He looked to Zak like a Sergeant Major; his wide square jaw seemed to sit directly on broad muscular shoulders. Zak could not work out how old this man was, nor where he was from. His cropped short, ginger hair could've been Scottish, but his accent was more American than anything. Zak decided that in Mr C he had been concentrating on fooling the wrong man, and that it was this large, powerful man that Zak should fear most. Zak didn't think that The Bodyguard gave Zak more than a passing glance at the party, and for that he was thankful. Zak decided that the less the man saw of Zak the greater his chances of escape, and made his excuses early that night.

This was The Bodyguard. Had Zak met him in different circumstances, he was sure he would joke about him looking like a Scottish Desperate Dan. The ginger stubble on his chin was now nearly as long as that on his head, but he was definitely the same man. Zak tried to swallow and found his mouth and throat too dry. The noise his throat made as it forced the smallest amount of saliva down seemed to be attached to a megaphone. Zak's eyes bulged at the image in the distance... huge. No black trousers this time, he was wearing jeans and a black 50's Fonze-style leather jacket, worn only to hide his holster. Checking all was in control, he tucked his gun back inside his holster.

The Bodyguard looked straight at the drums on the back of the truck and walked purposefully over. Zak could feel his breathing getting louder and decided his only chance of not getting heard was to hold his breath. Pointing to some other men and then at the dead bodies on the ground, The Bodyguard motioned for them to remove them.

"Get rid of them. Come on, we don't have much time."

He leapt onto the pickup and held out his hand for another man to pass him a crowbar. He caught it, and quickly began ripping open the wooden slats on the top. Zak looked up at the man's face. Cold brown eyes, knowing Zak was there, took no notice of him, his wide jaw grimacing as he fought with the wood. Zak felt a slight warming in his pants and immediately sucked his muscles in, to stop him wetting himself. This man was going to kill him, that was for sure, that was the penalty, and Zak knew it.

Finally the last of the wooden slats gave way to the strength of The Bodyguard and his crowbar, and the lid was quickly lifted off. Bursts of click clack noises echoed around the inside of the warehouse as the guns of the other men were being prepared to fire. Zak looked like a lost and frightened animal, cowering in the small space in the centre of the crate. The Bodyguard grabbed Zak by the back of the neck and hurled him effortlessly out of the crate. Clearing the back of the pickup, Zak would've been really hurt had he not had the gymnastic instinct to roll as he landed on the warehouse floor. He looked back at the pickup and watched as The Bodyguard jumped down, grabbed him by the back of the neck once again. He began to drag Zak like a rag doll towards the door at the back of the warehouse.

"We must talk, Mr Sharpe, you have some information I want."

Zak walked as best he could; the large hand holding him by

251

the back of the neck was forcing him double. An age-old joke about what a fly kisses goodbye when it hits a car windscreen disturbingly flashed through his head as he looked between his own legs. The other men were busily tidying the area. One man was throwing some fragments of wood into the back of the pickup, whilst another walked methodically around looking for what Zak thought must be bullet shells. They reached the outer door and Zak stumbled up the three metal steps. Zak heard The Bodyguard throw open the door and drag him through. The door came back on its spring and caught him sharply on his hip. He winced in pain and concentrated hard on the three steps down to the dockyard. Zak looked up into the night sky to see seagulls wheel and scoop in the night air, scavenging for morsels. Bright dockside lights glared down at them as Zak was led over to a portacabin.

Inside were a few chairs and a small table, on top of which sat a small portable TV blaring out some late night football game. Zak was turned to face The Bodyguard.

"Do you think you'd fuckin' get away with this?"

Zak could tell by the way The Bodyguard spat the word fuckin' at him that he didn't want a reply. The Bodyguard removed the small backpack on his back and checked him over. He threw it, without looking at its contents, on the table. Turning Zak around he opened a second door and pushed him to the floor inside, locking the door behind him as he left. A yellow streetlight outside shone through a single meshed window. Zak lay in shock where he'd landed, too scared to move. Zak heard The Bodyguard barking orders at the other men before picking up a mobile phone. Zak listened to the beep beep of buttons being pressed. A short pause. "Transmissions? Yeah, we have him. Contact The Group and ask what they want to know. Soon. We don't have much time, it will soon be dawn, and I must have

252

all the answers and this problem taken care of by then."

A small beep, and the call was over. Zak lay in silence, waiting. A short while later, two men returned.

"We have a problem."

"What?"

"Someone told dock security they heard gunshots. If we don't act quick, they're liable to call the coastguards."

"Shit. We gotta see these guys don't ring anyone. Where are they?"

"Main gate, but they're jumpy."

"You stay here, guard him. You come with me. We ain't havin' no customs mess this up."

Amazed he was still alive, Zak waited for a moment and looked around the room. The TV blared away in the room next door, and Zak slowly crawled to the door. He gingerly took a look through the keyhole. He could just make out a man, sat casually going through Zak's moneybag and backpack. He slowly, quietly, got to his feet and trod as softly as he could towards the window. He looked out and could see a deserted dockside. A McGuire advertising balloon swung high above the night sky, tethered by a rope.

Zak knew he needed to escape… and fast. He looked at the window and the screw-head bolt tops that held the mesh cover. Like a flash in his brain, he remembered that The Bodyguard had not removed his scuba knife from his leg. A smile of nervous expectation and elated hope broke onto his face. He quickly took it out and began using the sharp blade as a screwdriver head on the bolt heads. Sweating now, his face grimaced and eyes darkened to that of a madman desperate to save his own life, and knowing this was to be his only chance. Each small bolt was very stiff at first, but once he'd started them off they became easier to turn. Frantically turning to look towards the other room

253

every now and again, Zak could hear the man talking to the TV, urging one team on. One by one they were silently removed. His expectation of success growing inside him as he worked, Zak ignored the stinging of the sweat in his eyes until he HAD to stop and wipe his brow. Two more small bolts between himself and escape. Forcing the head of the one bolt too quickly, the blade of the knife slipped and seared the head off the bolt. Blind panic only a hair's breath away, he started on the other. Pushing the blade hard into the small slit, he was determined not to make the same mistake again. It turned.

More quickly now he turned the head of this bolt until it finally fell out. The mesh didn't move however. He put the knife back in his leg holster and pushed the mesh. The paint on the outside of the cabin cracked as the paint separated. The mesh swung down on the remaining one bolt, making a grating sound as it did so. Zak looked at the door. The TV sound was being turned down, but Zak was not going to wait to see what was going to happen next. Putting his hands onto the bottom edge of the window frame he jumped up and landed with a thump on his knees. Excruciating pain shot through his knees as the thin edge of the Portakabin window frame bit into them. Footsteps made their way towards the door as Zak tried to balance himself. Looking towards the ground below, and backside stuck high in the air, he wobbled too and fro trying to time his balance just long enough to release a hand. The key turning in the lock told him it was now or never, and as quick as a flash he let go of the bottom of the window frame and grabbed the side. Security. But the man was now walking into the room. Zak quickly got to his feet on the window frame and reached for the top of the high security fence that ran down the back of the Portakabin.

"Oi!"

The man ran towards Zak and missed Zak's feet by inches

as he jumped to get his body over the fence.

The steel spike dug into his chest just below his ribcage, but Zak for now didn't feel a thing. He swung his leg over and fell the eight feet down to the ground, spraining his ankle as he did so. He began to run away from the Portakabin, looking back to measure the progress of his captors. He heard more voices now as The Bodyguard had obviously just returned. He looked quickly down the line of the fence to see that it was a good 100 metres before the first opening. He ran into the darkness, looking for escape. He could hear a car or jeep being started and racing down the fence line for the opening. In front of him was little to hide behind. He noticed a large concrete block with a rope attached, and looked upwards. The advertising balloon was about 20 metres above him and tethered by a rope. With his ankle screaming at him to stop, he ran towards the concrete block and clumsily climbed on it. He wrapped his left leg and left arm around it and took out his scuba knife.

The Jeep was racing towards him as Zak hacked hysterically at the rope. With the Jeep getting nearer, Zak could see he was nearly through and held on tightly as he cut through the last tethers. Suddenly he was being lifted up high into the night sky and further down the dock. Zak's left arm howled at him that it needed help in holding on. Like a comic book pirate, Zak put the blade of the knife between his teeth and grabbed hold of the rope with his right arm.

Zak looked down at the fast disappearing men who had been tasked with his demise. Further still he rose. Now the distance between himself and land was starting to worry him. He started climbing the rope using his arms to pull him, and his one good foot to dig the rope into the shin of the poor one. His gymnastic background and enthusiasm meant he made light work of the rope and quite quickly climbed to the balloon.

255

Taking the knife out of his mouth he made a small incision. Being careful not to overdo it, Zak was keen to start descending, but knew that if the incision was too large he could hit the ground with a thump or worse. If it hadn't been for a small hissing sound, Zak would've been totally unaware that he'd even broken the surface of the balloon. He looked down and instinctively gripped tighter to the rope. He was really high now. The dockside had been replaced by some small factory units and he would soon be passing over a freeway.

Gripping as hard as he could, he decided to make safe his knife and put it back into his leg holster. The balloon didn't seem to be getting any higher, and after he'd crossed the freeway actually seemed to be slowly returning to ground. Zak hung on to the rope and watched the ground pass underneath him. As he returned back to the original height of the balloon, Zak put his hand over the slit in an attempt to stem any further leakage. The last thing he wanted was to kill himself now, after just about getting away from being killed! Helium seeped out and as it did so he drifted slowly back to earth. As he passed a garage, he decided to climb down to freedom. As he did so, the bottom of the rope started to catch on some small trees in a back garden. The earth seemed to be getting rapidly closer now, and Zak finally seized his opportunity by judging his height to that of the top of a playhouse. Running along the roof, he jumped to the ground. The ankle that had been hurt when he fell from the fence sent a shockwave of pain through him as he landed. As he lay there in sheer agony, he could hear the knurls of the rope drone over the pitch of the roof and across the garden as the balloon carried on for another few gardens.

Zak scrambled to his feet and made for the garden gate that led to the street. Looking nervously around, he hobbled along the avenue towards the main road. The nervous excitement suddenly

256

became too much for him and he decided to look for shelter. He made his away along the main road, keeping close to the bushes and trees. He arrived at the garage that he'd passed over earlier and walked around the side. A wooden bin park and Zak made a small shelter for himself using some discarded cardboard boxes. Little was Zak to know, but cardboard boxes were to be his main shelter for the next year. Zak ached all over and despite this, slept soundly till morning.

The Return

Glory is fleeting, but obscurity is forever.

Napoleon Bonaparte – (1769-1821)

"Hey… HEY!" Zak woke with a start.

"Come on… on your way. Y'can't stay here. Boss won't allow it, he'll have ya guts jus fur messin up his boxes. Come on now, get on yer way."

Zak looked up to see a young man in his early twenties motion him to stand. Dressed in shop overalls and sporting a baseball cap, Zak thought he looked a lot like a young John Travolta, save for a bulbous nose and a cluster of large, red zits on his forehead. Zak didn't move, mesmerized by them like a rabbit in car headlamps.

"Hey mister! D'ya hear what I sed? Come on, move it."

Zak flashed back to present day and rose slowly to his feet.

"Come on, if the boss catches ya he'll run you out!"

Zak looked back to the road and up and down, checking. He began his walk, urged on by the young shop assistant. "Jus rememba, don't come back now. He'll run you out." Zak lazily waved a tired arm over his shoulder as though he'd heard and walked on.

Zak had been bumming around for over a week now and without money he had found it hard. The fall during his escape had hurt his ankle quite badly and although he could use it, he was still limping. He hadn't walked more than a hundred metres along the sidewalk when a car slowly passed him. Zak looked nervously at it, hoping it wasn't The Bodyguard. A mum was driving her daughter in a car. The girl looked at him with interest.

Zak's nerves had been getting worse rather than better. The morning after his escape had been almost as eventful as the escape itself. Zak had woken up elated that he'd got away, only to be hunted down for the whole of the following day. He'd finally made his way into town and into the obscurity of crowds. Today, today was D Day. Declaration Day. The day he was going to go and prove his identity. He'd go into the labor office and make known who he was. He'd tell them and even give a DNA sample if they needed one. He couldn't possibly live like this, and this was the only way he could get back to England.

Zak limped up the disabled ramp and in through the rotating doors into the labor office. He looked around and saw a small ticket machine. Taking a stubb he sat near the entrance, watching others in the room. "Ping." 83 flashed up on the LED counter on the far wall. Zak looked at his ticket. 97. He'd wait, he had all day and besides, he didn't have a lot of choice. Time passed. The numbers slowly went up and Zak couldn't help but listen in to an orca fat black woman with a huge head of hair tell the teller how much she needed that money. Sleeping rough was bad. At times it had been really rough, but Zak had considered it a means to an end. This was different again. This was hell. Some people actually lived like this for most of their lives! Apart from a couple of youths in designer basketball gear, nobody seemed to have more than a few dollars to rub together. This was pitiful. "Ping."

Zak looked up for an empty booth. The black lady was still

giving her teller a hard time about what she didn't have to live between now and collection day. Zak shuffled to booth four and sat down. The frizzy-haired lady behind the thick glass pane looked at him through milk bottle glasses.

"How can I help you?" came the curt and tinned voice through the small speaker set in the booth window.

"Er, yes, I hope you can. My name is Zachariah Sharpe and I'd like you to help me get some money so that I may get home."

"Zachariah what?"

"Sharpe."

"Sharpe, y'say. Have you got a number?"

"A number?"

"Yes, a SIN number? What's your SIN number?"

"I don't understand. I don't have a number."

"Your Social Insurance Number! What's your Social Insurance Number?"

"I don't have one."

"Well if you don't have one, I can't help you."

"No, You don't understand. I don't have one because I'm English."

"You're what?" replied the tinned, puzzled voice.

"English! I'm English!"

"Have you a work permit?"

"No."

"Then you can't get money, honey." The teller smiled at her dip into the poetic.

"No. You see I don't need the money. I need to prove who I am, so I can get back home."

"Well I'm sorry, Sir, but I just can't help you."

"But you MUST help me," Zak urged.

"I'm sorry Sir, but if you're here without a work permit and no SIN number, I can't help you."

Zak could feel the anger and embarrassment rising in him. This stupid woman was not listening to him. "No. YOU don't understand. I don't need your poxy handouts. I NEED to prove to you WHO. I. Am. So I can go home!"

"Sir, there is no need to raise your tone at me!" A man in small silver glasses and wearing a shirt and tie walked over.

"Ah, can YOU tell this woman I'm English… from England! I'm stranded here and need to find either the money or the method of getting back home. I can prove my identity if only you'd give me a DNA or something. I need to prove to you who the FUCK I AM!"

Behind the glass panel the man took no notice of him and was listening to the teller. Unbeknown to him, she'd temporarily turned off the speakerphone. The man listened to her and looked at Zak. He turned the speakerphone on.

"… FUCK I AM!" demanded the bedraggled man in front of him.

On what he'd heard, the reception manager instantly decided Zak was going to be trouble. He'd get him in the interview room. People like that normally calmed down once they'd lost their audience.

"Could you make your way over to the interview room, Sir? I'd appreciate it if we could talk in there," he asked. He pointed to a door to Zak's right. Zak looked at it. The reception manager waved him towards it, eager to get this man out of the main reception area. His ankle aching, Zak limped over to the door and let himself in. Inside was a table, two wooden chairs and a door into the office area. Zak sensed something was not quite right. In fact he didn't like it at all.

As Zak shut the door, he looked back through the striped window, half glass, half mirror glass.

"Mr Williamson! We have a call on line three for you… it's

your wife," said the office temp.

Zak watched as the reception manager spoke with the teller, and then picked up the telephone. He spoke for a minute to someone and kept looking towards the room that Zak stood in. As the manager walked over towards the interview room, he considered what his wife had just told him. His brother and that pain of a sister-in-law were coming over that evening... what a bundle of joy tonight was going to be. Zak watched the manager approach, and his nerves began to get the better of him. Who the hell did he need to talk to on the phone, he considered to himself? 'Security? Police?' As the office manager drew nearer, it dawned on Zak exactly what had happened. 'THEM!'

The office manager walked in through the connecting door to the office area and beckoned to Zak.

"Hello Mr Sharpe, please take a seat. What can I do for you?" he asked.

Zak considered the situation in a microsecond. 'Take a seat!!! Did this man think that Zak Sharpe is mad! That's just so that THEY can get here. He's in on it! Look at the way he's sitting! He's rested only three fingers on the edge of the table... HE'S A BLOODY MASON! THAT'S what it is... A bloody mason, THEY must be in on it... well now, it's all fitting together.'

The office manager, who'd taken a seat himself, studied this dirty man who'd limped in off the streets asking for money. The man in front of him did nothing, didn't sit, but stared blankly at him. 'Oh Christ... I get em all', he thought. 'I hope he's not thinking this is some sort of bank. I wonder if he's packin' a piece?'

"Er.. sorry, can I go to the toilet before we start?" asked Zak.

'What the fuck?' thought the office manager, 'give me time

to let security know I've got a schizo in here'.

"Yes Sir, of course you can. It's down to the end of the reception area and turn right," replied the office manager, with a beaming smile.

"Thank you," replied Zak.

He turned quickly, and letting himself out walked across the reception area. He looked back and noticed the manager walk towards a security guard. 'He's not looking... OUT!' cried a voice in his head. Zak turned and fled to the rotating door. He pushed his way through, giving a woman a good shove in the process.

Through the door and out into the sunlight, Zak knew he was in the open but still vulnerable. He looked quickly around and, like some modern day Hunchback of Notre Dame, he limped quickly away from any limelight. He just knew they were either there already or very close. The office manager watched this farcical scene unfold before him and contemplated only momentarily that he should find out why this man scurried out the way he did. His indifference won and he simply watched as the eccentric stranger hobbled out of the building.

Zak walked on for several blocks, trying to blend into the crowds. He grew tired and sat outside a shopping mall to rest. He considered himself very fortunate indeed. That was twice he'd missed death by inches in the last week. He would have to be more careful next time. His foot and ankle were aching from the nigh on run that he'd just put them through. He undid his boot that although it was higher than a shoe, it seemed to be giving his ankle no support at all. He took it off and placed it between his legs, to ensure it didn't get stolen. He was hungry. Tired. Exhausted in fact. He let his head drop back whilst he thought about how he could let the world know he existed without getting killed in the process. He fell asleep.

Out and About

Obstacles are those frightful things
you see when you take
your eyes off your goal.

Henry Ford – (1863-1947)

Over the next few weeks, Zak faired quite well at first, making his way through Florida. His journey from the Keys up to Daytona was quite uneventful. Here, as he walked up North Atlantic Avenue late one night, some youths taught him two valuable lessons. The first was never carry cash where people can easily get to it; the second was to stay away from any main route where youths are likely to hang out.

So Daytona led to Jacksonville where Zak discovered, 'The Home of the Mustangs' had apparently moved from Daytona to Jacksonville, at the Mandarin High School. It seemed everyone wanted to be The Home of the Mustangs. The journey was full of too many signs and too many passing cars, without a lift. Zak lost count of the, 'Keep off Medium', and 'Florida Highway Patrol dial *FHP', or 'Fines doubled when workers Present', signs. In Augusta he sat for a clear two hours before his saviour stopped in a Freightliner Century. He was weary, but very grateful to grab a lift from a trucker who took him all the way to Rock Hill, quite fortuitous he thought. He had crossed South Carolina in less than a day. He begged once more for food and money, but had a lot less success. Zak's mental fitness became increasingly tested as tired, anxious and increasingly malnourished, he continued to be faced with situations and experiences well beyond his privileged upbringing. Increasingly, the days of determined travel spent on the road in search of a solution to his identity problem, were giving way to depressive, hesitant meandering through bins and back alleys. This is where Zak met Britt Fleming.

The March sky was white and the freezing wind blew thankfully softly across the bleak corner of Main Street East and Albright Road. Zak sat on an old copy of the Herald waiting for a lift; it provided mediocre protection from the frozen mud beneath. He could hear a train pass nearby and had thought about trying to jump aboard, but his ankle injury forbade him, complaining painfully if he tried to exert it. A huge Ford pickup pulled out of the car park opposite, and Zak held out his hand in despondent hope. It drove a short distance past him and waited. Elated, Zak stood up, and moved as quickly as his cold limbs and sore ankle would allow, towards the back of the pickup. A huge F350 on 24.4 inch wheels, he pictured its driver to be a burley farm hand or steel worker. This was a safe vehicle, Zak thought. For one, the Florida licence plate with the all too familiar orange in the middle, told him this was someone who was out of state, but being in such a monster of a truck, would hardly be someone from H^{e}aven.

He reached up to the door handle and pulled the door open.

"Where ya goin, honey?" asked a small, grey haired lady of about fifty. Zak's eyes were like saucers, and it was at least a second too late for him to make sure he did not look like a village idiot.

"North. New York eventually," Zak answered.

"Well ya better hop in then, I ain't got all day, and that

breeze is bitin','" replied the old lady.

Zak lifted his leg up as far as he could onto the floor of the pickup and grabbed the handle on the door.

"Thank you. Thank you very much," said Zak, as he closed the door.

"Quite all right," replied the lady. "No one should be out in this chill," she said with a smile.

Britt was a mother of four, and Zak had managed to get a lift from her as she drove her son's pickup from Lake Helen to Manchester, where he was working at the airport. Zak couldn't believe his luck when he learned how far up the coast she was going, however he still wished it was Manchester, England. Her son was a freelance engineer, and she was delivering some spares for a helicopter for him. The journey was to last two long days, and Zak learned more about American life in that time than he ever could. Britt was a talking machine, revelling in reminiscing about how she had raised her four children with their father, until he died of liver failure back in '82. She had let Zak sleep in the back of the pickup with the parts, whilst she had slept in the Ramada Inn. Zak thought she was quite pleased to have picked up a real English down and out, but still secretly feared she might be one of 'Them'.

***

Zachariah stood watching the stream of warm liquid hit the mud. As it did so, the stream started to gouge a small hole in the mud, slowly scraping away small fragments from the ground where it landed. As Zachariah watched this miniature excavation of the park he considered his daily takings, and the pleasures it could bring him. The liquid stopped. Zachariah tucked himself back into his trousers and re-fitted the zip closed. He'd decided on drink.

266

Zachariah walked back out of the park and towards his step. He knew from experience that the park was not especially welcoming at night. Kids, druggies and women all strolled around the park at night. They would sell him ass in for a splif. The Group would pay handsomely too… far more than a splif, and Zachariah knew his life and his secret would be the death of him around here for far less.

The small bell rung above the door as Zachariah entered the small liquor store. The man behind the counter had seen Zachariah on a number of occasions before, but still watched Zachariah intently. Zachariah hated him. An obvious informant. His shiny head would have been completely bald had it not been for the way his dark black hair was greasily pushed back over his ears each side. He never smiled at Zachariah.

"You ok, buddy?"

"Fine," replied Zachariah.

"What can I getcha?"

Zachariah looked down at his pockets as he ambled towards the counter, carefully making sure nothing fell out as he reached inside. He scooped out his money from his day, and laid it carefully on the counter. The bell rang behind him, startling him into turning around to see the figure of a small African woman walk into the shop and down the aisle that was signposted, 'Potato Chips, Candy & Snacks'.

He returned his gaze at the suspicious shop attendant.

"Bacardi."

"Your usual?"

"WHAT THE HELL DO YOU KNOW ABOUT MY USUAL?" Zachariah glared at him. Who was this man? The man looked taken aback by Zachariah's outburst.

"Sorry, Bud," apologised the man.

"I'm not your BUD! … Do you know who I am!?" declared

Zachariah.

"No! No! I just meant to be friendly... you'd been here a few times before, so I was just bein' civil!" explained the shocked attendant.

"Damn right you don't! I ain't no one YOU! know," barked Zachariah, pointing his finger angrily.

The shop assistant turned and lifted the cheap litre copy bottle of Bacardi off the shelf behind him and placed it in front of Zachariah.

"Fourteen Eighty."

Zachariah sieved through the change on the counter and whilst he re-counted the coins and swapped larger ones as change for smaller ones, the small African woman ambled up nearby. The shop employee had counted it with Zachariah and scooped up the coins and entered the amount in the till.

"You don't want to worry about me! YOU should worry what THEY'LL do to you when THEY find out YOU let me slip away!" and with that comment, Zachariah picked up his bottle and scurried out of the shop.

***

It took Zak another three days to make it from Manchester to South Amboy. Britt had indeed been a saviour and this is where Zak's luck ran out. Here he'd walked off the Garden State Parkway to the Christ Church Cemetery where he managed to find a quiet spot to sleep for the night. He found some old bushes someone in Portia Street had cut, and made himself a makeshift shelter in the corner of the cemetery, but the cold night air still bit through him. It took Zak a long time to drop off.

As unprepared as any man would be whose life had been cosseted the way Zak's had, his journey towards New York had left him physically weak. The long lonely nights in the cemetery, doorways and alleyways had cultivated a fear in him that made his actions and attitude appear schizophrenic. Had Zak not looked like a beggar and not acted like someone who'd escaped from the local asylum, his troubles would have been over much earlier. Unbeknown to him, The Group had other problems relating to President Clinton's sanctions on Cuba, affecting the island's resources.

Zak's arrival in New York was a very quiet affair. His bedraggled clothes and wavering communication skills had left him often unable to hitch lifts or even beg for food. Even when he could hold a normal conversation, many drivers of trucks often found his attitude change for a seemingly innocent conversational question such as, "Where you from?" They often let Zak out at the next diner or gas station.

During Zak's journey up America's east coast, he had become progressively more aware of the deterioration of his ankle. The throbbing in his leg whose strength and persistency demanded attention, was becoming unbearable. Finally he submitted to its cries for attention, and decided to take a risk and visit a library to look up his ailment.

Zak winced as he slowly climbed the steps that led to the large double doors into the library. He tried hard to blend into the crowds around him, yet unbeknown to him he stood out like a clown at a christening. People walking nearby studied him with the kind of interest that those with money have in those that don't. Zak tried pointlessly to straighten his crumpled, dirty clothes before entering. He wanted to look as normal as possible. Inside the library was a second set of glass doors. A brown-haired receptionist sat looking intently at her VDU screen whilst she typed. She looked up.

"Can I help you?" she asked.

Zak thought about his need for a book, and concentrated on his persona.

"Yes! .. I'd like to borrow a few books on medical problems, can you direct me to that area?"

"Are you a member, Sir?" asked the receptionist, eyeing Zak up carefully.

"No, but…"

"Then I'm sorry," interrupted the receptionist, "but the library cannot allow any books to be withdrawn without two forms of identification. Do you want an application form?"

Zak pondered for a moment

"No thank you… Can I still come in and have a look?"

"Of course Sir," she replied.

Zak walked on past the woman without another word, and pushed his way through the chrome turnstile. The fear of entrapment welled inside and Zak fought hard with his gremlins that were urging him to turn back. He turned and looked at the entrance; the receptionist was staring at him. Fearing he would be evicted if he did not act normal, Zak looked around and followed the signs that led him to the non-fiction section. He eventually found the section he wanted and began to flick through each book in turn. After reading the introduction or by flicking through some books he felt over informed. He eventually found a book he was happy with, and guessing that his ankle wasn't broken, merely badly sprained, he looked up muscular problems. Taking out his notepad, he made notes of his experience and reading.

'Library – I know I can't borrow books. But I'm still not sure of them.

<u>Diseases and Disorders of the muscle</u> (Courtesy of Encyclopaedia Britannica.)

Primary muscle disease, due to abnormality in muscle itself.

(Well mine was ok before my trip.)

Secondary muscle disease, due to abnormality in nerve supplying muscle.

Symptoms:

Enlargement (happens naturally in athletes and in muscular dystrophy) well I used to be fit – myotonia congonita and hypertrophia musculorum

Tetany – intermittent spasms (involuntary – I don't have these).

Atrophy – wasting (is it? I JUST DON'T KNOW!)

Weakness – Due to glycogen disorder (will have to get this looked at back in England – can be hereditary, check out McArdle's Disease).

One point I will promote and that is it's no mystery as to where all the sabotage – ALL – not just mine – is coming from.

Someone thinks that they (the paying guests) should all be lured to H^{e}aven. Unfortunately not all have the fare!

(That's why 'The Group' try to entice people with reserves in the bank)

I do think that if there are any other exiles of H^{e}aven in the USA, they must by now be thoroughly disillusioned or worse, living the life threatening thin line on which I find myself walking at the moment.

And the lesson? Now I know how American ancestors must have felt unable to escape from their log cabins whilst surrounded by hoards of yelling Indians with tomahawks!

Ps. I will give the Americans credit for one thing – they certainly believe in independence!

Zak looked around nervously, it was the first time in his diary that he'd used the words 'The Group' or 'H^{e}aven' and it made him nervous. But he supposed, if he were ever to be found he'd want people to be aware of who had ruined his life… and probably taken it. Sure that he'd discovered his ailment and made good his note for the day, Zak walked over to the steel book trolley and placed the book in the V shaped collection section. He hobbled slowly towards the chrome turnstile leading back out. The receptionist was typing away and didn't look at him as he passed through and back out of the doors into the street. He walked back down the steps and took the bottle of rum from his inner pocket. Taking off the metal cap, he swigged a good few mouthfuls to help calm his nerves. The neat rum did not make him wince and the bottle would last him less than a day.

The library trip had been a few months ago now, and neither Zak's leg nor mental constitution got any better. Feeling safer with people who had less, Zak found himself a doorway that didn't mind him sleeping there as long as he was on his way before they rose; a neighbourhood where he could earn enough from begging to feed his hunger for alcohol; and a bread shop owned by the Macnamaras where he could scrounge for food.

Epilogue

Buzz Anderson had drunk too much and had certainly spent too much. His cab fair home had been wasted on a brunette who gave him nothing more than a goodnight kiss. Buzz had a rented apartment on Eastern Parkway and now faced the not so welcome task of walking the four or so miles from the nightclub on 62nd Street back home.

Buzz could handle himself. He was quite streetwise. As he came within the last mile of his home, he could hear a down and out on the step up ahead.

"Bunch of fuckin tossers. I'll fuckin show em... bastards. Mess my life up, who do they think they are!!"

Buzz was a little worse for the drink himself, but this poor soul had had more than a skinful. He looked at him as he walked.

"Who do you think YOU are!"

Buzz looked at the bedraggled man on the steps and couldn't help smile at the way the man was comically slouching down them.

"Do you know who I am? DO YOU KNOW WHO I AM!?"

"No I don't, Mister... and to be fair, I don't really give a damn... I'm going home."

"I am a fuckin m-i-llionaire I am! An if y'don't fuckin believe me, its cossa THEM!"

"Yeah sure! And you know what? I'm only walkin home 'cause I like the air!" Buzz laughed at his joke and walked on.

Today was just another ordinary day for multi-millionaire

Zachariah Sharpe. Today was one of many in Zak's world, spent sitting in the streets of a big city hiding from The Group and himself. Evenings were traditionally spent topping up his alcohol content so he could face the schizophrenic fear that gripped his sober time. Would you give this man a second glance?... I did, and this was his story.